CHERRY BEACH EXPRESS

R.D. CAIN

CHERRY

beach
express

Published by ECW Press
2120 Queen Street East, Suite 200, Toronto, Ontario, Canada M4E 1E2
416-694-3348 / info@ecwpress.com

LIBRARY AND ARCHIVES CANADA CATALOGUING IN PUBLICATION

Cain, Richard
Cherry Beach express : a Steve Nastos mystery / Richard Cain.

ISBN 978-1-77041-005-3
also issued as:
978-1-55490-909-4 (PDF); 978-1-55490-977-3 (EPUB)

I. Title.

PS8605.A417C54 2011   C813'.6   C2010-906830-0

Design and typesetting: Ingrid Paulson
Printing: Friesens   1   2   3   4   5

The publication of *Cherry Beach Express* has been generously supported by the Canada Council for the Arts, which last year invested $20.1 million in writing and publishing throughout Canada, by the Ontario Arts Council, by the OMDC Book Fund, an initiative of the Ontario Media Development Corporation, and by the Government of Canada through the Canada Book Fund.

  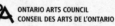

PRINTED AND BOUND IN CANADA

ECW PRESS
ecwpress.com

PROLOGUE

Six Months Ago
March 11, 2011

THE DENTAL BUILDING WAS A cool, dark place, lit by offset casts of amber streetlight that refracted between slats in the blinds. His shadow glided along the wall as he walked the hallway with measured, practised, maybe even rehearsed paces, to the utility room where two miniscule, green LED lights from the DVD recorder shone. They were reflective like cat's eyes, glaring from a lower shelf, from blackness. He took a disc out of the recorder and placed it in an empty case he obtained from a lower shelf. He put this disc in his pocket, then took a new blank disc from a drawer, placed it in the slot and put the now-empty case where he had retrieved the previous one.

Excitement wasn't the right word; it was hardly his first time taking a recording home and he was a man of strong emotional control. No, not excitement. Satisfaction or contentment maybe, as his collection of videos and veiled conquests was growing, slow but sure.

Dr. Irons was a six-foot-two, square-jawed man in his late forties with a lean, sculpted body from years of weight training. His greying hair, cut every two weeks, was kept trim and sharply angled.

He left, closing the door behind him, then proceeded toward the last room at the back of the building, his exam room. With the hallway door partially open, the vibrant Winnie the Pooh posters, colourful balloon borders and various children's trappings were lifelessly greyed down, looking no more alive than his silver, glinting dental instruments perfectly lined up on the chair-side tray. Sickle probes, excavators, operative burs, chisels — all waited eagerly for a patient, hopefully a child, to come in. Irons took a last moment to survey his operating room, then closed the door. He walked to the back door, keyed in the security code and left for the night.

He drove silently to his usual Monday stop: a corner grocery store. Inside, he grabbed enough vegetables, bread and cheese to last a week, placing them in his basket. Irons had begun walking to the cash when he noticed an attractive Latina mom with her five-year-old son in tow. Irons watched from a distance, considering the child, appraising his exaggerated movements. The blood in Irons' body came alive. How his face warmed and his heart thumped and thumped again like a bird testing its wings for flight. A welcoming smile slowly crept across his lips, his eyes remaining absorbed and predatory.

He considered how love comes as a gift and can be found anywhere at any time, always unexpected, and we never turn it away. How much saner would the world be if we could control what we love? When the boy's mother noticed Irons' interest, she unconsciously stepped between the two, blocking Irons' view. She looked back at her boy, then at Irons. Irons' smile became shy.

"Looks like my nephew, Charles," he said.

The mother's smile was no more sincere than Irons'. She grabbed her boy and walked away.

He walked into his condo. He carried his groceries in one hand and with the other he closed the door behind him, locking the deadbolt and putting a chain lock in place. Seeing only by the stove light, he kicked off his shoes, dropping them neatly in the floor tray, and placed the groceries on the counter. Pulling the DVD from his pocket, he went into the living room to the TV and put the disc in the player. The condo was minimally decorated: an efficient, modern look with matching black leather couches, chairs and an antique wrought-iron, glass-top coffee table.

He grabbed the remote from the table and walked back into the kitchen while he started the video. Irons took a steak that had been marinating in the fridge and placed it onto a wooden cutting board. It was a rib steak, less tender than a chateaubriand or a tenderloin, but far more flavourful. The delicacies of life were always worth a little more work.

A 60-inch flat-screen, big enough to be easily enjoyed from the kitchen, hung on the far wall. Video then audio came to life: his office and exam room. He was there with an assistant, a small child in the reclined chair. Irons couldn't take his eyes from the screen. He listened to himself speaking. The script he spoke was very important to him. It was all part of the ritual, like touching glasses before drinking wine.

"That little needle will help you relax, okay?"

"That did taste like banana," the child said.

His assistant Maggie spoke. "You don't mind doing the X-ray, Doctor?"

"No," Irons said softly, "we don't want to risk the little guy you've got growing inside." He smiled. "Actually, Maggie, I'll do the once-over as well, if you want to start the exam on Josie Nastos out there."

Maggie smiled, obviously relieved. "Okay, Doctor, let me know if you need me."

"You bet," Irons said. "Oh, and I've been watching Josie's spacing at two-four, so if you could measure it, we'll compare it to some old X-rays and see how it's doing. I won't be too long."

She left. White trash, through and through, he smiled to himself. Half the time she smelled like marijuana in the mornings and drank beer on weekends, but it was the X-ray that made her worry about her baby. Now it was just Dr. Irons and the boy.

There was a time on the video where nothing was being said. Irons glanced away for just a second, sprinkled spices on the steak, then took time to position it perfectly on the cutting board.

"Sammy, can you hear me . . . Sammy?" He absorbed the image on the TV screen. His face was that of a man in complete rapture. There were no sounds coming from the video, but whatever he was watching, he was completely under its control. His arms tightened: the tendons and muscles in his forearms slid under his skin like snakes squirming under a tight blanket. Slowly, then more deliberately, he began to bash the steak on the cutting board, beating his meat.

1

September 6, 2011

BEHIND THE FAÇADE OF THE crisp, dark suit, under a sharp haircut and behind pale blue eyes, was a place of anguish. Steve Nastos walked down the street, avoiding eye contact with various lawyers, court clerks and police officers in the court district of downtown Toronto. Not long ago, he had been a respected detective in the Sexual Assault Unit, a father to a seven-year-old girl and a husband to a beautiful wife. He now wondered what kind of a father or husband he could be in jail.

Nastos was flanked by two uniformed officers a step or two behind him. The shorter, older officer had his hand on Nastos' elbow and had a good grip, the way cops always seemed to. Nastos knew why, of course: if someone in custody was about to run for it, he would unconsciously become rigid in his upper body, and a good cop paid attention for any sign of tenseness in the arm or any other sign that the officer needed to wrench the handcuffs or slam the guy into a wall. Of course, Nastos was thinking of doing no such thing.

Despite his best efforts, his smile eroded at times as the natural walker's sway of his arms was constricted and squeezed from the handcuffs digging into his wrists behind him. His shoulders, aching for relief, burned from the weight of his increasingly heavy arms. The last time he had worn cuffs was in training at Police College, twenty-five years and thirty pounds ago; they were a little tighter and heavier now.

Nastos observed the court building, stone and marble coming together in an imposing, rigid and cold shell. Engraved on an archway was something written in Latin, probably a courtesy warning from the lawyers to have one's wallet ready if one wanted anything even resembling justice. And it was just like a lawyer to post it in a dead language. He wasn't sure he had ever noticed it before.

With a cool September wind behind him, he pushed a dream of freedom aside and walked up the steps, past an archway into the court building, transforming from a free man, a man of the law, to a man accused of a crime. He hoped for an imaginary wall to surround him, rendering him invisible to the crowd. With it he would drift into the back of bail court, anonymous in the audience. He'd say a few *yes sirs* and *no sirs* when called upon, then just float back out, unnoticed and unremembered. For that brief amount of time, he would just try to become someone else, a figment of his own imagination. No more perceptible than a ghost drifting through a thick, still fog.

His shoes hardly made a sound as he walked up the marble steps to the landing, past the pillars, through the turnstile and through security. He turned down the left hallway, weaving around and through the crowd. Years of pacing this very building, waiting for verdicts, allowed him to arrive at Courtroom 101 — the bail court — having rarely had to raise his eyes to anyone.

He made it as far as the double doors when he heard a voice from the side call out, "That's him there, roll the camera. Detective Nastos?"

In that moment, Nastos relinquished his hopes of anonymity, took a deep breath and braced for impact. His body became heavy. He was aware that his heart was racing, his cold hands were sweaty and his wrists were aching from the cuffs gnawing into him like an old dog's dulled teeth. He saw reporters and camera crews permeating through a deteriorating wall of courtroom derelicts as the media swarmed in around him.

"Detective Nastos? Detective Nastos, do you having any comments before you enter court?" a reporter asked.

He said nothing.

"Did he deserve what he got, Detective?" another tried.

Nastos thought it would be best to shut down. It was easier just to abandon a part of his humanity, to give up his sentient, communicative being and accept his fate. Questions came in a wall of noise from the dozen men and women wanting their quote for the day. *Just shut down, let it all go.* What could have gone on for an eternity ended when one of the police officers behind Nastos grabbed the door handle and directed him to the temporary safety of the courtroom.

Long immune to the odours, filth and scum of courts, Nastos stood still, looking for a place to sit with his small entourage of officers. The older of the two officers pointed to the defense lawyers' desk and without a word Nastos headed directly for it. *Looks like I move to the front of the line.*

On his way down the walkway, he passed a young white man dressed like a black gangster. With a quick glance, Nastos saw the real gangsters in the back of court. They were probably here for aggravated assaults, attempted murders — real violence. For the white kid, dressing up like them was about as authentic as a Walmart Halloween costume, and more than a little insulting. Hopefully for this kid they'd see the humour in it rather than feel the need to stick a knife in his throat.

A sudden, violent stench identified the white kid as the very epicentre of the vomit and stale sweat odours filling the cramped room. The feeling of it settling into his mouth and lungs was as offensive as if someone had stuffed a rag soaked in gasoline down his throat. He suppressed a gag and moved past, shaking his head. *Pretty soon, when this makes it to the front page, people are going to see me in the same light.*

Slowly pushing the gate that separated the general gallery from the front of the room, Nastos approached the defense desk. Three lawyers eyed each other, then slid over to create a space. The two officers who had escorted Nastos took seats directly behind him, but made no attempt to pull his chair back. Obviously, they hadn't been handcuffed in a while themselves or they might have known it was basically impossible for him to do it himself. Nastos shook his head, rolling his eyes, then began sliding a chair back with his foot. Quite surprisingly, the youngest of the three lawyers saw his efforts and reached a hand back to get the chair for him.

"Thanks," Nastos said.

"No problem," he replied without looking up, taking his own seat.

Nastos recognized him as Kevin Carscadden. He was barely thirty-five. Carscadden had only been in town for a few years. In that time, he had begun making a name for himself as a reluctant mob lawyer. How someone gets into that line of work was anyone's guess. It was a good way to wind up dead, in jail or to become the media go-to guy every time they needed a sound bite from someone who talks like he's spent the last ten years with his head up his ass. Of course, this seemed a little hypocritical in light of Nastos' current predicament.

An officer sitting behind Nastos surprisingly removed the handcuffs from him. Nastos began rubbing his wrists. The acidic burn slowly began to clear from his shoulders and arms when he rolled his upper body forward. He tried to raise his elbows to stretch his back, but his body was not ready for that one yet.

One of the other lawyers leaned forward, past Nastos to Carscadden and spoke. "Looks like your guy's up first." The man slid a copy of the court brief over to Carscadden, then he and the other lawyer took seats next to the two cops in the row behind, leaving Carscadden and Nastos alone in front.

Nastos watched the brief sliding along, past him to Carscadden.

8

"Are you the duty counsel for me today?" Nastos asked.

"Looks like it." Carscadden checked the other two lawyers. It was pretty obvious that he had just pulled the short straw. "Kevin Carscadden," he said, extending his hand. "And you are?"

"Nastos. Detective Nastos."

Carscadden appraised him directly for the first time. His eyebrows tightened when Nastos said "detective." And it was obvious that he saw the exhaustion on Nastos' face.

"You going to be okay?" Carscadden asked.

Nastos answered, "I just really hope to make bail. I'd like to see my family again before I go away."

"I can't promise you that one; all I can do is try." Carscadden wasn't too convincing. He kept eye contact until Nastos diverted his gaze down at the table. He was probably wondering what a detective was doing getting arrested and held for a bail hearing.

"Just do what you can," Nastos muttered, almost to himself.

Nastos' gaze fixed as if he were looking through the desk into nothingness, his body slumped forward and still. The table's wood-grain veneer was nearly imperceptibly pitted, capturing the fluorescent lights almost like a kaleidoscope. The din of voices in court allowed Carscadden to lean closer to Nastos and they shared a private exchange.

"Detective, did they question you all night?"

"Since nine last night."

"So you haven't slept?"

"No. I sat with my arms crossed reciting 'I want my lawyer' over and over again. They never got tired of hearing it."

The obvious question had to be asked. "Are you guilty, Detective?" Nastos didn't respond. Even thinking he'd answer that question, here in court was an insult to his intelligence.

He had gone twenty-four hours or so without sleep and it had brought him a certain mental fluidity, a tendency to drift off into daydreams and digressions as easily as a person passes from one nightmare to the next.

He was nowhere near the lawyer who was sitting right next to him in court. Nastos was leaving the front door of his house on a hot sunny morning in July. He, his daughter and wife were walking into furnace-orange sunshine that warmed their faces when they stepped from the shade on their driveway. Josie was swinging from his left arm, springing up and down with each step. His wife, Madeleine, was dressed for work, wearing a dark blazer and skirt. Her hair was back in a ponytail, making her appear younger than forty-two. She'd been a jogger since college and her habit still kept her thin.

The three of them walked to the minivan. Madeleine got in the back passenger seat next to Josie. Nastos took the driver's seat.

"Hey Jo, let's wipe the rest of the toothpaste off your face, okay?" Madeleine pulled out a Kleenex and started cleaning her daughter up.

"You're pressing too hard, Mom," Josie squawked.

Nastos spoke from the front seat. "Relax, Jo, we don't want the dentist thinking you have rabies." When he saw everyone was buckled up, he started driving. Traffic was light and through the length of the subdivision they were the only car on the road.

"Mom, is he going to freeze my face? I don't wanna talk like Grampa."

"Grampa only talks like that when he's tired, Josie." Madeleine glared right at Nastos through the mirror.

Oops. "What?" he asked, as if he had no idea that he had poisoned her mind.

"Nice one, Nastos" was all she could say, shaking her head.

Let's try a subject change, he thought. "Should we pick you up afterwards and go for lunch? We can try Italian, Frankie's place."

"I wish you had asked me yesterday; today I have to list Jackie's house, take a few pictures and do some running around. How about tomorrow instead?" She already had her BlackBerry in her hand, opening up the calendar.

"It's a date, with the two cutest girls on the planet."

◦ ◦ ◦

HE LED JOSIE INTO THE DENTAL OFFICE'S RECEPTION AREA. THERE WAS a waiting room with a wall of kids' toys and books. A video game system—probably a Wii—was running on the big-screen TV with no one playing. Three moms flipped through magazines while awaiting their children's return and Nastos' nose was invaded by that dental smell. Baking soda and antiseptic odour filled the suite. Josie realized that she had all of the toys to herself and, not waiting for a personal invitation, she dove for the video game. Nastos went to the reception desk and the next time he saw Josie, she was boxing the computer.

The receptionist was an older woman, who, despite working bankers' hours and though her most critical decision was to make a cancellation for an appointment, still found some reason to be cranky. The dental assistants and hygienists seemed welcoming enough while they grabbed or dropped off files on the reception desk or picked up equipment from the storage cabinets, but not this woman.

"Name?" she snarked.

"For Josie Nastos, please, nine o'clock." He tried to sound upbeat.

"Nothing for Mazitoze, are you sure —"

Nastos pointed to the scheduling book on the desk. "No, it's Nastos, it's written right there in front of you, for nine o'clock."

The receptionist didn't sound much happier when she replied, "Well, you can have a seat, it won't be long."

"Thank you." Some people were just always pissed about something. This was the first time Nastos had brought Josie here, though she had been seeing Dr. Irons for three years. He hoped to make it his last and let Madeleine deal with this bridge troll from now on; she was in sales and had a knack for it. He turned and walked into the waiting room, took a seat and went through a *Reader's Digest* magazine. He found one with a cover story about a trekker lost in the winter woods for a few days. It was sure to be a real page-turner. Josie was totally engrossed in her boxing match. She had the footwork going and her arms swinging. Somewhere, Oscar De La Hoya had the cold sweats.

Soon enough, Dr. Irons came out from the hallway. He was tall and lean, with short, greying hair. He had a slightly reddened tan, likely from the business next door. Irons was wearing a t-shirt–style scrub shirt, like the kind seen on every medical show. Nastos noticed Irons' veins and muscle tone; he was clearly a fit guy.

As Irons came into reception, a smile broke over his face. He stepped past Nastos, glancing from him to Josie on his way by, and it was the strangest thing for Nastos. Something struck the detective right away as being out of place, but he couldn't think of what it was at the time.

We may not always remember what people say, but no matter how much time passes, we always remember how people make us feel. Despite Irons' pleasant mannerisms, smile and polite request for Josie to accompany him — despite these things, Nastos felt uneasy. A feeling he later wished he had listened to.

"Josie Nastos?" Irons asked.

The future lightweight champion turned around, smiling and ready to go. "Hi," she said.

Irons reached out his hand and Josie took it. He smiled again to Nastos. "I can't imagine I'll take over half an hour, but sometimes it takes a while to get all the edges of those tiny little teeth during the cleaning."

"Great, thanks," Nastos said. He glanced at the moms in the room. They were appraising Irons. Nastos could see why they liked him: good looks, fitness, money.

◻ ◻ ◻

AS HE REMEMBERED WATCHING HIS LITTLE GIRL SKIPPING BEHIND Dr. Irons, hopping from place to place in an imaginary hopscotch game, he felt that nagging feeling that he had left the house and had forgotten something, or like there was a merry-go-round in his stomach that he just noticed had begun to go too fast. He should've stood up and shouted *Stop* or taken his daughter out of the spinning room. But he did nothing. He told himself that there was nothing to worry about, that little Josie was as safe as she could be. And by doing so he made the biggest mistake of his life.

Nastos returned to the reality of the courtroom. He was discreet when he wiped his eyes dry. He was aware that his shoulders and wrists felt raw, then noticed that everyone else in the room was standing.

Nastos stood up next to Carscadden who eyed him as if to say, *It's about time.* The judge was just taking his seat with a sucked-in

12

lower lip, a little put off that Nastos was slow to stand. The judge shook his head and for just a second glared at both Nastos and Carscadden. His Honour slid forward in his chair, smiling broadly for the court and gallery to see. He was an older man in his sixties with grey hair. His smile was practised, insincere and not particularly comforting.

"Good morning, everyone. Madam Prosecutor, are you ready to proceed?"

Nastos didn't hear the court officer ask everyone to rise or say the judge's name. He glanced to his left and saw the prosecutor standing to address the court. Seeing that it was Angela Dewar almost made Nastos smile, in spite of everything. No matter how overworked and frazzled she was, her effortless rigid posture and sharp facial features made looking elegant come natural to her. She was dark-skinned and spoke with a refined Indian accent.

"Your Honour, the accused before the court is here for his bail hearing. Mr. Nastos, a detective for the Toronto Police Service, is charged with murder."

Six Months Earlier
February 21, 2011

DETECTIVE NASTOS OPENED THE door and walked into the central office of the Sexual Assault Unit. A dozen cops sat at cubicles, ignoring ringing phones on their desks in favour of the TV screen, shouting at the Maple Leafs for losing another hockey game while they sipped their Tim Hortons coffees. Play-by-play commentary was accented by shouts from the detectives filling the room. *It's not a crime until it's overtime,* Nastos said the common police motto to himself. All day you do your important personal stuff, catch the hockey game, visit a girlfriend, avoid your boss, then just before you're supposed to go home, you find something plausibly urgent — get a witness to come in for a scheduled interview or follow up on a tip you got hours or days ago. By the end of the year, it was an easy way to make a few thousand in overtime. A hockey game was as good an excuse as any because, for full enjoyment, it required assistance from other detectives.

Nastos went to the cubicle farthest from the door in a back corner. He sat at his desk, turned on the table light and flicked the mouse to bring the computer screen to life. It was five in the afternoon and he was beginning his night shift. The phone rang and he picked it up.

"Nastos, Sexual Assault Unit." With the phone jammed between his ear and shoulder he logged into his email and started deleting junk.

"Yeah, I have all my files here, where else would I keep them? Umm, that one's not really standing out by name. Yeah, that is pretty gross, but this is the Sexual Assault Unit — all of these stories are disgusting. Those circumstances aren't really standing out for me. Harper file? What can I say, the guy's not a productive citizen. Listen, I've got four uniforms and a road sergeant helping me with a warrant in an hour to bust that guy. Tell you what, I'll call back when I'm done with this mess tomorrow afternoon, okay? Yes, Inspector."

He hung up without taking his eyes from the computer screen. He turned to the officer seated at the desk behind his.

"Hey Jacques, where'd the new inspector come from, Walmart?"

Jacques Lapierre had been Nastos' partner for two years. He was scrawny with black hair and spoke with a deep voice. He appeared one hundred percent native, although his mother was Irish. Jacques was promoted to detective at thirty-five for his work in the robbery unit and considered working sex crimes to be punishment. Hearing haunting stories of child abuse wasn't his idea of a good time.

Jacques turned to meet Nastos, saying, "The guy's half-retarded, Nastos. He belongs in the Safety Village."

"Can you come with me for a warrant? It won't take long."

Jacques started closing off his computer and putting a few files away. "I've been itching to get out of this frigging place. I hate hockey. I'll give Jen Baker a call; I'm sure she'd love to get out too."

Nastos turned back to his phone and began dialling a number. "I'll tell the roadies that we're on the way." Nastos spoke into the phone, "Hey Sarge, it's Detective Nastos. Can your guys meet me a little earlier at the convenience store on James Street? Okay, see you then, thanks."

The noise coming from the hockey fans obscured the sound of Detective-Sergeant Koche approaching Nastos and Jacques' work area. Koche like the first part of the word *kosher*. He resembled a somewhat taller and uglier Napoleon. He had penetrating blue eyes, made creepier by the fact that they bulged out of his head slightly. It likely wasn't genetic, Nastos had decided. He probably developed it over time from being wound so tight. It was like a release valve and you could probably tell the barometric pressure in his head by measuring how far out they stuck at a particular time. When he got mad, he would stare in a way that was probably not supposed to be comical. Like all perfectionists, he was a micro-manager as well as imperfect. "Where the hell have you been?" he began.

Nastos turned around and watched as he tried to puff his chest out. But with that shit-locker of an abdomen running at max capacity, it wasn't very intimidating.

"I'm sorry, what did you say?" Nastos asked.

Jacques turned back to his desk and tried to put the show on of being both very busy and very invisible. "Here we go," he muttered under his breath.

"Listen, Nastos," Koche began, "I had a conversation with Sergeant Lister not long ago. He said that he and a few of his guys had a warrant with you today, but that you two hadn't talked yet. It's unprofessional to leave him in the dark, don't you think?"

"It's for an hour from now," Nastos said, trying to hold back his anger. "I just got off the phone with him. It's all under con —"

"If it was under control, Nastos, I wouldn't have to take your phone calls."

Nastos slowly stood up, the backs of his knees pushing his chair back with a loud scrape. He took a slow deep breath, which was completely ineffective in calming him down, and clenched his hands tightly into white-knuckled fists. He considered whether this was finally the time to just beat the shit out of Koche and get it over with. With some people, there is just no talking and this goof was one of them. Nastos brought his face close to Koche's, whose eyes became filled with a stupid wonder.

Koche did what Nastos expected: he flinched. He took a step back then a long slow gulp. Nastos noticed that although the sounds from the hockey game were still going on, the shouting and jeering from the spectators had stopped. All eyes had turned to him and Koche.

He strained to speak softly, barely controlled. "I don't know what your problem is, Koche, but I've been doing this job since long before you got here and I'll be doing it long after you're gone. I don't need to be micro-managed, so why don't you just back off?" He looked directly into Koche's eyes.

Koche's face was flushed red. Veins stuck out on his neck and forehead and he did all he ever knew to do: he yelled. "You think you're being micro-managed? No, you're being babysat. There's more to this job than arresting people; you have to treat people with courtesy and respect, especially superior officers. I could have you in the bicycle unit writing parking tickets by the end of the week, if you don't smarten up."

Nastos needed Koche to throw the first punch so he could respond in kind. "Is that an image that runs through your mind from time to time, me in tight bicycle shorts? Guess what I heard about you was right."

Koche screamed, "I can't believe what you just said, Nastos."

"Actually," Nastos corrected, "it's Detective Nastos, Detective-Sergeant Koche." *That ought to do it. He's going to throw the punch and pave the way for me.*

Koche got to the level of frustration that he often reached and stammered a lame response. "Make sure *Detective* is on your resumé when you apply to the SPCA. And get the fuck out of the office."

Koche turned and fumed out of the room. A dumbfounded wayward detective accidentally found himself in Koche's path and was greeted with a cordial, "Move the fuck over," as Koche shoved his way past.

Nastos noticed the faces in the office; shocked but not entirely surprised. A few detectives shook their heads as if to say, *Nastos, you're playing with fire.*

Jacques spoke as he stood up, grabbing his coat. "You know, you should probably chase him down and un-fuck yourself before it's too late."

"It's just not in me to suck ass. Who could possibly have any respect for that moron? Screw him."

Jacques swung his coat on and locked his cabinets. "Nastos, if not because he's our boss then maybe because he's the Inspector's puppy dog. The two of them can send you anywhere in the police service, you know that. And they hold grudges, Nastos; they'll keep you on their naughty list till they get you. He'll get you kicked out of here if you're not careful."

Nastos shrugged. "And get me away from child molesters and perverts? A big part of me thinks they'd be doing me a favour."

They walked to the door, past the other detectives who rediscovered hockey. He overheard one snicker to another, "There goes Nasty Nastos," followed by a few laughs.

Jacques ignored it and spoke quietly. "Nastos, see it from Dave's point of view. One more promotion and he gets the company car, golf membership, probably even the ceremonial helmet with the antlers. If he identifies and corrects a problem employee, he looks like a hero. His rank can be dangerous."

Nastos knew that Jacques was only trying to help. It only took the first week of working together for Nastos to figure out that Jacques was the most trustworthy partner that he'd ever had. "Well, my plan is to do my thing and soon enough he'll get his promotion and some new blowhard will be here trying to make a name for himself so I can get a fresh start."

"Well, as far as team building goes, you at least have style. Really, who goes up to their narcissist boss and implies that he's gay in front of a squad of detectives?"

Nastos smiled. "Yeah, let's get out of here. Maybe we can find the chief and call him a cross-dresser."

◻ ◻ ◻

NASTOS WALKED UP TO THE FOUR UNIFORMED OFFICERS WHO WERE standing in the parking lot of a convenience store, sipping coffees. It was barely above freezing with no snow on the ground. All of the cops were men: three were fairly young, in their twenties, and Sergeant Lister was at least thirty-five, well over six feet tall—a not-so-gentle giant of a man. Jen Baker and Jacques got out of their car and joined them. Jen was the best sexual assault officer he had ever heard of. At barely five feet tall, maybe 110 pounds, with long blond hair and a youthful face at thirty-two, Jen could connect with victims when other detectives failed. Standing near Sergeant Lister, she looked like a child herself.

Nastos smiled as he got close enough to address the officers. "Hey guys, thanks for coming early."

"No problem, Nastos," Lister said.

He began, "Okay, I know you're busy, so I won't waste too much of your time. I've got a copy of the warrant for everyone to read and sign." Nastos passed it out. The officers signed it with barely a glance. Nastos continued, "Basically it's an entry and arrest warrant. Page two is search and seizure. We want computer files, disks, camcorders and tapes and anything else like that. Dude's name is Sean Harper; this is his picture." Nastos passed out some photos. "You've all read the file. He works at a video rental store. He lives alone and has no kids of his own. He's raped three kids who will go to trial and six that we know of who won't."

Lister was the only one to speak. "Child molester, eh — he's probably going to resist arrest, then I'm probably going to kick his ass." A few of the officers exchanged smiles. Watching Lister jackhammer that special someone could be a thing of beauty.

Nastos had to try to give the appearance of wanting them to take it easy. "While I certainly can't disagree with your thinking, sir, my name is going on the arrest report so if it's all the same, I'd like to take this guy in all in one piece. Any questions?" They all shook their heads no, disappointed.

He could have confirmed the officer's suspicion about the man becoming combative with police, could have said he's resisted police before. It was part of policing jargon, the code words to say, "Beat him into a coma, I'll fix the paperwork and buy you drinks after." There were times when Nastos had given the pack of wolves the scent of blood, but not this time. With

19

Koche's eyes on him, he couldn't take risks like trusting anyone except his partner, Jacques.

Nastos directed the last of the troops. "Detective Baker, you're first one in the door."

"Sure thing, Nastos."

"And you," he pointed to a lanky rookie in the back with a nametag that read *Post*. "Take the fastest guy from your shift here with you around back in case buddy bolts. The rest of you come up with me."

Despite having one hundred percent confidence in Baker, Nastos still felt a certain amount of protectiveness for her. At her size, if Harper was going to make a stand Nastos would rather she not have front-row tickets to a brawl. But the shortest officer usually went in first so the guys back in the line could see what they were walking into. And she signed up for this job and never asked for special treatment, so he wasn't going to offer her any.

◻ ◻ ◻

IT WAS A FOUR-STOREY BUILDING. THE ENTIRE FIRST FLOOR WAS MIXED commercial places: a Chinese food place, dry-cleaners and massage parlour. The elevator was too small to hold all of the cops so they wedged the door open to put it out of service, then took the stairs. The line of officers trudged up the winding staircase, led by Sergeant Lister and Detective Nastos. The smell of stale sweat and damp hung in the air. Nastos consciously avoided scraping against the walls, which were coated with a kind of filth best not contemplated.

Sergeant Lister read Nastos' face. "You miss working on the road, Detective?"

"I miss kicking down doors; I don't miss the shit-hole apartment part."

"You got to take the good with the bad and the ugly." Lister opened the door into the third floor hallway.

Nastos, Lister and the other officers took positions a few doors down from Harper's apartment. Nastos keyed the mic to his radio and spoke to Post. "You in position at the back?" There was a pause. *Poor skinny kid's likely looking for something to eat.*

"It's all ten-four on this end." The radio crackled.

Jen crept up beside Nastos. They smiled dryly to each other. Nastos moved to the suspect's door. They all withdrew their pistols, pointing them down to the floor.

The door had a walnut veneer with a peephole; it smelled of urethane and piss. Nastos knocked. "Pizza guy." There was a noise, a movement. "Pizza guy," he said again. "Hey pal, you want your pizza or not?" This time the movement sounded rushed, reckless. Glancing at the sergeant, Nastos whispered, "Someone's in there screwing around," then nodded sideways at the door.

Lister put his gun away and shouldered the door open. There was a loud crack as the jamb split followed by the thud of the door swinging into the back wall as the officers, led by Jen, exploded into the apartment shouting, "Police, search warrant!"

Shouts of "Clear," or "Nothing here," came from the officers as they fanned out through the apartment. From a back room one of the uniform officer shouted, "Hands *up! Get your hands up!*"

Nastos turned from the back washroom and headed for the shouting officer.

Nastos recalled how people always say that responses to stress are either fight or flight. This, in his experience, was totally inaccurate. Anyone who has ever gone on YouTube and watched civilian responses to terrorist bombings, ever witnessed a car accident happen right in front of them, or even been startled by an evil niece or nephew from behind a door, never reacted by punching the first person they saw nor by running full speed in a random direction. No, what they do is what everyone actually does in such an instance: they freeze in place, staring wide-eyed, and in that time of hesitation police are trained to charge aggressively.

Harper was standing in a back laundry room with his hands over his head. As scared as he was, he was also pretty scary. Tall and broad with long greasy hair, forearms sleeved-out in faded prison ink—he almost certainly had hepatitis. Harper obviously hadn't bathed in a few days and he stank of stale cigarettes. In fact, the whole apartment stank of stale smoke, Nastos now noticed. There was no need to check with the photo in his back pocket.

"Yeah, that's him," he said.

"I think he tossed something out the window," the officer said, not taking his eyes or gun from the man. Nastos shoved past Harper, pushing him against the wall, and peered out a small half-open window covered with a dingy blind. He keyed the mic to his radio again. "Hey, Post, you see anything fly out this window?" He stuck his hand out and waved it around.

Through the radio he heard Post say, "Yeah, some DVDs and a memory stick. We'll pick it up and meet you upstairs."

Sergeant Lister walked into the small room. Having put away his gun, he had two hands free, so he grabbed Harper, turned him around 180 degrees and handcuffed him as painfully as he could. Harper made no effort to resist. His eyes were wide open, pupils as big as dinner plates. He was breathing quickly but was trying to slow himself down.

Harper's voice cracked. "What the hell is this, who the fuck do you people think you are? You've got no right to come in my home like this—"

"I don't need to take any bullshit from a child molester," Nastos interrupted. "If you had any brains at all you'd close that hole in your face till I read you your rights."

Harper said, "You lay one hand on me and I'll sue your ass off." It wasn't very convincing.

Nastos turned to Lister. "On second thought, Sarge? Can one of your guys read this guy his rights in here? I want to have a look around."

"Sure thing, Nastos." Lister pointed to one of the officers, then followed Nastos out of the room.

They searched the apartment, going through cupboards, drawers, laundry baskets. Nastos went over everything again, this time

searching jacket pockets in closets, the toilet tank, the freezer—
everywhere idiots think you're too dumb to check. When Jacques
found that the home computer was turned off he unplugged it and
started packing it up. "I love when we can take their stuff," he said
to Lister. "It's just so satisfying."

Lister replied, "I'm happy enough just seeing their faces when
we smash their shit to pieces right in front of them." He smiled.

"Yeah, it must be how firemen feel when they rescue drunks
with the jaws from fender benders."

Jen had a uniformed officer following her around as she took pictures with her digital camera. "Hey guys," she called out to everyone,
"continuity is key, gentlemen, so if you hit a jackpot, let me photograph
what you found in place before you move anything. And who's the
rookie so I know who is getting screwed with the property reports?"

An officer got Nastos' attention. "Check this out here, Nastos, I
think I'm going to puke."

Nastos walked into the room and found a cop flipping through
Polaroids. Looking nauseous, he handed them over to Nastos.
Nastos began flipping through the pictures, his hands moving
slowly away from his face as he lost the strength to make himself
go through any more pictures. It wasn't long before he couldn't bear
it. His hands dropped down to his sides; he took a deep breath. He
put all but one of the pictures in his jacket pocket. Nastos shouted
to the officer with Harper.

The officer came into the living room, guiding the prisoner in
front of him by the elbow. Nastos rotated the photograph he was
holding so Harper could see it.

"Tell me who these guys are with you in this picture."

Harper evaded eye contact and ignored the picture. "No, I don't
know."

Nastos moved closer to Harper, close enough that he had no
choice but to look back at him. While there was every sign of fear,
all Nastos saw was a deranged man. *He probably tells himself that
he really loves them.*

"Can you follow me while I take him down to my car, officer?"

"Sure thing, Nastos."

"And can you ask Jacques to deal with things here?"

"No probs, boss."

3

THE AIR WAS COOL AND FRESH
and after the day he'd had, after the disgusting apartment building,
not to mention his current company, it was like a cool bath on a
smouldering hot day; he welcomed it into his lungs. Outside, it had
begun to darken and in the slow mist, streetlights cast cone-shaped,
amber pools of light on the sidewalks below. Nastos directed Harper
into the back of his caged, unmarked police car, secured the door,
then got into the driver's seat. Nastos turned the car on and cleared
the mist from the windshield with the wipers, leaving them on a
slow intermittent scrape.

He pulled the car away from the curb and entered the sparse
city traffic. Brake lights refracted through the moisture on the
windshield, collecting like blood splatter before the wipers glided
across the glass, scraping it clean for the time being.

"I've never been arrested before," Harper said, breaking the silence.
He tried to sound confident, but he had a long way to go.

Nastos made eye contact with Harper in the rear-view mirror.
He spoke in a neutral tone. Some people just needed to be treated
with respect. Playing Harper the right way was critical in getting anywhere with him. Nastos wanted the other men in the picture who
shared Harper's disease. *I'll ask a few questions*, he thought. *Harper
won't know it, but he'll be telling me what has to happen next to get
him to talk. Is it going to be good cop, bad cop or worst cop?*

25

He checked the roadway, then glanced back to Harper through the rear-view mirror. The man was nearly shaking with fear. Pale, taking deep rushed breaths, with sweat pouring down his forehead, it was like he'd had a hit of acid and was on a seriously bad trip. Harper's gaze met his. As the car's mirror vibrated, the narrow slit revealed something more. Nastos knew this happened to him. He knew that he projected evil onto the offenders he arrested. It made what was coming easier.

He saw the dark, sunken eyes of a sexual sadist strobing to life under the passing yellow streetlights. Officer Friendly checked out, leaving something behind that more closely resembled Frankenstein's monster. "Who's in the picture with you?" Nastos asked.

"I don't know who he is — I already told you that." Harper looked away from his reversed image. Nastos had no sympathy for Harper, who squirmed vainly to get comfortable in the cramped back compartment of the car. Poor guy had to turn his feet sideways because of the intrusive metal cage that divided the car in two. He couldn't lean back into the seat without crushing his twisted wrists in the handcuffs. Nastos drove slowly, allowing the imposing environment to become part of his psychological warfare. *Let the pain burn into your memory, Harper. You just made your first mistake. Two guys in the picture but you say you don't know who he is? You know one of them. That's a good start.*

"Well, I've got to say, Sean, you do some pretty disgusting things with complete strangers. You know, I have a daughter about that age."

Harper shrugged. "Wish I could help, sorry." He chewed his bottom lip then tried to get comfortable by leaning his head against the fogged window.

The Impala smoothly drove past the Gardiner Expressway, south on Cherry Street. Nastos turned left, following a sign for Cherry Beach Park. Away from the streetlights, on the north side of Lake Ontario, a person can look south and see not much of anything but open water. Although there was a tree line about a mile south of shore from the Toronto Islands, the combination of thickening mist and blackness

26

from overcast skies erased any contrasts in the black of night. It was as though nothing existed beyond a fifty-metre radius.

"I don't recognize this part of town — where are we?" Harper asked.

Nastos put the car in park, turned the lights off and sat there. The outside world had disappeared. The detective turned and spoke to Harper in hushed tones. "Listen, I'm going to make this really easy for you. Tell me who those two guys are in those pictures, the pictures where you're raping that little kid."

Harper let out an awkward laugh with a *this guy is kidding me, right?* expression on his face. Then his twisted smile froze as he wondered what was going to happen next. This was about the time they all did that. "My lawyer's going be all over this guy if he touches me," he said, barely audibly, as if ready to confront the fear signals his body was no doubt sending him. More forcefully, Harper said, "Get me my lawyer. Take me to the police station so I can make my call."

Nastos nodded his head to himself gravely. He turned off his cell phone and put it in the glove box, from which he grabbed something else, a small hand-held device that he slid into his pocket. He got out of the car, closed his door and approached the back window; Harper's face wore a mask of pale fear.

In one motion, Nastos pulled the door open, grabbed a fistful of hair from the back of Harper's head and began dragging him out. Harper dropped onto the cold ground in a heap, face first, getting a fist-sized wad of sand in his mouth. He kicked and squirmed, trying to bring his knees up under him as he tried to spit and clear his mouth, but the cuffs held his hands behind his back and the sand choked his breath. He took as deep a breath as he could through his nostrils, vainly trying to suck in air.

Nastos took the hand-held device out of his pocket and engaged it. A rapid-fire series of loud clicks burst through the air as he drove the taser's electrodes into Harper's testicles. Harper bucked and squawked as if his throat had been squeezed in a vice. He spat most of the dirt from his mouth in a strained puff, gagging. By pulling a knee up, he was able to roll partially onto his side and there he tried to use his teeth to scrape the filth and sand from his tongue.

Nastos spoke calmly. "I need to stop those other guys, Sean; who are they?"

Harper's guts rolled audibly, as if the contents of his stomach were churning with filthy clothes during a washing machine's spin cycle. Harper's forehead found a cool smooth rock. He tried to lean against it and ignore the detective, but Nastos would have none of it.

"You like raping defenseless little kids, Sean. It stops now. You're going to talk. Do it now rather than later and save yourself a lot of misery." Nastos kicked Harper again, this time in the stomach. Harper, in turn, immediately spilled his guts all over the ground, then rolled away onto his back. Using his legs, he wiggled back and actually pulled himself into a sitting position.

"What the fuck are you doing?" Harper sputtered. "There's no way you can get away with this. Those other cops saw me, they're witnesses."

He stood in front of Harper, about six feet back, and engaged the taser. Neon blue electricity rattled between the terminals, with a sound like a million sets of insect teeth gnashing on flesh. Nastos' voice remained calm. "I don't want to leave any marks. You're prob- ably not going like this part too much."

Harper shouted, *"Wait — wait — wait!"* then felt a hot-cold convul- sion rippling throughout his stomach. Muscles twisted and contorted, contracting so hard he couldn't breathe or speak. Then the pulsing stopped. He gasped in a long full breath and collapsed onto his back.

"Make a mental note of how good you feel right now, Harper, 'cause in about five minutes, you'll be begging to feel this good again."

Harper's head rolled around. "Please stop," he said between laboured breaths.

"You know the price to get off this ride. Who are those two other guys?"

Harper's head darted around like he was lost. The fog remained thick at the water's edge, only the slightest of waves from the weakest

of wind differentiated where the land ended and water began —
tones of black on black.

"You ready to start helping me, Mr. Harper?"

Harper wasn't exactly Navy Seal material; they both knew that.
It was just a matter of time. All Harper had to do was figure out
that Nastos wasn't going to give up until he got an answer. No one
in their right mind would endure this for two hours, or even ten
minutes, then cave in anyways.

"Okay, okay," he began. "One guy is my brother-in-law, George.
The other guy I met on the internet. He lives in town. I don't know
his name, but I have a phone number, a cell."

"See, that wasn't so tough, now was it? Where does George live?"

"He has a photo studio; he lives in the upstairs."

"Okay, the other guy, what's his number?"

"It's on my cell, under the initials W.G., W.G. for weird guy."

Nastos figured that whatever Harper had decided was weird
was something best not pondered. "Let's get you back in the car," he
said, helping the man up to his feet.

Harper collapsed into the soft leather back seat. The air was still
warm from the heater. Nastos dampened a rag with lake water and,
after cleaning Harper up, threw it into the lake. Harper reacted to
the cool, clean water by exhaling deeply. He obviously felt a lot better with all of that bullshit behind him. Nastos watched periodically
from the front seat as Harper sat emotionless, reflecting on what
had happened. He probably wondered what he had done to deserve
such violence and pain. Even the worst of animals were heroes in
their own stories. Harper was trying to decide if he was still a hero,
or if maybe he had that coming. Nastos could have told him how the
taser would leave only minor marks and no lasting damage, but he
chose instead to remain silent, to let Harper stew in his juices.
Harper sat hunched forward with his knees apart, trying to comfort
his aching balls.

Nastos hadn't kicked him full force, just enough to get his point
across. And whether that moment was past by a tenth of a second

29

or a million years, it was just as gone, just as irretrievable. Nastos wished he had kicked him harder.

"You know, Detective, in places like Thailand it's basically legal. Even in western cultures, girls got married at thirteen only a hundred years ago."

"Things have changed, Harper; I guess you're just not a man of the times."

"Yeah, I was just born a hundred years too late."

"And too close to me."

◦ ◦ ◦

NASTOS STARTED THE CAR AND CIVILIZATION RETURNED WITH LIGHTS from the dashboard and sounds of talk radio ragging on the mayor about something. Nastos said, "You may not know this right now, Mr. Harper, but I just did you a favour."

"How's that?"

"That kick in the balls, that pain will go away. You got a little scared but that was all I tried to do, scare you, and you'll get over that too. What you should remember here is that you did the right thing by stopping those other guys that you helped identify. You're protecting other people's babies."

Harper slumped forward. He was making laboured snotty noises, like he was trying to suck back some tears.

"How you feel right now is how those little kids felt after you raped them. And now you have felt a little pain so they don't have to feel pain anymore. Now, you can tell everybody that I beat it out of you — no one will believe you anyway. When we get into the police station, you can just tell your story and try to reclaim some of your dignity. You must have done some good things in your life, Sean, surely; let's try to get something positive out of this too. Learn to control and suppress this small part of your life. Don't let that be the only thing that defines you as a person."

30

Nastos tried to ignore the irony of what he had just said and Harper wasn't yet convinced that the cop had done him a favour. "People will want me dead; my picture is going to go everywhere."

His concerns were probably justified, but Nastos wanted to minimize them. "Sean, you're going to be a flash on the screen. This is a big city with big city problems. You won't even make the six o'clock news. It's time you reinvent yourself and leave the monster someplace like the Dark Ages."

Harper's gaze dropped to the floor; he appeared lost in thought. The car pulled away from the river's edge, turned around slowly then moved toward the city lights of Toronto.

4

September 6, 2011

NASTOS RELUCTANTLY RE-
turned to the reality of the courtroom. He was still sitting next to
Carscadden; Dewar was just across from him. The judge's voice
brought him out of his digression.

Judge Ryan raised his hand to stop Prosecutor Dewar mid-
sentence.

"I'm sorry, did you say the accused is a police officer charged with
murder?" Ryan picked his glasses up from his desk and reviewed a
piece of paper.

"Yes, that's right, Your Honour," Dewar said.

"And did you say who the alleged victim is?" he asked.

"Sir, the alleged victim in this case was the Nastos family dentist.
The accused discovered that the dentist was molesting children."

Judge Ryan seemed to be trying to put it all together but was
obviously missing large pieces, so Dewar continued.

"Yes, Your Honour, Detective Nastos discovered that Dr. Irons was
molesting his own daughter. Not long after, Dr. Irons' body was found
floating in the lake at Cherry Beach; he had been beaten to death."

Judge Ryan opened a notebook and began scribbling notes.
"Okay, well, let's continue on, then I have to make a statement for the
record. Go on, please, Ms. Dewar."

"Certainly, sir." She glanced at Carscadden and then turned her
attention on Nastos for the first time. She looked him right in the eye.

Nastos was unsettled by the direct eye contact with Prosecutor Dewar. She was the one who could take him away from his family. She toiled in this place daily among the gallery's swarm of degenerates, the filthiest of street criminals. It was her job to put away the worst society had to offer and despite this, she had an elegance about her that Nastos thought he had put out of his mind.

She was pretty. While his wife was blond, slightly freckled and socially talkative, this woman was dark, of few words and — despite their past together — a complete mystery. Of all people Dewar just had to be the one who was going to try to take him away from his family by putting him in jail for the next twenty-five years. He tried to gather himself, to read anything the prosecutor's face might reveal, but missed his chance. An elbow from Carscadden broke his train of thought.

"Detective, yes, I could check her out all day too, but I need to ask a few questions."

Nastos lowered his head and leaned over to Carscadden. "Fire away."

"I've very briefly read over the file here. Is your union going to cover your court costs?"

"No, I wasn't working when I allegedly murdered this guy, I was off duty."

"*Allegedly*, nice one, Detective. Now, can you get a surety to supervise your release? Your wife, a work buddy, your mom or dad?" Carscadden likely assumed that Nastos' wife would be arriving at any moment, and failing that, cops are tight with each other. He probably thought Nastos' parents might even drop by, but he was wrong.

"No, I don't have anyone who will do that. The guys from work all disappeared; they would face consequences for supporting me and they all just want to stay clear for the time being. My wife can't do it."

"Why can't she?"

It was obvious to Nastos that Carscadden had not read much of the file and the way he flipped through the pages didn't inspire much confidence. "Kevin, my wife can't do it because my daughter will be

33

a witness against me. I can't associate with a prosecution witness, so I can't live at home. Both of my parents are dead. Looks like I'm going to go to jail. If I go to jail, even overnight, I lose my job, whether I'm convicted or not. I have no money to fight this, and we both know a guy only gets as much justice as he can afford. I'm screwed."

Carscadden said nothing and to Nastos, he appeared not to care. He scratched a few notes in his legal pad, like he was trying to work something out.

Rubbing his wrists, Nastos caught up to where Dewar was in her opening remarks.

"Your Honour, the accused is also charged with lesser included offences subsequent to the murder. The prosecution asks for remand in custody, for concerns to the public."

Ryan nodded to Carscadden. "Mr. Carscadden, anything to say?"

Carscadden took his cue, getting to his feet to address the court. He had a strong but tired voice and spoke like an actor who had recited his lines in the mirror so many times that the script became as unemotional as reading the obituaries of strangers. It was a passionless drone of words. "Last name Carscadden, initial K for the record, Your Honour. Since I plan to only help the accused obtain bail, then pass the case along, I request that I have a few days with him to get a position together for whoever takes this on. I would then submit, sir, that we revisit the necessity for court-ordered detention at that time. While I agree with my colleague that these are serious charges, the defense's case will reveal that the prosecution's case is very weak." Carscadden glanced at Nastos and decided to say something positive, even if he felt it was a lie. "In fact, my client is innocent of this crime. We ask that the court allow the accused at least forty-eight hours to get some affairs in order either way." Nastos barely reacted. *When you need John Wayne, you get Pee-wee Herman. I hear the jails in Vancouver are okay.*

Dewar stood, and both she and Carscadden began an exchange with the judge. Nastos gave up and tried to tune it out. He decided he was better off thinking of the future, hoping for a nice protective custody cell, maybe something in a corner with reduced hallway traffic and a roommate in for tax evasion or failing to buy his yearly dog licence.

"Your Honour," Dewar said, "I don't want to spend all day on this. We can't show special consideration for a police officer. He's supposed to uphold the law; he should be held to the highest standard."

Nastos noticed how Carscadden winced and his face flushed at the words *highest standard*. It was about time he started taking this seriously.

"Your Honour, despite Ms. Dewar's revealing beliefs that the police deserve fewer rights than the rest of the public, I wish to remind you that Detective Nastos has not been convicted of anything. A week, how about a week, Your Honour? Detective Nastos has an exemplary record of public service."

The judge asked, "Just to understand you, Mr. Carscadden, you mean because your client was good at his job?"

His face flushed red; he flipped through the blank pages on his desk like he might find answers there. Carscadden was getting flustered. "To speak very bluntly, Your Honour, if this man had molested the detective's daughter, it sounds to me that the only member of the public that need fear Detective Nastos need worry no longer. My client is a risk to no one and the only real issue here should be, if my client has an appropriate surety, to post bail, surrender his passport and be allowed some time to get his personal affairs in order."

Nastos appreciated Carscadden's directness. He'd seen judges listen to the same prefabricated arguments from the same lawyers day in and day out for years. He'd learned that if one can generalize and say there is one trait shared among all judges, it's the unbridled excitement they feel when a lawyer actually goes off script and opts for plain-spoken truth.

"Mr. Carscadden, I'm going to grant bail, let's move on to the issue of a surety."

"Your Honour," Dewar interjected, "the defendant cannot reside at home since his daughter's a witness. Who is Mr. Carscadden suggesting be a surety, himself?"

35

Carscadden had no time to say how bad an idea he thought it was, but Nastos did have the time to read the serious aversion on his face.

"If you want your client to have bail, sir, unless you have a better option, you will have to monitor his whereabouts, for the time being."

"Me, sir?" Carscadden couldn't sound less enthusiastic.

"Well, for the time being, you're his lawyer. If you want him to have bail you'll have to monitor him, unless you find another volunteer."

Nastos watched incredulously as Carscadden turned around from the judge and surveyed the gallery like he was searching for someone to bail *him* out. His gaze fell on the little wanna-be gangsters, street prostitutes, crack addicts — how long before he would realize that a miracle wasn't going to happen? Then his eyes settled nervously on Nastos. "It would be an honour, sir," he said unconvincingly, like it was his plan all along.

Judge Ryan continued. "The accused can only leave the residence of Mr. Carscadden for court purposes or to deal with legal matters while in the company of his surety, Mr. Carscadden. Mr. Nastos will also be afforded two hours per day to attend to personal matters, but under all circumstances the accused will have a curfew of six p.m., seven days a week. Further release conditions include no communication directly or indirectly with any witnesses that the prosecution is to call. I'll provide you with the complete list on the recognizance."

"Thank you, sir," Mr. Carscadden smiled.

"Now a few words for the record," the judge began. "Since the accused is a police officer in this court jurisdiction, we'll need to make arrangements with the trial coordinator to get an outside judge. I won't be able to take this myself since I have to clear my docket completely for personal reasons. Ms. Dewar, what dates do you have in mind to start the Prelim for the trial?"

Dewar opened up a paper notebook and flipped through the pages. "Sir, Chief Crown Attorney Scott has some dates highlighted." She flipped some more pages. "Monday, May seventh, 2012."

Nastos considered the prospect of arranged and supervised access to his daughter for the next eight or so months. They may as well just convict him. It would give the people working against him more time to manufacture evidence, discard the evidence that could clear him. Time would work against him. *There's another way.* He leaned over to Carscadden and spoke softly.

Carscadden recoiled and spoke loud enough for the judge to hear him. "Are you crazy?"

Judge Ryan said, "That date doesn't appeal to you, Mr. Carscadden?"

Carscadden stood up to address the court. "Sir, my client is offering to waive the pre-trial and go directly to trial."

It was an unusual request but Ryan didn't flinch. "Ms. Dewar?"

She flipped through the book some more. "It looks to me that there is time available beginning September twenty-sixth for a trial but that's short notice for defense to prepare."

Nastos nudged Carscadden's arm. "Let's do it."

"This is a seriously bad idea, Detective." Carscadden addressed the court. "That's fine with us, sir. The sooner we can start the sooner my client can clear his good name."

Carscadden sat down next to Nastos. "What the hell are you thinking?"

"I'm calling their bluff. If they want to fight, let's fight. I'm not giving them months to get their shit together."

Judge Ryan mumbled something to himself as he shuffled the papers on his desk. "Madam Clerk, if you could formally read the charges into the court record, then the accused will be remanded into the custody of Defense Council Carscadden as his surety."

The judge banged the gavel. Nastos and Carscadden slowly rose to their feet. Dewar began digging out another court file for her next case.

The charges were formally read: on the night of August 14, Steve Nastos did, knowingly and with premeditation, commit the murder of Dr. Jason Irons, DDS, of Toronto, by beating him to death in the City of Toronto.

"How do you plead, sir?" the judge asked.

"Not guilty, sir." Nastos hoped he sounded confident, self-assured, but he didn't think that was the case. With a bang of the gavel, he was free to leave.

The two police officers who had escorted Nastos into the courthouse not long ago said good luck and left. Nastos wanted to say something — *hey thanks*, or something a little less lame — but was distracted by Carscadden, who grabbed him by the arm. "Follow me, Detective, we'll get the releases signed, then we need to talk someplace private."

◻ ◻ ◻

AS CARSCADDEN LED NASTOS OUT OF COURT THROUGH THE SIDE DOOR, another man left through the main doors. He was shorter than Nastos, with a beer belly, and his blue bulging eyes were narrowed and angry. He knew he couldn't talk without shouting, so instead he typed into his BlackBerry. *Jeff, your dyke prosecutor just let Nastos get bail, she's useless. We'll have to come up with something else.* The man stuffed the BlackBerry back into his pocket. A court security officer approached him in the hallway, intending to take away his phone — its use was barred from court — but when the angry man, Detective-Sergeant Koche, thrust his badge up, the court security officer backed off with an apology.

Koche stormed down the courthouse steps two at a time. He jogged across the street into the coffee shop on the corner. It was quiet and warm inside, with only a few customers — there was a Tim Hortons down the street that got a lot more business. There was a man waiting for him in a booth, and Koche took a seat to join him.

"Thanks for coming, North," he said, wanting to get right to business.

"Thanks for asking," North replied. He was a gaunt man in his forties. To Koche, with his slowly exploding waist line, North was the kind of thin only drug addicts and movie stars attain through starvation. When he reached for his coffee, his sleeves pulled back enough to reveal faded, green-tinged tattoos on both forearms — some kind of Chinese symbols that were meaningless to Koche. Immature crap from that Chinese or Japanese phase a lot of metal-heads went through in the '80s. North's eyes were sunken with dark circles underneath and his face was lined with wrinkles deeper than expected for a man his age. Koche had no idea that it was because North had just come from the gym and was dehydrated from a ten-mile run. Koche wasn't interested in North's hobbies or interests; it was all about business.

Koche knew that North was becoming popular. It was called the Old Boys' Club, a private investigation and security resource company that worked the grey areas of the law. They obtained information where the police would be hampered by warrant requirements and other procedural speed bumps. They stalked, intimidated, extorted, harassed just about anyone, for whoever paid the bills. Lawyers and police used them regularly and they were beginning to get a lot of work from the general public and franchise stores as their reputation grew. Only current and retired police officers knew the full extent of their services, though. It was an industry dependant on discretion, something North knew well and had proven to Koche first-hand while he was still a police officer.

"You don't mind looking after this, do you?" Koche asked.

"We both know I don't turn down much business." North ran his fingers through his hair and scratched the side of his head. "We both know I got the time," he added.

Koche sat in an awkward silence. There was something between them that needed to come out, but he didn't want to be the one to start it.

"It was your plan, your cash and your drugs," North's eyes fixed on Koche.

"I know, I know," he replied, trying not to be the first to look away, but he was.

"They took my life from me. I was a good cop. And where were you? Where the fuck were you?"

Koche knew the topic was a minefield and tried to turn the conversation away. He comforted himself, thinking, *If North had any other options, he would have either left already or shot me dead.* The detective-sergeant, a man with twenty years of police experience in drugs, robbery, intelligence and the street beat couldn't help himself for checking North over. Koche knew all the behavioural characteristics of armed persons. Aside from obvious signs like a jacket or sweater hanging heavy on one side, there are the nearly unavoidable idiosyncratic movements. Armed people frequently tap, pat or otherwise move and wiggle to make sure their weapon is still in place — the same way a person might touch sunglasses on top of their head to see if they're there, people with guns also got used to pressure and weight from the weapon and had to remind themselves by touching it or moving that it was still there. Koche saw no sign that North was making any such movements, but that was not enough to put him completely at ease.

"North, listen," he said, "I've got something in the works; if it pays off, I'll bring you in. I owe you."

North obviously didn't have much trust in Koche. "What do you want me to do this time?"

"You remember Steve Nastos?"

"Yeah — arrogant fuck, thinks he's the best cop that ever was. I worked robbery with him years ago."

"Well, it's him. He's up on charges. I want you to follow him. Catch him breaching. I want him to serve some time."

"Receipts or no?"

"Not a chance."

"Two hundred a day plus expenses." North produced a BlackBerry and dialled through to a memo pad. "You screwing him like you did me?"

"No," Koche said, "with Nastos it's Shakespearean; he did this one to himself."

"You owe me a lot more than a week's work and you know it." North put both hands on the table and got ready to push himself up, but he slumped back as if trapped between two bad choices. Koche decided to throw something in to tip the balance. Lies were only harmful if people ever found out about them.

"You know it was Nastos, right?"

"What?" North asked, confused.

"Holy shit." Koche tried to feign a *you poor stupid bastard* look. "You know it was Nastos who ratted us out years back."

North's face went pale and he froze, expressionless. *Yup, that got him.*

He didn't leave. Instead, his fist tightened around his coffee cup.

North looked Koche in the eyes. He was probably trying to figure out if he was being played, but the newly directed anger was exhausting his ability to reason. Koche had sufficiently poked the bear; now he just had to make sure he wasn't the slowest runner.

North surprised him with an abrupt response. "Okay, I'll do it. But I want the first week in advance, Koche, cash."

Koche didn't realize he had been holding his breath till he exhaled. "I'll get it to you tomorrow. Call my cell anytime, especially if you get anything good. Got it?"

"And if I need to bring someone else in, that's on your dime too," North added, meeting Koche's stare.

"Listen, this is sensitive, I don't want some druggie—"

"I'll tell you what I want. I'll get this guy for you, but I can't do 24/7 surveillance myself. I assume you want pictures or video of this guy breaching, which would be easier with backup. You know this. I started this business from ground level. If you want to hire the Old Boys' Club, you leave it up to us, to me, to decide how the job is done." 41

"Use your best guys," Koche relented.

"Just like old times, boss. Except this time, if you fuck me over I'll saw your hands off, then light your face on fire with gasoline. It would be worth the twenty-five years I'd get. Be the easiest time of my life reliving your screams every night. I'd even videotape it and put it on YouTube."

Koche tried to gulp, but his mouth was too dry.

"So, it's a deal, then. Here's his current picture. He'll be coming out in the next twenty minutes or so." Koche pressed *Send* on his phone to email a picture of Nastos and Carscadden to North. "That's his lawyer. He's going to be staying at his place for a while. I'll send the address by text. Like I said, five grand. Sound good?"

"Good enough for now."

◻ ◻ ◻

WITH THE DEAL DONE, KOCHE LEFT NORTH TO SIP AT HIS COFFEE AND consider the direction of his life. And North did that for a little while. Then he took out his cell phone and called the most irrationally dangerous goons who worked for the company. They often referred to themselves as the Inhumane Society. They were self-aware enough to know that they lacked any vestige of conscience. Their names were Shawn Eade and Michael McCort.

5

CARSCADDEN LED NASTOS past a security kiosk to the court services department. Nastos' arms and shoulders ached as he walked, still stiff from being bound behind him for so long. They stopped at the bullet-proof glass wall, the kind with thin wire running through the panes. Shielded from the public view and with no government workers in sight, it made for a quiet place to talk.

Carscadden was certainly making every effort to be a no-bullshit guy, getting right to the point. *He must be getting antsy for a drink.*

"Okay, Nastos, I'm going to make this really easy for you, okay?"

"Sure thing, Carscadden, what?"

"Did you do this thing?" He looked right in Nastos' eyes, searching for any eye movement, any wavering of confidence.

"What the hell do you think?"

"That's a bullshit answer, Detective. I'll give you one more chance at it."

43

Nastos tried not to shout. "What kind of idiot do you take me for?"

Carscadden took a deep breath and exhaled, glaring at the ground. He began nodding to himself, agreeing with whatever the hell he was thinking. "I'll tell you what I'm going to do for you," he said. "I'll do what I said in there. I can help you get a decent lawyer suitable for the kind of client you are. I'll even start the procedural foot-dragging to buy you some time out of jail."

"What do you mean, more suitable for the kind of client I am?"

"One who doesn't care if you win or lose, one who doesn't care if you co-operate. I defend co-operative clients because I don't want to make a fool of myself in there."

Nastos sounded madder than he intended to. "Hey, I need you, I'll pay. What else do you want from me?"

"Co-operation. I can only help if you're honest," Carscadden pleaded. "That's the only way to make things as good as they can get. The last miracle I worked was paying my credit card."

Nastos tried to be as convincing as he could. "I didn't do it. If I did, I would just say so. Everyone knows I wanted to kill the asshole, but I didn't. Looks like I'm going to be the next David Milgaard, the next wrongly convicted. I'll rot in jail for a decade before this all gets sorted out. By then Josie will be in university and I'll be a stranger to her. When I heard he was dead, I was elated. I watched the TV footage every chance I got. I even wanted to call CityTV and get a copy of the newsreel. Then out of nowhere it came back on me."

Carscadden replied out of his vast legal experience. "Well, of course you'd at least get asked about it. They'd go through the whole patient list searching for red flags."

"Yeah, well, I didn't get asked anything until I was arrested. Koche and whoever else, Clancy Brown I guess, they started working the evidence to meet the theory instead of the other way around. And once somebody gets arrested, investigations stop cold." He slammed his hand against the wall. "Bang, it's over, I was the guy."

Carscadden didn't respond verbally; he just let out a breath. Nastos observed his young face, soft, boyish. He needed a better lawyer, but that wasn't going to happen. He got another idea. He said, almost in a whisper, "I'm going to have to sort this one out myself."

"Pardon?" Carscadden asked.

Nastos made the decision. *It's the only way out.* "I said I'm going to have to solve this one myself."

Carscadden mentioned the obvious. "You're on bail, you have a curfew. You breach, you're in jail."

"And what if I don't breach, where am I then? In jail." Carscadden didn't seem to have an answer. "If I just sit around and do nothing, I'm essentially losing my life. Worse, I'm giving it away. Madeleine, Josie, gone. I'm not the suicide type."

"That's what's wrong with you cops — with your high school education, you still think you know as much as lawyers. I'll tell you, at no time did any of my law professors tell me to listen to the cops because they have their grade twelve diplomas mounted on their wall so they really have their shit wired tight. If you're innocent, I can win this."

Nastos wasn't convinced. "I know it sounds stupid, but I just don't think anyone is going to look out for me better than me. I'm facing life in jail."

Carscadden shook his head. "If you're innocent, we can win; if you trust me, co-operate."

Nastos was barely listening as he consciously stopped the circular loop of *but I didn't do it* and began running through last night's interrogation. *What did they ask me, what did they not know about the murder?* He noticed Carscadden staring at him, wanting an answer. He knew he was going to need a lawyer, and there wasn't a line-up begging for the job. "I can't promise anything when my family is on the line. But I'll try my best to co-operate and tell you everything I'm doing."

Carscadden didn't seem too happy with the answer. "I'll tell you what is about to happen. I'm going to go out and deal with the media. You stay here. When I'm done and the coast is clear, I'll come back in and get you. We need to go to my office before we go back to my place. I have some stuff to do there. It won't take long."   45

"Okay, sure, I'll stay here."

"But one thing, Nastos. Why the hell did they bring you right in the front of the courthouse? They could have brought you in the back like everyone else."

Nastos shrugged. "Just to embarrass me, I guess, turn it into a circus. They have a lot riding on my conviction. Maybe give me a taste of how bad it can get if I decide to fight this."

"Who?" Carscadden asked. "Who would make that decision?"

"I already mentioned Detective-Sergeant Koche. The other is Jeff Scott, the chief prosecutor."

Carscadden stood there, appraising him. He sounded like Clint Eastwood when he said, "Well, it looks like you pissed off the wrong guys."

"At least I got a decent judge. At least it gives me *some* hope."

Carscadden seemed a little confused. "You mean Ryan?"

Nastos thumbed toward the courtroom. "Yeah, you just saw him."

"Yeah, well, maybe you missed it, pal. Ryan passed it off. He got promoted to the Appeals bench, so he's clearing his schedule. I heard Dewar say Montgomery is taking it as a favour. He's retiring afterwards so he doesn't give a shit about who he pisses off."

Nastos felt his face turn pale.

"What?" Carscadden asked.

"Montgomery. He's got a nickname—the hanging judge."

◙ ◙ ◙

CARSCADDEN STOOD OUTSIDE THE COURTHOUSE, HIS BACK TO THE wall and a semi-circle of reporters standing on the steps just below him. In his past life as a corporate lawyer, he never had to deal with media. Reluctantly, he decided to select from the idiotic reporters shouting at him, to avoid tougher questions. The closest reporter, a young woman of maybe twenty-five, held out her microphone to him like it was a fistful of free candy, like she was doing him some kind of favour. *This poor girl*, Kevin thought. *So young and pretty — she probably lives in a bubble where every guy treats her like gold, patiently patronizing her till they get her pants off. This should be an easy one.*

"Mr. Carscadden, Mr. Carscadden," she began. "Last month your previous client, Mr. Kalmakov, was acquitted of multiple murders. Now you're defending a police officer also charged with murder — are you trying to set a reputation as a last-chance lawyer?"

"Did I hear you right?" Kevin said incredulously.

"It's no secret about your past troubles, Mr. Carscadden. About how Mr. Kalmakov and you—"

"Don't bother finishing that question, don't bother—" Carscadden held up his hands, stopping the reporter mid-sentence. He hoped to find someone with a legitimate question. "Does anyone else have questions about *this* case?" With his hands back in his pockets, tightening into fists then relaxing, he took a breath and pointed to another reporter, inviting a question. This older woman pushed her way to the front after the previous woman retreated, satisfied with her soundbite.

"Mr. Carscadden, there is a general opinion out there that you saved a mass-murdering gangster, Kalmakov, from multiple life sentences. People wonder if you're going to be party to another miscarriage of justice, in this case that of the corrupt cop. Any thoughts on the matter?"

Deep breaths just aren't enough sometimes. Carscadden considered the question before answering. It was important that he didn't make any attempt to mitigate the detective's possible crime. That would be like pleading guilty with an excuse. Saying *no comment* was worse. He took a moment to get his thoughts straight. He prepared himself, then answered, slowly at first. "Listen, no one thought I would win the Kalmakov case, but I did. I won because the facts weren't strong enough to convict him. For all of you—and I mean you, and you," he pointed at certain reporters, "who did not sit in court every day, did not read the transcripts, did not weigh the full set of facts and circumstances in the case, to arbitrarily decide that Mr. Kalmakov was guilty, based on the lampooning that he took prior to the commencement of the trial by other reporters, is repugnant and basically not worth much more consideration than that which you failed to give my client in the first place.

"I should hope, if any one of you were every charged with murder, that the evidence be completely overwhelming and convincing before any of you would want to be thrown in jail for life. The government owes us all that much. Mr. Kalmakov is not a crime boss, he

47

happens to be a Russian guy who inherited his dad's trash business and bought a restaurant; as cliché as it is, it does not make him a mass murderer. The real story should be that I went fifteen rounds with all of the resources of the prosecution and got a TKO. Too bad you, the conspiracy theory contingent, just don't want the facts to get in the way of a good story. I mean holy, holy crap."

The reporter carried on like she had not even heard a word he had said. Another shouted another question. "So, is Nastos your client or isn't he? Are you going to defend the disgraced Detective Nastos in his murder trial?"

"I was the duty counsel today, that's all. It was just my turn for prelims. I was basically the guy left standing when the music stopped. Let's try not to taint the jury pool by implying he's guilty on accusations that have not had the benefit of being tested under oath.

"As far as defending him, the detective is a smart man, I advised him to get counsel that is congruent with the position he plans to take with his case. I told him I just had a long trial with Mr. Kalmakov, which took me away from other clients. A case like Officer Nastos' is not readily appealing to me. Sorry, but I have to get to my office to finish some work I have here. If I stay any longer I'll have to bill you my hourly rate."

The scrum drastically changed direction when another man came out of the courtroom. He was about five-nine, in his fifties, with a pudgy face and a salt-and-pepper moustache. The cameras turned to him and Carscadden waited to see what the fuss was all about. He asked one of the reporters, "Who's that guy?"

She said, "The spokesperson for Dr. Irons' other victims. He's a total hothead."

A reporter asked, "Mr. Whitmore. How do you feel about a man being arrested for killing Dr. Irons? Does that provide some closure in this travesty?"

Whitmore became incensed. Hs face went red and blotchy. "Closure? That cop deserves a goddamned medal. He'd make a good police chief as far as I'm concerned."

Another reporter asked, "You don't think he should be punished at all?"

Whitmore's eyes darted left and right like he was looking for words. "Well, I guess maybe a reprimand for not televising it. I'm sure there's a large demographic out there that would pay big money to watch a child molester get beaten to death 'cause our legal system is a fucking gong show."

The first reporter got another question in. "You've had legal problems in the past, have you not, sir?"

Whitmore stood tall. "Two little punks busted the wrong car window. Why don't you track those kids down and ask them if they've ever done that again?" He began pushing his way through the crowd. "That's it. I'm done."

Carscadden left the steps of the courthouse, heading back inside to get Detective Nastos.

◘ ◘ ◘

WHEN THEY LEFT FOR THE OFFICE IN CARSCADDEN'S CAR, THERE WAS only silence. Carscadden tried to recall very specifically when exactly he'd lost control of his life. Once successful by most standards, he'd had money, what he thought was a happy relationship and a good reputation in his legal community. He blew the whole mess in less than a year. Now he was an alcoholic and a bottom-feeding, last-chance lawyer to gangsters and nobodies, vainly trying to save them from the person they should have feared the most: themselves. *Moving here from halfway across the country to reinvent myself was supposed to be better than this. I could use a drink.*

With a sideways glance, Carscadden watched Nastos sitting silently in the passenger seat. *He must be exhausted. And it has been a long enough day for me too. It'd be nice to get away somewhere warm, some all-inclusive with a poolside bar and just forget everything. But, there's no way that can happen, not now.* Maybe it was the stress of the day, the low blood alcohol or who knew what, but he thought that a car about one hundred metres back seemed to be following them.

49

6

CARSCADDEN'S OFFICE WAS IN A
red-brick Edwardian row house in the Garden District, across from
Moss Park. It didn't look much like an office and the area wasn't the
greatest, but Nastos wasn't complaining. His wife, Madeleine, had
been a real estate agent for just over ten years, so it was second
nature to consider properties the way she did, as resale. This place
seemed to have little hope on its own. It would take the entire strip.

Carscadden led Nastos in the charge through the double front
doors. A secretary, maybe forty-five years old, sat at a desk. She had
thin brown hair cut just at the shoulders and the square, black-framed
glasses that were in fashion these days. The office space was neat and
clean, much more her influence than Carscadden's. He barely even
acknowledged her on his way past but stopped in his tracks when she
said, "Mr. Kalmakov is waiting in your office, Mr. Carscadden."

Carscadden turned back to her, eyes wide with surprise. "You
said Kalmakov? In my office?"

"Yes," she said, "he said he'd be more comfortable in there rather
than the waiting room. He kind of just walked right in."

Carscadden eyed the closed door to his office and rubbed his
hands on his pant legs. "Do you mind having a seat here, Detective?
I won't be too long."

"Sure, take your time."

"Thanks. Ms. Hopkins here will bring you a drink if you like."

Nastos took a seat across from her. "I don't need a drink, but thanks," he said.

Hopkins smiled coyly, speaking to Carscadden but watching Nastos for a reaction. "If I hear a hacksaw, I assume I have the rest of the day off?"

Carscadden replied without missing a beat. "Yeah, just hire a new lawyer and carry on without me." He walked into his office, trying not to appear terrified.

Hopkins stood up from behind her desk, reaching her hand out to Nastos. "Nastos, is it? Are you a new client?"

Nastos quickly stood up, reaching his hand out and shaking hers. He saw that she was wearing a snug, long dark skirt with a white blouse — conservative choice — but it did show that she was lean and curvy.

"Yes, ma'am, I am."

She smiled broadly. "Is it a divorce?"

"Pardon?"

"Is that what brings you by, you're getting a divorce?"

"Actually, no, I'm on trial for first-degree murder."

"So, you're married then, umm." She sat back down and went back to her work.

◊ ◊ ◊

A MAN WAS SITTING ON THE CORNER OF CARSCADDEN'S DESK, SMOKING a cigar and flipping through a magazine. He was wearing an expensive suit and an overcoat. He was a little shorter than Carscadden, but was wearing a hat that made him seem taller.

"Nice to see you again, Mr. Carscadden." Kalmakov's voice was warm and deep, like that of an old friend who knows you better than you know yourself. He smiled, placing the magazine on Carscadden's desk and reaching out his hand. Kevin took it apprehensively, saying, "You too, Mr. Kalmakov."

"Viktor," Kalmakov said, "call me Viktor." If Carscadden had not been so concerned he might have read Kalmakov's smile as admiration, but being familiar with the man's reputation through his colleagues, he was seeing warning signs in the most benign of places. "Well, I've got a little something for you, sir."

Kalmakov used his left hand to open his overcoat slightly and with his right he reached into his breast pocket. Kevin was happy to see a piece of paper rather than a nine-millimetre Glock appear. Kalmakov passed him the paper; it was a cheque. It was for him and it was for a lot of money.

Kalmakov filled the silence. "I added a little bonus on there."

"I see that. What for?" Kevin asked.

"To put you on retainer; you're still my lawyer and I am still in your confidence. Got it?"

"Of course, Viktor, but you didn't have to—"

"And hey, if you ever need anything you give me a call. I owe you one. Actually, I owe you a few. Anything."

"Greatly appreciated, sir. I hope I don't need to call. I mean I can't imagine . . ."

"Well, I can show myself out. You know, it feels good to help you out after what you did for me. I won't forget it. Good day, sir." They shook hands again.

"Good day, sir." Kalmakov left the office. Kevin stood still, with his eyes on the cheque for a moment, then placed it on his desk. He opened the briefcase he had placed on the floor, pulled a file out and spread it on his desk.

◘ ◘ ◘

52 NASTOS GLANCED UP AT THE MAN WHO WALKED INTO THE WAITING room from Carscadden's office. Kalmakov was a little surprised to see someone with Hopkins. He began to excuse himself as he walked past, but stopped, his eyes squinting at Nastos. "Excuse me, sir—hey, aren't you the guy who killed that molester?"

Nastos set aside his *Reader's Digest*, as gripping as the story was, and recognized the man: Viktor "The Saw" Kalmakov.

"That's what I'm charged with." He still couldn't believe it, but he was getting better at saying it.

The man stuck out his hand. "Victor Kalmakov. Pleased to meet you."

Nastos shook the hand of The Saw.

An intercom buzzed and Carscadden's voice interrupted. "Ms. Hopkins, can you come in here, please?" She got up immediately and walked to the door. She certainly seemed to enjoy the attention that she got from the two men as she squeezed between them to get by. When she went into the office and closed the door behind her, Kalmakov turned back to Nastos, broadening his stance as if settling in to talk a while.

"I'll tell you what; they should have given you a medal and put your statue on the courthouse steps."

"Thanks, I guess." Nastos had no idea where this was going.

"You know, I don't have a problem with you cops. You have a tough job, dealing with the black kids shooting up the neighbourhoods, drug addicts robbing banks, gooks kidnapping each other — you catch one and what happens to them? Nothing. And don't let the fact that he's broke bother you about Carscadden; he's a good lawyer."

"He's really that good, Kalmakov?"

He nodded confidently. "He is. You know, Detective, after going through the process of being wrongly accused of murder myself, it's reminded me of how lucky I am in this life. I have a nephew with autism and I see how hurtful and how much work it is for my sister. It would mean the world to her if just once, she could have a conversation with her little boy, to hear him say that he loves her for how she has sacrificed her life to take care of him. I find myself thinking of that all the time now. Then I was charged with those heinous murders where everyone thought I did it, but Carscadden saved me."

"That's a shame about your sister's boy. I can't imagine how hard that is." Nastos crossed his arms in front. Kalmakov unconsciously did the same.

"I'm just a small businessman. I own a waste management company picking up and dealing with people's trash all day and have a little restaurant as a hobby. I think we have a lot in common. So, trust me to mean it when I say that if there is anything you think I can do to help you, have your lawyer give me a call, okay?"

"That's a generous offer, Mr. Kalmakov."

"And tell you what; my restaurant is Frankie's on College and Manning downtown. Drop by anytime, on me. Carscadden knows the courtesy table."

"I've been there once with my wife; it's a nice place. We love Little Italy."

"When you're on the other side of this, all I ask is that you pay it forward. Be kind enough to let me pass it on to you, so you can pass it on when it's your turn."

"I've got a bail curfew at six p.m., but nothing beats an Italian lunch."

"Good. Well, I have to go. Don't give up." Kalmakov swept out of the office, leaving Nastos alone. He recovered the discarded *Reader's Digest*, but he couldn't seem to focus on the story. He presumed that Carscadden was looking for a way off the case and he wasn't so sure that it was a bad idea.

◊ ◊ ◊

CARSCADDEN SAT WITH HIS ELBOWS PROPPED ON HIS DESK, HIS HANDS on his forehead. He looked up only briefly when Hopkins entered, then turned his attention back to the files in front of him. She pulled a chair up alongside Carscadden and slid close to him. She had a way about her, how she moved: confident, open. Carscadden was oblivious.

"Is this all the disclosure we have received so far for Mr. Nastos out there?"

"Yes, the last fax was a few hours ago."

"I just need to clarify something in my mind." His eyes closed and squinted as he searched his memory.

"What's that?"

"So we never actually got a patient list from the dentist's office?" Carscadden asked.

"Sure we did, that's the blue file on your left. Some of the names have been vetted out by the prosecutor." Hopkins slid the list out, showing her boss.

"Yes, thanks. But, I just don't get their strategy here. They should be making the list of children's names longer, to demonize the victim and further the motive for Mr. Nastos. It's just basic tactics."

"I thought sex assault victims, especially children, have the right to privacy. Disclosure is illegal, right?"

"True, but I'd get access to properly defend my client. Maybe I'm just suspicious by nature, but I wonder why she would do that. For us at this stage its all about Charter motions and disclosure requests. We bury them in delays to have time to develop a better overall strategy. Of course, at some point Nastos is going to have to tell me his side of things. I don't want this trial to get past the next hurdle. We're also missing a copy of the police force's Policy Directives on Internal Investigations, the Arrest Procedures and the booking video for Nastos."

Hopkins asked, "How are they relevant?"

"Just by their absence so far, really. Why would they not turn them over?"

"I have no idea; they're likely just overworked like everybody else in the country. We should be glad that they're sloppy."

"Check this out." Carscadden held out a sheet for her. "A drug inventory of the dentist's office — like I care how much banana-flavoured analgesic they had handy." Carscadden tossed the sheet aside, but Hopkins took a glance at it. 55

"Well, Kevin, it does seem like there's a lot of OxyContin missing."

"What's that?" he asked.

A sympathetic smile spread across Hopkins face. He felt that she thought he was naive about something. She'd be in her mid forties — not that he was going to ask — making him ten years younger than her. She seemed to have intuitive knowledge about how things operated on the other side of the street. He probably couldn't tell the difference between a street hooker and a go-go dancer, but at least he'd be honest about it.

Hopkins explained, "It's called hillbilly heroin. It's a narcotic analgesic that a lot of people get prescribed for whatever reason — back injuries, dental surgery — but a lot of people get addicted. They resort to buying it or some replacement drug on the street because there aren't any treatment programs."

"Umm," he said, thinking. "Okay, well, we'll look into that at some point, but first is the list and the usual disclosure stuff."

"Anything else missing?" She put her hand gently on his shoulder.

Carscadden didn't notice. "What about the dental assistants? Why weren't they interviewed? They should have statements here, even if they didn't have much to say."

"Sure, Mr. Carscadden. I'll send a fax in the morning requesting everything. Maybe they have the interviews with the assistants, but for whatever reason, they just never sent it."

"The last thing is a synopsis on the investigators themselves. I want their workplace history. Start with the lead investigator, Clancy Brown. Find out what type of guy he is."

"Where do you expect me to get that from?" Hopkins smiled.

"The same place you got all of your stuff for the Kalmakov case, which I'd probably be better off not knowing," he said, without smiling.

Hopkins rubbed her chin, her lips pursing as if trying to work it all out. "I think I can do that one."

Kevin sloppily flopped the pages back together and wrapped an elastic around the folder to hold it all together. "This case is a mess. Good luck to the poor bastard who takes it."

"You're not going to?" She looked at him like he was crazy.

"This is a loser case, plain and simple. Which is fine, can't win them all, but I don't see this helping me attract high-paying clients."

"Listen, it's a paycheque, how can you afford to turn it down?"

"The Kalmakov payment will help out for a while, won't it? Take a gander at that fat, juicy bastard." He slid the cheque in front of her so she could read it. He gave her a smug smile.

"You need to read over the books, boss, we're dirt poor. You can barely even pay me this month, so you must have developed a taste for cat food."

"I thought this had us above water?" He deflated back into the chair.

"Kevin, when we first started here, you were the one that gave me the big speech. 'What do we call something with a nickel in its back pocket, a sob story and a heartbeat? A client,' you said. Take the case. We need the money."

"You blowing all our cash getting your hair done?"

"I know this case now — this is the cop who killed the molester. This is the guy who goes to work every day hearing the most disgusting stories, seeing the most disgusting things. Finally, it gets to him and he kills one of these pieces of shit. Don't you think he deserves someone in his corner?"

"A good man, who did a bad thing?"

"And needs some help."

"And needs some help. And we need the money?"

"Yeah, we need the money."

"Umm."

"Think it over." Hopkins got up, sliding her chair back against the wall. She watched Carscadden as he turned his back to her to put the file in his briefcase. He was the man who'd given her a job she wasn't qualified for, gave her the office basement apartment for free and asked for nothing in return. Of course, that didn't mean she didn't want to give him something. If only he'd make a move.

7

"IT'S NOT MUCH, BUT IT'S ALL mine. And, for the time being, all yours." Carscadden invited Nastos into his apartment with a wave of his hand. It had mercifully been decorated well enough by previous occupants, but Carscadden seemed not to notice. He had been using his couch as a place to fold laundry—probably during the hockey game—a recycle box was on the floor in the kitchen and there were dirty dishes and glasses all over the living room. Carscadden was a helpless bachelor.

Nastos took his coat off and handed it to Carscadden, who had just put his own coat away in the closet. "Carscadden, I haven't properly thanked you for what you are doing for me. I can't tell you how much I owe you for this." Nastos was tired. The events of the last twenty-four hours were catching up to him.

"To be honest, Nastos, I've never heard about much charity coming from lawyers either. They'll argue charter rights to help some businessman off an impaired driving conviction, but they wouldn't cross the street to piss on you if you were on fire." He produced a twisted, sarcastic smile, shaking his head. "Hungry?" Carscadden went into the kitchen and opened the fridge. He pointed vaguely down the hall. "Hey, have a look around; you can take the room down on the left."

Nastos kicked his shoes off and checked out the room that was offered. Carscadden shouted from down the hall, "So, is it Steve, or Nastos, or Detective?"

The room was smallish, ten by ten with a spare single bed that seemed never to have been used. "Better call me Nastos. Everyone does. The only one who calls me Steve is my wife. You start calling me Steve, I . . . I just don't think it's a good idea, especially since we're sharing your condo. How about you? Do people call you Kevin or Carscadden?"

"Friends call me Kevin."

"Okay, then I'll call you Carscadden. Nothing personal — just to remind us that we've got a business relationship."

A quick check of the closet revealed a set of spare sheets and a few extra pillows. Nastos tossed them onto the bed for later, then returned to the kitchen to find Carscadden rummaging through the cupboards as if he had never gone through them before.

"What's for dinner, Mother Hubbard?" Nastos asked.

"Looks like ketchup sandwiches and rock soup, Nastos." Carscadden closed the cupboards and went for the phone. "I'll order some pizza. I've been meaning to get groceries, but I can't cook, so I haven't really got around to it."

"Is there a store around?" Nastos wanted a good meal after the day he'd had.

"Yeah, there's a decent grocery place down the street. It's a good one with a sushi bar and everything. Hey, let's get some of that, a few California rolls."

"I'll tell you what. I love cooking; it's what I did to get through university. I'll zip out to the store and pick up something decent. You like fish, steaks, pasta?"

Carscadden did a bad job of suppressing his enthusiasm.

"Hey, it's not a big deal, we can order in — I wouldn't want to put you out." Carscadden raised the phone again, but Nastos was already taking his coat out of the closet and putting his shoes on.

"I get two hours of ROR a day, and it's 4:30 — I have enough time to pick up something good."

Carscadden put the phone back in its cradle and walked over to the front door.

"Want me to come with you? In case the press or —"

"No, I'm good, but thanks. I need to clear my head."

◻ ◻ ◻

THE SIDEWALKS WERE BUSY WITH PEOPLE COMING HOME FROM WORK to Toronto's gentrified Queen and Spadina area, known as Queen West, full of upscale boutiques, chain stores, restaurants. It's also the entertainment district and walking distance to the Hockey Hall of Fame. It was the perfect place for a single guy like Carscadden — too bad there was no way he could afford it.

Most people at this time had either got off the city buses, or walked up the dank stairwells from the fluorescent world of the subway system. Narrow side streets were busy with commuters trying to avoid the larger clogged arteries running through the heart of the city, resulting in smaller backlogs that were just as time-consuming. But to Nastos, it was paradise. He wasn't in the back of a paddy wagon going off to the Don Jail, just across town; he was, for the time being, free.

All he wanted was his daughter on one side and his wife on the other. Being between the two of them was like being between the poles of two magnets. They had their own family language with inside jokes born from inside jokes.

Visual segues flipped through his mind. Where he was born, what his parents were like, his grandfather telling stories about shipwrecks, lost treasures, lost lives and lost souls — none of those things defined him anymore. His years pursuing child molesters — everything was overshadowed by the new story of his life. His daughter had been molested and would never be the same again. That's what defined him as a person now, the factoid that people would whisper about him after he left a room or was introduced to someone new. He was the guy who let a monster get his daughter.

He sucked in the cool downtown air through his teeth, tasting the diesel exhaust of city buses, driving people on the brink of poverty to their dead end jobs. It was still better than the inside of the unventilated interrogation room where he'd spent most of the night. It helped clear his mind to recall step by step how he had come to identify Irons.

He found the photograph when he arrested Harper, of two guys with a kid. Harper had eventually had an *a-ha* moment — courtesy of jolts from a 50,000 volt taser blast into his nuts — and identified one man as his in-law. The other one, *Weird Guy*, remained elusive.

The picture got tagged, put into evidence and forgotten. That was in February. The first time he ever took Josie to Dr. Irons' dental office in July, he got the creeps from Irons and didn't know why. It had been months since Harper's arrest, and he had seen hundreds of pictures and faces since then. After Harper pled guilty, Nastos checked the picture to see if it had any investigative merit before ordering its destruction. This time he recognized *Weird Guy*. It was Dr. Irons, the dentist Josie had been going to since they had moved to Port Union three years ago.

Remembering back, she seemed unaffected on the first few visits. Then there were slow changes. He tried to tell himself that warning signs weren't there because she had been knocked out when it happened, but he knew that wasn't the entire truth. She had been sore; she had had a tender abdomen, and she began to have nightmares. He was supposed to be an expert, and he had missed it.

He realized that he had clenched his fists, his finger nails digging into the base of his thumbs. He made himself relax.

He walked into the grocery store, relieved to see it was new and clean. There was a good fresh selection of just about everything and when the waft of fresh naan bread came from the bakery, Nastos knew it was going to be Indian food for the night. He got everything he needed for Tandoori chicken, naan, curried vegetables. He grabbed some breaded shrimp for an appetizer and something to drink. He took a few moments to pick up some bread and eggs, not trusting Carscadden to be much of a breakfast guy.

By chance, he passed a phone kiosk. He grabbed a blank Pay-As-You-Go phone and a few phone cards, knowing that an untraceable

61

cell could always come in handy. He glanced at his watch. It was 5:40. *Time to go, I have to be back at six — it's going to be close.* He paid for his things at the cashier and began walking back quickly to Carscadden's place.

Nastos passed store fronts, some with angled glass. A reflection caught his eye — a man holding a Sony camera. At first, he was concerned when he realized he was being followed. Someone, likely Koche, had someone following him right now to catch him out late so his bail would get revoked and Nastos would go to jail for the rest of the trial. But automotive surveillance was very easy to spot once you knew how, and even easier to defeat. Nastos didn't have time to backtrack, cross the street or go into stores to aggravate whoever might be following him, though. He had a deadline and had to make it. If anyone really wanted to catch him, they could also just randomly go to Carscadden's door at all hours and knock. If Nastos was not there, he could kiss his freedom goodbye.

Near the apartment, he saw a commotion on the sidewalk involving a small crowd of half a dozen people and a homeless man. As Nastos got closer, he saw that the homeless man was spinning in circles, shouting to the universe and swinging an empty liquor bottle at anyone trying to sneak past him. The road was too busy with traffic to get around that way and the only other way involved plowing through a cedar hedge and climbing over a four-foot fence. The man was wearing a greyish overcoat and looked surprisingly clean. His drug-addict-like gauntness stuck out to Nastos, since many homeless people were far from emaciated.

62   Nastos read his watch. 5:58 p.m. Screw this. He put all of the grocery bags into his left hand and charged forward at a fast walk. Nastos thought he caught the slightest smirk from the man's lips and for the briefest of moments he thought that he had seen the man before. But all homeless people acted and smelled the same, didn't they? The man's teeth clenched and he swung the bottle directly at Nastos. A woman from the crowd of blocked pedestrians shrieked while Nastos flinched, taking the strike across his shoulder and face.

The glass bottle careened to the ground and smashed to pieces. Nastos charged the man, shoulder-ramming him to the ground. The homeless man reached up to grab Nastos' collar and pulled him to the ground on top of him. Their eyes met. Nastos realized that he wasn't homeless and that he seemed familiar.

The man gasped and caught his breath, smiling at Nastos.

"Looks like you're going to be late for your curfew, Nastos." The man checked his watch.

Nastos pushed himself up to his feet and grabbed the bag of groceries. The man on the ground held up his hand and took a picture of Nastos with his watch in the foreground. Nastos gave him the finger. "Whoever the fuck you are," Nastos began, "stay the hell away from me, if you know what's good for you."

"I'm just getting started with you, Detective."

Nastos backed warily away from him and turned to walk down the street. He never noticed the Buick parked at the curb where a man was recording everything with a video camera.

As Nastos approached the apartment, he did see a squad car parked out front. There were two cops sitting in the car and an ominous vacancy in the back seat. Nastos went right to the front door of the building.

A voice shouted from the cruiser, "Hey Nastos."

He turned to see an officer he didn't recognize. He didn't need to check his watch to know it was after six. "Yeah?"

"We got a call that you were out on your own and were going to breach; looks like someone finds you interesting."

The officer was in his late thirties. Word was likely out that whoever caught him breaching was probably making a good career move. "Thanks for the heads-up."

"Anytime." That was one cop not interested in making a name for himself; the last solid cop in the entire country. Nastos considered that he was probably supposed to have gotten into a longer confrontation with the man disguised as a vagrant; if he could just put a name to the face. Whoever it was, it was a set-up.

He trudged up the stairs, glancing back briefly when the squad car pulled away. If different cops had been called and he was found out past curfew, in a fight just hours after being released, he'd already be on his way to jail for the rest of the trial. *Going to have to be more careful, Nastos.*

□ □ □

CARSCADDEN HAD THE APARTMENT MOSTLY CLEANED AND WAS sitting on the couch in front of the TV by the time Nastos walked back in with the groceries. Clothes had been packed away, the dishes washed and stacked. Carscadden didn't seem to notice any marks on Nastos' face, but his cheek still hurt like hell.

He smiled at the full bags of food being dropped on the kitchen counter. "The hockey game's on in an hour."

Nastos began emptying the bags. "Good; you like Indian food?"

"Oh yeah, I love that stuff. You can make it?"

"Yeah, I dated a girl once — she was a pro. She taught me a thing or two."

Carscadden reached forward to the coffee table, cracked open his briefcase and started going through Nastos' court brief. "There's beer in the fridge."

Nastos was getting dinner started when Carscadden walked over to the bar stool, bringing the court brief with him.

"So, Detective, what do you know about the prosecutor here, Ms. Dewar?"

Nastos opened the fridge and grabbed a beer. "She's from Appeals, probably pretty smart."

"Do you know anything about her personally?" Carscadden flipped through a few pages.

"No, nothing personally. I mean, I think I heard she's dating a woman, so if your defense strategy included sleeping with her you might want to save yourself some trouble and go right to plan B." Nastos washed his hands and started separating the chicken meat from the bone on the cutting board.

"You kidding me? She dresses like she's on the hunt for a man."

"She used to date guys way back, so I guess she's bi. Maybe she just likes to dress for success. I guess you haven't taken her on before?"

Carscadden shook his head. "I wish. It would be nice to know her better. I'm wondering if she smells a promotion in this mess?"

"Forget about Dewar — the problem is the other two. Jeff Scott and Dave Koche, they're political. They smell blood in the water and want to get the biggest bites out of the bloodbath." Nastos rinsed his hands again then put the chicken in a wok. He put the cutting board in the sink, then started on the potatoes. "Carscadden, how did you get Kalmakov off his charges?"

Carscadden shook his head, putting his drink down. "I got lucky. There were no witnesses and forensics was sloppy. Plus he had a rock-solid alibi; the prosecution eventually had to seek a stay in the proceedings and after a year the charges were withdrawn. There was also no compelling motive for Kalmakov; he barely knew the guys that were killed. Kalmakov thought I was a miracle worker though.

"Your mess, on the other hand, is a dream motive as far as the prosecution goes. It's nearly justifiable homicide, for Christ's sake. They must be thinking that if our case is weak we'll pull that card and beg for the jury's mercy. It might even work, you know. But I think it would be premature to go that way. Let's see what the prosecution is able to prove first."

"Did you ever have kids, Carscadden?" Nastos spiced and oiled the chicken, flipping the wok, and put the cubed potatoes in a pot, starting the burner.

"No, thank god. Not that I don't like kids, I love kids, but not with that bitch. You must miss your little girl."

"My father told me that when I first held a child of my own, the first thing I would think would be the first thing that all fathers think."

"And what is that?" Carscadden finished his Coke, then went back to the fridge to get another.

"That I would do anything to protect her, that I would do anything for her. He was right. I didn't even need to complete the sentence for myself. I just held her and this feeling came over me. I felt this connection when I saw her little face. Her eyes opened and she looked up at me so calmly — she was so content, she didn't cry or fuss. I guess she was exhausted from being born. I would do anything for her. I had doubted my ability to have that instinct but I guess it's in all of us just waiting to come out." Nastos wanted to have her with him now, to smell her skin. *Even if I couldn't do much to make her feel better, at least she wouldn't have to be going through this without me.* "She's not doing very well," he added. "I should be there."

"I can't even imagine. All I can say is I'm sorry."

Nastos blinked and avoided eye contact. "If I had only come across this guy a few months earlier —" Nastos did not want to finish the thought, not even for his lawyer.

"Isn't that the foundational regret of mankind: if I only knew then what I know now?"

Nastos agreed. "I guess it is."

Carscadden spoke as if he'd finally made the emotional connection to the case. "I'll do everything I can, Nastos, whatever it takes."

During dinner, they talked about everything except court. How the Teacher's Pension Fund ruined professional sports in Ontario. They talked about politics and both answered what they would do with ten million dollars. Kevin Carscadden never asked his client if he had murdered the man, and Detective Nastos never made any declarations of innocence.

While Carscadden watched the last period of hockey, Nastos went to his bedroom. He called home to speak to his wife but there was no answer. She was either out showing a house or she was at a counselling session with Josie — or she was just avoiding him. He didn't leave a voice message, deciding to send a text instead. *Call me when you can,* he typed.

He lay back in the stiff, narrow spare bed, but after an hour or so he knew he couldn't sleep. Despite being up all night being interrogated and sitting in a sweaty courtroom all day, it was impossible to lay back and do nothing. Anxiety about going to jail was eating him alive. It was time to do something.

He returned to the TV room and found Carscadden asleep on the couch. At the front door, he put on a jacket, took a house key from the man's key ring and locked the door behind him.

◊ ◊ ◊

MR. WHITMORE WAS AS GOOD A PLACE TO START AS ANY. THE REPORTERS didn't have to scratch too far beneath the man's surface to find free-floating hostility. Every time he was on TV, he was losing his mind. While he waited for the elevator to take him to street level, Nastos thought about the ridiculous interrogation Detective Clancy Brown had tried. *Defective* Brown's secret to success, Nastos knew, had been joining the local Masonic Lodge. Lacking imagination was a career limiter in the police service — unless you made the right friends. Nastos couldn't think of a relevant question he had asked during his entire interrogation. Brown just repeated the same thing a hundred times too many, "Just confess, Nastos, you'll feel better."

He left Carscadden's condo through a back door, jumped the fence and walked through the back alley. He saw a city bus coming and took it to the subway station. He'd rather have walked or taken a cab, but the TTC was better for anonymity. Unlike a taxi company, no one could call the TTC later and ask if they picked a guy up in a certain area at a certain time. He took the northbound train to St. George, then headed east to Kennedy where he caught the 86A Scarborough bus east along Lawrence. After about an hour he found himself in front of Whitmore's. It was a detached house on Lawrence Avenue near Meadowvale, just a mile from the closest police station, Forty-Three Division.

He took out his pay-as-you-go phone and dialled the number. No answer. He dialled again. No answer again, until the third ring.

"Hello?" It was a woman, Whitmore's wife.

Nastos said, "I need to talk to your husband."

"Who's calling?" she asked.

I should have had something ready to say. "It's work. We have a situation." He hoped that Whitmore wasn't retired, or laid off.

She didn't speak to him again; instead he heard the phone being jostled around and some muffled talking.

"Yeah?" asked a groggy voice.

"I need to talk to you."

There was the sound of movement, some creaking, then the click of a light coming on. "Who the hell is this?"

Nastos took a breath. "I'm out front right now, take a look."

There was more noise, then a curtain was pulled back and a face peered out. Nastos was standing under a streetlight. He waved.

"I thought you were under house arrest?"

"That's why you're not going to tell anyone who you're speaking to. Not even your wife."

The phone went dead. The face disappeared from the window, and the light turned off. A moment later, the porch light came on and the door opened. Whitmore was wearing a bathrobe and construction boots. He walked up to Nastos, who met him on the porch.

Whitmore pointed around the back of the house. "By the garage, out of the wind."

Nastos walked there, then turned around just in time to catch a heavy punch to the jaw. He collapsed to the ground, banging the back of his head on the garage's brick wall.

Whitmore was on him immediately. He ripped Nastos' jacket open and frisked him down. "You wearing a wire, cop? This some kind of fuck-over?"

Nastos let him finish his search. When Whitmore began to back away, Nastos pushed the man's hands off and pulled his jacket closed. *What does he have to hide that he asks if I have a wire? Who calls it a wire anymore?*

"Get up," Whitmore said. "Now what the hell can I help you with?"

Nastos got to his feet, deciding whether to reply to the man in kind. He adjusted his coat. "I'll make this quick. Where were you on the night of August fourteenth?"

"You asking me if I killed that asshole? If I feel like taking your place at the defense table?"

"Yeah."

"You've got a lot of nerve, my friend." Whitmore stuck his chest out and raised a defiant chin, daring Nastos to come at him.

On my own terms, jackass. Nastos began, "I couldn't care less if you killed him, it's just that I didn't and I don't feel like spending the rest of my life in jail."

"And?"

"And if you can point me in a direction, on my daughter's life, I'll make sure you're never implicated."

Whitmore softened a little, his shoulders dropped and his lower lip pursed; he was considering. "I must have read you all wrong, Nastos. I just figured that you did it."

"Part of me wishes I did," he said.

"Me too," Whitmore agreed. "Me too. I mean I wish I did it, but I didn't."

There was a silence during which neither knew what to say. Whitmore held a hand out. "Sorry about the greeting; I had no idea what a cop was doing at my door."

He's guilty of something, just not this. Nastos shook Whitmore's hand. "You deck all the cops that come by?"

"No, just the ones under house arrest who can't say shit about it." He spat on the ground and glared at Nastos. "Don't think that what happened to my boy makes us pals. I just don't think you need to go to jail."

A car came to a stop at the end of the driveway. A squad car. Nastos felt his blood run cold. Whitmore shrugged. "I told my wife to call if I wasn't back within two minutes. Guess she jumped the gun."

Nastos rubbed his jaw. "Runs in the family."

Whitmore pointed into blackness. "Go through the backyard. Watch the wife's garden."

The cruiser's spotlight flashed past them, then came back to their position. Nastos took off into the dark. He was still seeing stars from the intensity of the spotlight when he stumbled through the small garden, knocked down a panel of cheap metal fencing and crashed into a wooden shed.

He heard Whitmore shouting as a cop shoved past him, treating him like he had dealt with him before. Whitmore had a certain disdain for the officer and it seemed mutual.

Nastos half-climbed, half-broke through the fence and plowed into the next yard. From here there was more light. He twisted his upper body and barely squeezed between two houses. Grit from wet bricks scraped the front and back of his coat. He looked back into the dazzle of a flashlight. The cop on foot was thinner and faster than Nastos. He was closing the distance.

It was tough, but he made himself slow down, feigning more fatigue than he felt. Out on the street, he ran to the light so he'd be backlit, his face obscured. When he heard the officer's footsteps closing in, he zagged suddenly to the left so that the officer would be on his right side. It was all about the timing. He hit the brakes and drove his elbow back at face level. Contact. The cop's feet flew up in the air as his body careened past. He hit the ground hard.

The anti-authoritarian streak in Nastos took a little pleasure in hitting a cop, but really it was just about getting away. Trying to hide was not an option. If the cops wanted him badly enough, they'd get the dog out and he wouldn't stand a chance. All he could do was run. He crossed Lawrence Avenue — four lanes of well-lit roadway — and jumped the fence leading down to Colonel Danforth Park. It was a nearly sheer drop-off, one hundred feet down, over earth covered in pine needles and low foliage to a river below. Reluctantly, he crossed through two-degree, thigh-deep water after finding no other option, then took a trail south to the shore of Lake Ontario. By this time, he was good and cold. He wouldn't be warm

until he could get himself dry, which meant getting new clothes —
and that wasn't going to happen until he got back to Carscadden's.
He pushed himself another two miles east to the Port Union Plaza,
the whole way expecting a helicopter, police dog or a pissed-off cop
to find him.

The plaza was mostly dark, except for street lighting and a few lit
Closed signs. There was a pay phone in the corner near the liquor
store. Soaking wet, tired and cold, he stood at the pay phone. There
was no sign of cops; they must have given up the chase and gone back
to waste their time interrogating Whitmore. He dialled a number.

"Hello?" the voice said.

"Carscadden, it's me."

8

AT CARSCADDEN'S, NASTOS LAY in bed, warm, dry and tired. He'd be asleep soon. His body felt heavy, as if it were being pulled back into the bed by a force stronger than gravity: hopelessness. Court was weeks away but if he didn't get into the habit of sleeping he knew he'd look like a blood-thirsty vampire by the time the jury saw him. Dewar was going to see the toll it was taking on him. There was a lot he could have told Carscadden about his history with her, but he didn't trust him and he wasn't sure he ever would. It had been nearly a year since he had seen her last. Things had changed so much.

Eleven Months Earlier
October 30, 2010

NASTOS HAD WALKED INTO JOSIE'S CLASSROOM, MAKING NO ATTEMPT to keep track of the chaos. Thirty grade fours and fives dressed up for Halloween were running around fuelled by sugar, playing games and shouting. From the hallway, he saw her teacher standing at the door. In her early thirties, she was talking to a few parents who had arrived to pick up their goblins and axe murderers. Nastos had arrived at a good time and was not too far from the beginning of the line of parents.

"No, Mr. Jackson," the teacher said, "it's not a bother. Emily and David are great kids."

"You're the first teacher ever to do this for them, Ms. Liuzzo," Jackson replied, "and they really appreciate it, so thanks." Jackson, the single dad, was striking out big time. Ms. Liuzzo shrugged it off — she could smell desperation.

Jackson and his two kids left the company of Ms. Liuzzo. The next parent in line began talking to her. Nastos leaned against the white painted brick wall, waiting his turn. Seeing all of the lone guys in the line-up, Nastos considered that by the end of the year, she probably got more offers for dates than coffee mugs.

Nastos felt a new presence next to him. For all the men there, it was like the centre of gravity had moved from the teacher to someone else.

"Detective Nastos," a voice said.

He turned to see a woman standing next in line. She was a tall, thin Indian woman in her late thirties. The long black hair curled slightly at her shoulders, then hung down her back. He felt his breathing stop and hold as his eyes scanned her face. It was awkward to see her, so Nastos said the first thing he could think of. "Ang Dewar, long time no see. You have a kid here? When did that happen?"

"I adopted Abby when I was downtown working Appeals."

"I didn't even know you were married. Maybe we should have reconnected on Facebook or something. What's your husband do?"

"My husband, he did his secretary. He's yesterday's news." she replied archly, shaking her head.

"Sorry." *You're a class act, Nastos.*

Dewar paused only briefly. "I've got someone else in my life now; it's all for the best." Her eyes gently slipped all over Nastos' face. She suppressed a small smile, noticing the effect she still had on him.

"Do I know him?"

"Her name's Nicole." She continued, "She's great with Abby and Abby's dad has gotten over the shock. He's a good dad, so that's all that matters."

"Nicole?" Nastos had never heard Dewar say the name before. "And now you live around here?"

73

"When Matt and I split, he bought me out. I moved in with Nicole about six months ago in West Hill. Matt and I had talked before about how good a reputation this school had, so when her school shut down it was a fast decision to have her transferred. Nicole usually drives her, actually. Last I knew, you were in Etobicoke."

"Madeleine and I have been here in Port Union for three years now. So you're working Appeals downtown, right? You're making quite a name for yourself as far as prosecutors go. You ever going to come uptown and get back on the front line?"

She turned back to the kids acting up. "They rotate us every few years. If a good opportunity comes up, maybe. Otherwise I'd like to stay where I am."

"Too bad we never ran into each other sooner."

Dewar smiled like she didn't believe him. "Are you suggesting we start meeting at the park to have the kids play together?"

Nastos reconsidered. "I don't think my wife would like that too much. Maybe if you had three eyes and weighed six hundred pounds."

"She doesn't trust you?"

"She knows that we dated. To her, if you don't hate your ex, then a part of you still loves them."

Dewar paused to think about that. "Do you agree with her?"

"Only when she tells me I have to." He smiled.

Her attention was drawn to something in the room. She turned her body to match the direction she was looking, and took a sideways step toward Nastos so she was right next to him. Nastos was trying to figure out what was interesting to her. She leaned closer to him, touching his arm, and whispered in his ear.

"See the guy just finishing with the teacher? That's Judge Montgomery."

Nastos whispered back to her. "Oh yeah, I did a trial with him last year. He's kind of old to —"

"His grandson," she interrupted. Before she could continue, the judge smiled at Dewar and headed over to them. He was a shorter, balding white guy in his early sixties. He moved easily, with a little Spiderman holding his hand.

"Ms. Dewar, how are you?"

"Fine, sir," she said. "And you?"

"Better, now that I have Spiderman to protect me." He rested his hand on the boy's head. "You seem familiar somehow, sir — Thad Montgomery, pleased to meet you." He extended his right hand to Nastos, who took it reflexively and smiled in return.

"Detective Nastos, sir, Sex Crimes."

"Oh, I see," the judge replied. "Well, I guess we should keep this brief then; that's too bad. If I could impose, though, briefly," he continued. "If either of you knows of a kids' clothing store you could recommend for my grandson here, I'd appreciate it. He grows too fast for me to keep up with. I want to grab a few things on the way home. I wish I had been a little more prepared." His voice trailed off, his eyes glossed over as he felt himself slip into a memory.

"Must be tough on everyone, sir," Dewar said.

"Well, at least I have Spiderman here to protect me now."

"Well, there's a strip mall off Lawson Road," Nastos offered. "They have everything in there. Kids' clothes, a pharmacy, a dentist — all right there. It's pretty handy."

"I'll swing by there, thanks. See you two in court." Montgomery walked slowly, moving his hand to the child's shoulder.

When Montgomery was far enough away, Nastos asked, "What happened to his daughter?" They remained right next to each other, although the line had moved and they did not have to be so close. Nastos noticed the other men were still making sideways glances at Dewar, admiring her.

"It was a car accident. Some drunk guy crossed the centre line. She burned to death."

"Holy shit. I have a list of about a hundred people that I wish could take her place."

"In Sex Crimes, I'm not surprised."

"Well, that's the thing. No judge will send someone to jail for life on the word of a four-year-old. We're lucky to get probation orders."

Dewar shook her head. They reached the front of the line. They moved ahead again, staying right next to each other, her arm still around his. Nastos couldn't help but enjoy the touch. They had always felt physically connected to each other. It was just everything else that was a mess.

"Which one of these little monsters is yours, anyways?" asked Dewar.

Nastos took a good breath in and straightened up. He surveyed the room quickly. Pointing to the back, he identified his daughter Josie. "See that other Spiderman in the headlock, getting his ass kicked?" Dewar saw the senseless violence of these kids playing.

"That little guy is yours? How cute." Dewar pointed to a far table. "Abby's the astronaut colouring at the table."

Nastos smiled. "No, not the Spiderman, the fairy princess administering the beating, she's my little angel."

Dewar couldn't suppress a smile. "Talk about a chip off the old block, eh?"

"What's that supposed to mean?"

"Well, Detective," Dewar spoke with a tone of mock admonishment, "this may come as a surprise to you but your reputation precedes you, you know. Clients talk to their lawyers and tell some interesting stories about how you interview people. You beat them up."

"Well, I wouldn't necessarily believe what those upstanding members of the public have to say. Complaints have been made, but none of them went anywhere. I deal with the worst of the worst, and they try every angle they can to stay out of jail. It's pretty easy for them to make false allegations against me — it costs them nothing and takes some of the attention from what they've done."

"If you say so." She shook her head. "Most of those guys deserve a lot more than they get, especially in Sex Crimes. Their own lawyers would be the first to admit it too, after a few drinks of course."

"Yeah, I don't know what I'd do if anything ever happened to Josie. Make her testify in court only to watch the guy get away with it? No, thanks. He'd just fall off the face of the earth one day, wouldn't even make the news."

"I have no idea what I would do, Nastos, I don't want to even think about it."

It was like Josie felt that she was being watched. She scanned the room and when she saw her dad, she came running over to him, hugging him.

Nastos barely had time to crouch down and catch her. "You ready to go there, peanut?" His fingers found her little ribs and tickled their way in for a second.

"Okay, Dad, let's go." She stopped at Dewar's feet and stared up at her without losing her smile. "Hey, are you Abby's mom?"

Dewar leaned forward, smiling at little Josie. "Yes I am, how did you know?"

"'Cause the boys all say Abby's mom looks like a movie star and you do."

Dewar's smile broadened and she knelt down, matching Josie's height. "You can come over and visit Abby anytime you want, okay, Josie?"

"Okay," she said, grinning back to her dad.

Nastos stood up, grasping Josie's hand as he did so. "We better get out of here, Mom's waiting, isn't she, Jo?"

"Yeah, let's go, Dad."

"Bye Ang, see you next time." Nastos smiled.

"See you later, Nastos."

77

Josie waved bye-bye with her magic wand as they disappeared down the hallway. Dewar stood, watching the way he carried her, like she was the most important thing in the world. He'd always made her feel the same way. He was something that she wished that life had not taken from her.

September 26, 2011

NORTH ARRIVED FIVE MINUTES late for his meeting with Madeleine Nastos and was happy to see that she was gracious enough to wait for him. He had changed from his homeless garb and bottle of Scotch to a business suit and briefcase. He walked to the front door of the house, where she stood in the archway.

She was wearing dress pants and a business jacket that was thankfully high enough in the back that he could get a good look at her behind when she turned to unlock the door. She was in her forties, blond, tall and slim. He wondered what the hell she was doing with a guy like Nastos.

"Sorry I'm late," he said, "I'm not used to what the traffic is like in this part of town."

"Don't worry about it," she smiled, "I just got here myself. Mr. Sitler, right?"

"Yes, Sitler," he smiled. He had forgotten the alias he had provided her office.

She led him through the house in which he of course had no interest. He had all but forgotten about Detective Nastos after he saw the man's delicious wife. He surmised from her physique that she obviously worked out and that she was either gullible, stupid or naive to show strange men around vacant houses without doing much of an investigation into who they were.

"What's the kitchen like?" he asked. "I enjoy cooking and enter-taining."

"Let's go see," she said. She led him into an open concept kitchen and living room, oblivious to the fact that he was studying and com-mitting to memory every aspect of her appearance. Her long elegant fingers when she reached out for a light switch, her wrists. He fanta-sized about those hands grazing on his chest and running through his hair. He made note of her full lips when she spoke, barely catch-ing a single word she said. He'd just wait till she was done, then smile when she smiled. He noticed her hips and behind again, when she walked into the living room to flick the light switch. Again she seemed to notice nothing.

He almost felt sorry for her — almost. The sad fact was that what was coming her way she likely in some way deserved, she likely actually wanted. When her husband was gone to jail, she was going to need someone there for her — and North had decided that he was going to be that guy.

"So is this going to be just for you, Mr. Sitler, or do you have a family?"

"I have lady friends in my life, Madeleine, but no one special. I'm still keeping my options open." He smiled at her and caught the first hint that she felt something unusual about him, proba-bly his raw masculinity, his pheromones, heating up and distributing his scent to her below her consciousness. He read her facial expression as being aroused. Smiling, he asked to see the fireplace.

"You must be thinking of another listing; they don't have one here." Her eyes wrinkled in a way he thought was particularly cute. "Having you been dealing with another agent? Are you familiar with implied agency?"

"Oh, don't worry. I haven't been out with any agents — I must have been thinking about a place I saw on MLS. I'll sign a release if you want; I'll deal only with you."

Madeleine produced a form and North signed it, pausing for a moment to remember how to spell Sitler. She showed him the rest of the house, then they spoke briefly outside the front door.

"So you think you're interested in the neighbourhood, Mr. Sitler?"

It was so nice to hear her call him *mister.* He let her keep doing it and decided that he wasn't going to give her a first name. He'd even like her to call him *mister* when they had sex later. He made a mental note of it. They said their goodbyes and he watched her walk down the street to her car noticing the way her hair wisped back in the wind. He took down her license plate then walked to his own car. *Till next time, baby-doll.*

◊ ◊ ◊

NASTOS SAT NEXT TO CARSCADDEN AT THE DEFENSE DESK. CLEANERS must have been through the place the night before — the smell of Pine-Sol was nearly successful in masking the stench of bodily odours that were soaked into the worn, concrete-coloured carpet. Air conditioning was fighting the good fight in a no-winner against stale body heat trapped in a windowless room. The only decorations were the two Canadian flags on either side of a large gold, embossed coat of arms, complete with lions, lances and doves on either side of a shield filled with meaningless symbolism. The dead language again, with its extinct virtues like truth, integrity and equality — virtues that only ever existed in fairy tales or as punch lines to any of humanity's greatest tragedies. Nastos checked his watch. *Let's get this over with.*

Judge Montgomery was watching Dewar with the mild interest only possible in a half-blind man in his sixties. A younger man would not be able to take his eyes off her. He barely held on to a trace of the Irish accent that made him sound distinguished and deliberate in his speech. He was making notes, typing into his laptop as Dewar spoke; he was straining to keep up with her. Nastos considered whether a half-blind, half-deaf judge was good or bad for them.

"Members of the jury," Dewar was saying, "the accused is a detective with the Toronto Police Service. Officer Nastos investigated cases of child abuse and child pornography. During one of his investigations, he stumbled on a new suspect. Dr. Irons, the victim in this trial, was alleged to have committed a series of repugnant sexual attacks on children. Officer Nastos did not conclude his investigation; he never arrested the suspect. He never brought him into the station for an interview. Instead, he made a plan: he coerced the victim to go to a secluded area — then," she went to her desk retrieving a baseball bat, "with this baseball bat, he beat Dr. Irons to death and dumped his body in Cherry Beach. It was slow, torturous, evil. The motivation in this case is possibly the most universally obvious; you could probably even guess it. Officer Nastos' daughter was one of the alleged victims."

Nastos saw the jury's reaction and it wasn't good. Many were subtly nodding their heads in agreement; it all made sense. *Of course, that's why he did it. Can we vote and go home now?*

Dewar allowed them a moment to run those thoughts through their minds, then continued. "He acted out of vengeance, beating to death an unarmed and defenseless man. I don't mean to portray the victim as anything less than cruel or evil, but Dr. Irons was not convicted of any crime. Our society does not condone the actions of police officers who take it upon themselves to administer the death penalty at their whim.

"That is the issue here in court. In many trials, the defense will try to blame the victim and attempt to justify murder. It is very easy to taint a dead man who can't defend himself. Let's focus on the facts of this case. A defenseless man was brutally murdered at the hands of the accused; with forensics and the work of the investigators this will be proven beyond a reasonable doubt."

Nastos saw that the jury was immersed in her words. There was no way that she could not be effective. She came across as obviously intelligent, poised and well-spoken. Nastos glanced at Carscadden, who met his gaze. Carscadden took a breath that seemed to be an apology with just a hint of surrender — a ghost of things yet to come.

"Good morning, everyone," he said, getting to his feet. "My name is Kevin Carscadden and I've been a defense lawyer here in Toronto for about two years. Before that, I was on the west coast, where I practiced law for ten years. In all of that time, I've never seen a police service and prosecution office so determined to get a conviction. It's pretty simple to figure out why. They learned a long time ago that the *appearance* of justice being done matters more than justice actually being done. The shame about this is not just that an innocent man who dedicates his life to catching criminals is now wrongfully accused, but that he has been taken away from his daughter—the real victim in all of this, not Dr. Irons. The fact remains that Dr. Irons participated in high-risk behaviour, much as if he were running drugs or drinking and driving. What happened to him was the result of his lifestyle and had nothing to do with my client. Officer Nastos is completely innocent of these charges, as will be proven very clearly."

He took his seat next to Nastos, who was still watching the jury to determine his effectiveness. Male jurors seemed more interested in the ruminations that involved Ms. Dewar and probably never heard a word Carscadden said. One younger and very muscular guy in the back row was trying to see down the top of a young girl in front of him and off to the side. She had breast implants that he found particularly interesting. There was a middle-aged man, heavy-set wearing a denim jacket—an East York dinner jacket—and a baseball cap. Nastos named him Trucker Billy-Jim.

Some of the women scratched a few notes down on the pads of paper that the court provided. One woman, the oldest, in her seventies with a pink-tinged elder afro, enthusiastically wrote down every word like some crime fiction fan who had finally gotten the call-up to the big leagues. All the Agatha Christies on her bedside table were finally going to come in handy.

Montgomery had the floor after Carscadden sat down. He paused a moment as if to consider his words, then spoke softly. "Madam Dewar, are you ready to call your first witness?"

"Yes, sir," she began. She stood and took up a position at the podium with her notes in front of her. "The first officer on scene please, Constable Thomas."

The young officer made his way up to the stand. Tall, a little too thin, with black hair, he seemed too young to carry a gun—the recoil would likely knock him flying backward. He entered the witness box, the small gate creaking shut behind him. He stood firm, facing Dewar, waiting to begin. The bailiff approached, a plump woman in her forties. Her uniform was ready to burst at the seams. She barked loudly in case the guys three courts over had hearing problems. "State and spell your name for the record please, Officer."

"Thomas," he replied, "Gary Thomas, T-H-O-M-A-S." The officer was calm and smooth.

"Do you swear or affirm?" the bailiff asked.

"Swear, ma'am."

"Place your left hand on the bible, raise your right hand. Do you swear to tell the truth, the whole truth, so help you God?"

"I do."

Dewar finished absentmindedly flipping through her notes, then smiled warmly to the officer. "Officer, how long have you worked for the Toronto Police Service?"

"Six months, ma'am."

"And on the fourteenth of August of this year you became involved in an incident; can you tell us about that, please?"

Thomas took a moment to get his thoughts in order then began. "At 0745 hours I received a radio call from Communications that a body had been found floating in the lake in Cherry Beach. I pulled into the park and went up to the gazebo. A man was standing there with his dog. I walked over to him and he led me to a spot where I could see a body floating face up near the shore."

The crime fiction fan in the jurors' box was leaning so far forward Nastos thought she was going to tumble out onto the floor. Even the men were able to concentrate on the facts, maybe because when men eventually tire of ogling a beautiful woman, the only thing that interests them is gore.

"Did you have any immediate thoughts or observations?" she asked.

"It was a male and he was code five. Sorry, I mean, that he had been dead for some time."

"And what did you do then?" she asked.

"I called Communications, told them to get a coroner on the way and the homicide unit."

"That's it for my questions here, Your Honour. Thank you, Officer Thomas."

Once Dewar was sitting, Judge Montgomery asked Carscadden, "Do you have anything, Mr. Carscadden?"

Carscadden stood and walked to the podium slowly. "Yes, sir, just a few," he said. Then, turning to the officer, he asked, "Constable Thomas, how long had you been a police officer at the time of this event?"

Thomas took some time to do the math. "It was six months at that time."

Carscadden smiled condescendingly then smiled to the jurors' box, shaking his head. "So you really had no idea how long the male had been dead. What did you do before joining the police service, pump gasoline? I can't imagine you see many dead people under those circumstances."

"Not exactly, sir," Thomas replied. He appeared a little insulted.

Dewar lifted herself just barely from her wooden chair. "Objection. Relevance, Your Honour? What's the relevance to how long Officer Thomas has been a police officer?"

Montgomery stopped typing and peered over his laptop.

Carscadden took the invitation and began, "Your Honour, the officer's initial decisions were not based on experience or knowledge. It set in motion the chain of events that brought us here. Without that decision, none of the subsequently obtained evidence would have been available for the prosecution to taint against my client. It boils down to witness reliability, if the officer had no more experience with murders than the average guy on the street."

The judge seemed about to speak, but the officer gently interrupted. "To clarify, Your Honour, before joining the police service I was a paramedic for five years, so I know a dead body when I see one."

Montgomery smiled broadly. "That satisfy you, Mr. Carscadden?"

Carscadden's shoulders drooped and he chewed a little on his lower lip. "No further questions for this witness, Your Honour." He took his seat next to Nastos. "Not off to a great start, are we?"

Nastos wished he shared Carscadden's levity.

Turning to the officer, Montgomery said, "Thank you, sir, you may step down," then back to Dewar: "Next witness, Madam Prosecutor?"

"Yes, Your Honour, I'd like to call the lead homicide investigator in this matter, Detective-Sergeant Clancy Brown."

Carscadden watched Clancy Brown as he was sworn in on the stand. He was the man who had interrogated Nastos for nearly twelve hours when he was arrested. Carscadden had read the brief on him that Ms. Hopkins and Nastos had prepared. He had a reputation for being a robot. The only self-generated thought he ever had was when he first joined the police service, and from then on he decided to just do whatever the hell he was told. He had no ability to think for himself. He was the perfect detective to investigate Nastos because he made sure the investigation reached the conclusion he was told to reach.

Watching the jury, Carscadden could see that many of them seemed to regard Detective-Sergeant Clancy Brown as royalty, the cumulative hero of all of the TV shows and movies that they had ever seen. Brown was six-four, with short brown hair and a lean, muscular build, in his late forties. He resembled Rock Hudson and had an easy, friendly smile. The old lady in the front of the jurors' box, the crime fiction fan, had her elbows on the railing and her head resting in her hands. She had put down her writing pad and seemed confident that she could just hang on his every word. Carscadden winced, not liking his appraisal. *We're fucked.*

Nastos knew he had to think of a way to separate the humble, unshakable exterior from the arrogant company man who was bereft of independent thought. He considered the history of the police service, the history of scandals. The most obvious scandal was the Cherry Beach Express. He reached out to Carscadden's notepad, picked up the pen and wrote a few thoughts.

"Detective Brown," Dewar began, "can you please take us through your thoughts and impressions upon arriving at the crime scene?"

"Certainly." Brown patted down the front of his suit, then began. "Your Honour, I was called to the crime scene by the radio dispatcher. I arrived at around nine that morning. The uniformed officers had cordoned off an area and I was able to walk right in. I immediately thought that it was a homicide when I saw the body. I observed trauma to the head and face. A forensics team was arriving, so I touched nothing and walked out the way I had gone in to disrupt the scene as little as possible."

"And you had some thoughts as far as what you were dealing with?" Dewar asked.

"Well, it seemed the man was beaten to death. He was well dressed, low body fat, seemed fit. I would imagine that he would hold his own in a fight against one to two men unless he was drunk or taken by surprise or the assailant was armed. The toxicology screen turned out to be negative. He had suffered fifteen to eighteen direct and glancing blows with a rounded blunt wooden object. It seemed the suspect decided to break the victim's arms and legs before taking any head shots. A few teeth had been smashed out. He could have used some of his own dental work, actually. A baseball bat was found nearby in the water. It was stained with what appeared to be, and turned out to be, blood and had a tooth embedded in it. The bat was initially perplexing."

Carscadden saw that the jury were listening intently.

"Why was it perplexing?" Dewar asked.

Brown arched his back slightly to stretch. "Well, it occurred to me that the killer chose a good enough location for the murder, had a good hour of night, but discarded the weapon recklessly. I began to think that the killer might have been exhausted and careless at that point."

"And at what point were you actually assigned the homicide?"

Detective-Sergeant Brown paused for a second, thoughtfully considering his answer. He leafed through his notebook to reference something. "Yes, my, umm, supervisor in Homicide spoke with the DS of Sexual Assault and they told me to run with it. When the lead suspect turned out to be the defendant, Detective Nastos, his supervisor, Detective-Sergeant Koche, reiterated that I should go with the investigation no matter where it led."

Brown explained the link to Nastos for them. "Nastos arrested a molester named Sean Harper. In his apartment, Nastos found a picture of Harper and two other men standing there with a small boy with them. The second man was George Costello, a horse farrier of no fixed address who was out on probation for sexual assault. The third man was later identified as the murder victim, Dr. Irons. Nastos had submitted a brief property report listing the names of the two men with Harper, but nothing else.

"A name check of the police database linked the name Irons with the Harper case, of which Nastos was the lead investigator. Nastos was almost perfect at covering his tracks, but he was just sloppy enough to get himself caught."

Nastos saw the way the jury was reacting — the trucker nodding his head, the crime fiction fan concentrating on the second draft of her manuscript, the ending already written. He felt that they'd lost the jury right at the start of the trial and getting them back was going to be like turning the *Titanic* around.

Carscadden leaned over and nudged Nastos from his thoughts. "Why did Brown check with Sexual Assault before you were a suspect?"

"That's the million dollar question. I told you this whole thing is bullshit."

Carscadden fidgeted with his pencil, then scribbled something on his writing pad.

Dewar took a sip of water from her glass; it tinkled against the jug when she put it down. "No more questions for now, Your Honour, but I would like to recall if necessary for different aspects of the case." Dewar was beginning to tire; she was ready for a break.

Judge Montgomery looked at Carscadden, who was just getting to his feet. "Granted, Ms. Dewar. Mr. Carscadden, to cross?"

Nastos slid his pad of paper over to Carscadden.

"What's this?" Carscadden asked.

"It's a suggested approach for Brown."

Carscadden glanced over the page. Nastos continued. "He's a company man and a robot. Make him have to think for himself. Put him in a position where he contradicts the police service."

Carscadden considered those words, then read the page over quickly.

Judge Montgomery glowered at Carscadden. "Any time you're ready, Mr. Carscadden."

"Yes, Your Honour." He took his position at the podium and placed some papers on the face for him to reference.

"Now, Detective Brown, how would you have disposed of the murder weapon?"

10

"SORRY?" BROWN'S EYES SQUINTed in confusion.

Carscadden tried again. "Use your imagination, sir. You've been a policeman for eighteen years and in Homicide for the last five. From what you have learned in that time, how would you dispose of the bat?"

Dewar stood to object. "Your Honour, that's speculative."

Montgomery flipped back a page in his notebook. "Fair question. Ms. Dewar, the witness may answer."

"Well, let's see," Brown began. He pursed his lips, trying to imagine a scenario. "I would either dump it in another body of water, cover it in peroxide or bleach — or both and bury it someplace or possibly burn it. No one would find it, I'll tell you that much."

Nastos thought it was a decent plan. That's what he would have done, too.

Carscadden continued. "As would anyone with experience, such as yourself or my client here. Certainly a detective with Mr. Nastos' experience would do a better job of disposing of the weapon. Aside from making sure the body is never found, it's got to be the most basic instinct a knowledgeable killer would have."

Brown responded condescendingly. "Well, like I said, maybe he got so tired after swinging it and killing Irons that he got careless." Then he turned directly at the jury to emphasize his next point. "Or he knew it did not have his prints, so he didn't want to take the chance of transporting it and contaminating his car or clothes with the victim's blood."

Carscadden countered. "So none of the evidence ever linked my client to the bat? Is that right, Officer Brown?"

"No." He corrected himself, "I mean yes." He took a disappointed breath. "It didn't link in any way to your client."

"So, really, that would make two things that do not link the crime to my client: no forensics linking him to the weapon, and my client would be too experienced to let it even be found."

Dewar stood to object. "I did not hear a question in that last statement, Your Honour."

Carscadden put his palms up in surrender and clarified what he meant. "Isn't that true, Officer Brown, two things that do not link to my client?"

"Well, it's my experience that most pre-planned murders seldom take place where there are witnesses or video cameras. Your client had the most understandable of motives. There is just no denying that. There is not a person in the world who would not consider killing the man who assaulted his daughter, me included. And that's the God's honest truth. On top of this motive, Detective Nastos had a unique perspective into what was going on. As far as we can tell, he was the first to learn of the assaults. He had come across the victim during another investigation. No one else knew that Nastos was connected to Irons; no one else knew Irons was a molester. On top of that, the murder happened in a place where the detective had obtained numerous excessive force complaints. We didn't just pick his name out of a hat."

Carscadden turned to Nastos, appraising him. Maybe he didn't believe what he had just heard. Nastos didn't realize that he had missed something.

Carscadden continued, "Excuse me, Officer, did you just say that *we* did not pick his name out of a hat? Who, besides you, makes up the 'we' you speak of?"

"I meant to say I, *I* did not pick his name out of a hat."

"So it was you alone that felt that there was enough evidence to pursue my client?"

"It was my decision and I made the right one."

Carscadden, shaking his head from left to right, was totally unconvinced by Brown's answer. Nastos read the jury. They saw Carscadden as incensed. Unlike them, Nastos was used to it, the way lawyers responded incredulously to mundane testimony, trying to impart by body language that a comment is scandalous. Classic lawyer bluster. It was a last-ditch move, right before you'd admit that, oh, my client did it, but he had one hell of a reason. Brown stood tall and stoic; the jury seemed confused.

"Now, sir, you've already testified that you've been a police officer for nearly two decades. Isn't it true that Cherry Beach is notorious among petty criminals as a place where police in general get rough with career criminals, drunks, the homeless?"

Brown's lips tightened briefly. He was obviously reluctant to engage the line of questioning. "Sure, maybe fifteen years ago. Policing isn't done like that anymore."

"Isn't it true that a late-night trip to Cherry Beach was often referred to as the Cherry Beach Express among officers and the street community to this day? I think there was even a rap song titled 'The Cherry Beach Express.' The band was called Pukka Orchestra; I could sing you the verse —"

The jury seemed mildly amused by Carscadden's threat to sing. Brown was becoming less confident and somewhat confused by Carscadden's approach. "I wouldn't really know about the Cherry Beach Express; it was before my time. It's like an urban legend." Clancy tried to sound authoritative, trying to close the line of questioning.

"So, to recap for the jury, sir, you readily admit to knowing how to dispose of the murder weapon efficiently, a skill not in the domain of general public knowledge, yet you deny that the Cherry Beach Express routinely takes troublesome street hoods for street justice, a fact which is general knowledge to anyone who has lived in the city — teenagers, old ladies, postal workers — everyone who has lived here for more than a few years."

Dewar's lips began to purse. Nastos thought she was trying to decide whether to object or not. She did. "Again, there was no question, Your Honour." She sat.

"The question, Judge, is whether Officer Brown expects anyone here to believe that."

Brown tried to get back on track. He cited a line police use all the time in testimony. "I can't testify to what other people know. I can only testify to what I know."

Carscadden did a quick scan of the jury, making sure they were paying attention to him and his next question. "Well, I can say that you've been on the stand for a short period of time and already people wonder if they should doubt your credibility —"

Dewar stood to object again, but Carscadden finished. "Shouldn't they, Officer?"

"I couldn't say," Brown replied.

"No more questions for this witness, Your Honour — seems he's out of answers." Shaking his head from side to side and even rolling his eyes, Carscadden took his seat, trying to project as much disappointment as possible in Officer Brown, as if the detective-sergeant should be ashamed of himself. No lawyer was above the most pathetic games when nothing else was working. Carscadden was so involved in his high school drama revival that he missed it when Dewar appraised him. Nastos saw that she was at least a little impressed.

She got to her feet. "Redirect, Your Honour?"

"Please, Ms. Dewar," Montgomery said, graciously.

"Your Honour, something that came up in my friend's questioning of Detective Brown; did you say that no one else knew of this investigation into Dr. Irons?"

Brown cleared his throat. "Yes, ma'am, that's right. Detective Nastos only wrote one property report about Irons, just that he had come up from another investigation and he should be looked into. That was the last of the paper trail. Irons was never even questioned. Someone just skimmed the surface with him, and next thing we see he's doing the backstroke in — sorry, deceased in the water."

"Did he ever come to anyone else's attention in the Sexual Assault office?"

"No one. I asked Detective Nastos that question when he was interviewed —"

Nastos nudged his lawyer to stand up, to stop the incoming hearsay evidence. Carscadden began to rise, but Dewar redirected Brown. "And as a result of asking that question, were other leads pursued?"

Brown said, "I asked Nastos very specifically about that point, but no other leads came up, Ms. Dewar."

"Thank you, Detective-Sergeant."

"Thank you."

Judge Montgomery smiled to the officer and waved his permission for the detective to step down.

As Brown left the witness box, Nastos followed his gaze toward the back of the courtroom, where Detective-Sergeant Koche was standing. Nastos saw the conspiracy in their eyes. Brown gave a smug smile to the jury, pleased with himself. Brown opened the low swing gate, heading from the front of the courtroom to the gallery. When he did, Koche's eyes set into a hard stare, his face flushing red as he looked from Brown to Dewar. His lips tightened. He cast his stare down at his phone and started dialling a number.

Montgomery leaned forward to his microphone. "Okay, it's three-thirty. I'd rather not have to interrupt the next witness in the middle of their testimony, so let's call it a day and be back ready to go at nine tomorrow."

"Thank you, sir," Dewar said.

Carscadden was the first to his feet, quickly saying, "Yes, sir, thank you."

Nastos leaned back in his chair, watching Dewar as she put papers in her briefcase and closed it up for the day. She didn't seem to revel in prosecuting him, but it didn't seem to bother her too much either. Carscadden nudged Nastos' arm, distracting him from his appraisal of the prosecutor, so he missed it when she turned to appraise him.

Carscadden flipped through the pages of his briefing notes, and saw the notation about the dentist's secretary. *She must have access to the patient list,* he thought. *I should just drop by and see her. It would only take an hour.* Nastos would just be getting dinner ready. "Nastos, I just got a text message from Hopkins."

"Oh yeah?" he replied, only half-interested.

"She needs to see me after court. It should only take an hour."

"Sure, whatever. I'm going to get tired of feeding your face every night anyways." Nastos' eyes narrowed. "What's going on?"

"I dunno. I asked her to check into something, now she wants to meet."

"So what's the dinner plan?

"This time it's on me."

Nastos smiled, "You're going to cook?"

"Jesus Christ, no. Meet me at Frankie's. Hey, it's good food and we'll be home by six. There's a game on tonight too."

"Okay, see you there." Nastos tried a smile, but it didn't seem to fit very well on his face.

◊ ◊ ◊

94 BEFORE THEY LEFT, DEWAR OBSERVED HOW NASTOS SEEMED TO HAVE paled and wrinkled around his eyes in a way she had not noticed before. His hands were red and raw from the wringing and clenching they had been taking. Many people on trial for murder were much more apathetic than Nastos. In her experience, accused murderers often just sat back, watching the show of their lives unfolding around them like they were in a nightmare, where they had only the vaguest understanding that it was their lives on the line. Others

had resigned themselves to being convicted at the outset and considered the trial a formality delaying their transfer to the more civilized federal prison for the gone and forgotten.

To Dewar, Nastos seemed acutely aware of his surroundings and knew what was at risk. He didn't seem like he was ready to give up and accept the inevitable. She gathered her things and left for the office.

11

CARSCADDEN REGRETTED LYING to Nastos about having to meet Hopkins, but it was necessary. The last thing he needed was Nastos out with him — he'd cause a scene. Besides, the thought of doing something out of court, investigating this mess on his own, felt liberating.

He tapped the address into his GPS and started driving. Flemingdon Park wasn't the worst area of Toronto, but parts of it were pretty bad. Carscadden thought back to the privileged area of Vancouver where he'd grown up — although at the time he had not realized how lucky he was. His dad had worked two factory jobs to help him get a university education, despite the old man's contempt for neighbourhood people he considered the snobby elite. Life in Kitsilano was nothing compared to life here, the ghettoized apartment complexes and row houses. Garbage and other litter were all over the place as though there had been a garbage strike for the last few years. Thankfully, it didn't smell too bad; scavenging raccoons, skunks and dogs probably ate any table scraps or loose trash. It was the type of neighbourhood that was more likely to scramble into action to welcome a patrolling squad car with a stone-throwing riot than to work together in the garden for the May tulip festival.

Carscadden stopped at the curb. It was small house with run-down caged-metal fencing around the perimeter, missing shutters and cobwebbed windows. Partially chewed-through bags of garbage and recyclables sat on a sagging porch with an empty dog bowl and filthy *Welcome!* mat in the wrong place. His jacket snagged on a loose wooden railing studded with protruding nails. The thing would come right off if bumped the wrong way. The doorbell rang without much enthusiasm and while he hoped that no one would answer, he had the sneaking suspicion that the occupants would not be at work. Soon enough, the screen door creaked open and a black man's grimy, unshaven face appeared.

"What?" he asked.

"Yeah, I'm here for Maggie." He said, trying to sound nonchalant.

The man's Jamaican accent revealed itself. "Fucking lawyer, eh?" He sized Carscadden up. "What do you need her for?"

Carscadden didn't like being pegged as a lawyer so easily. He didn't think he fit the stereotype. "I need to ask a few questions about her last job," he replied.

"Like what?" The man's teeth clenched and his lower jaw jutted out defiantly. A voice shouted out from behind him. "Troy, who is it?" Carscadden noticed that the door opened slightly when the man turned back into the apartment. Troy was shirtless, with bruises and red patches all up the inside of his right arm. Tattoos covered the outside. Troy was nearly sleeved out — nearly every square inch of both arms was covered in prison ink, faded indiscernible markings.

A woman came to the door and Carscadden recognized her as Maggie, the dental assistant. She was a little gaunt but pretty, despite the greasy, lifeless blond hair and dark patches under her eyes. She saw Carscadden's suit and naively optimistic face.

"You'll have to excuse Troy; he's a little suspicious of lawyers." Troy grunted and retreated into the apartment, leaving Maggie at the door. She opened it halfway and squeezed out onto the porch, closing it behind her to stand next to Carscadden.

How can they tell I'm a lawyer so easily? He hesitated only briefly, then extended his hand. Maggie took it.

"Yes, I'm Kevin Carscadden, and I'm a lawyer."

Maggie, with her arms crossed, drummed her fingers impatiently.

He continued, "I understand that you used to work for Dr. Irons — is that right?"

"Yes, what a mess that turned out to be." Maggie took a cigarette out of her pocket and lit it, making Carscadden take a half-step back to get away from the stench.

"Yes, well, we represent the man who was charged with murdering him, and we're trying to get a copy of the complete patient list from the office. You wouldn't know how we could get one, do you?" Carscadden watched the woman closely for any sign of deception in her answer.

"I'm sorry, I can't talk about that." Maggie moved to go back in the house but Carscadden touched her arm, stopping her.

"You can't talk about it? Why not?" he asked.

"Well, I signed the form, the non-disclosure agreement. I can't say anything about anything."

"Who would ask you to sign that?"

"Some lawyer. He said it was all pretty standard. That it protected me from having to talk to the media or anyone. Easiest money I ever made."

"He paid you?"

"Five thousand in trust. Two thousand for me right now — the five goes to my son's college fund. It's all done automatic."

"Can you get me the lawyer's name? I need to talk to him." Carscadden pulled out his notepad, but it was no use.

"No, I don't have it. The money all got deposited and that's that. If I say anything I get sued and lose all the money from the trust. He said that if he gets one single phone call mentioning my name the deal is off."

Troy shouted something from inside the house and then a child started to cry. Maggie squeezed the door open and turned away. "Sorry, I have to go, nice talking to you." The woman disappeared back into the house leaving Carscadden on the porch by himself.

He saw a few young men from the street corner watching him. He got the creeps and left.

◘ ◘ ◘

KOCHE OBSERVED THE GREY AND HEAVY SKY AS HE WALKED TO THE Crown attorney's Case Management office. He had let her leave before him while he was on the phone and now he followed discreetly, not wanting her to think he was following her like some kind of stalker. She probably attracted more than a few of those.

He allowed himself to check her out. Nuances like the gentle lilt of her hips as her small, tapered waist twisted to accommodate the easy stride of her heeled shoes escaped him just as much as how her loose hair unfurled behind her in the gentle wake.

Koche was an ass man and his eyes barely left his target.

He did see her confidence, the smug superiority and entitlement. Like her team had all of the cards stacked in their favour now. He knew that women got promotions and raises because not to do so would invoke lawsuits and more bullshit than it was worth. It was better or cheaper to promote them and just let them screw everything up. And if they were beautiful, they really had the world by the balls. Because now, not only did they have the old guys scared of lawsuits, they had the young guys rubbing their feet and cooking them dinner every night — basically becoming wives. The world was going to hell.

Koche entered the building, and when he saw Dewar in the elevator, he took the stairs to Jeff Scott's third-floor office, sucking air most of the way. He walked down a hallway until he found Scott's door and walked in without knocking.

Scott was sitting behind his desk. He was wearing a suit, shirt and tie. The shirt was denim blue with a white collar and cuffs. He was in his mid-forties, skinny, but flaccid and pale. He was severely balding with tufts of curly hair and large clunky glasses. As the chief prosecutor for Toronto, he was Dewar's superior and was a political player.

Koche got right to the point. "I don't like the way the trial is going. That cunt of yours isn't aggressive enough."

Scott rolled back from his laptop and put his feet up on the desk. He took a breath, and interlocking his fingers behind his head, said, "She's taking the soft approach—it's too slow and indirect. You'd think after ten years she'd lose patience for that and go for the jugular. You fart around, try to be cute, and it can backfire."

"Truer words have never been spoken," Koche began. "So light a fire under her ass, Jeff. We need this guy to get convicted fast. If the media think we're dragging it out, reluctant to pull the trigger on this guy, it'll reflect poorly on the police department and the justice system even when he does get convicted. We go way back, Jeff—"

Scott cut him off with a raised finger. "He'll get convicted, and when he does we'll make sure everyone knows that it's because of our efforts, not Dewar the Indian window dressing." Scott exhaled. "We'll get the credit we deserve. The police chief will see how tough on corruption you are for starting this investigation, and the Attorney General will see the same in me."

Koche added, "So will the public, when you run for mayor."

Scott smiled. "Remember, Dave, not a word about that till the time is right. Most of the voting public in this town are socialists and cop-haters. When we get a cop convicted of murder and vindicate every allegation of the Cherry Beach Express that any homeless freak has ever made, that's when it comes out that I'm a candidate."

Koche allowed himself to become optimistic again. He took a breath and found himself agreeing. "If Dewar gets with the program, I'll make Inspector, Jeff."

"Just remember, Koche: Dewar is a woman lawyer. They don't play nice with others; she'll oppose any suggestions I make because I'm a man, just to prove a point. I'll be honest with you—she's tough to manage. But she's the best."

Koche took a seat in the chair opposite Scott. He leaned forward with his elbows on his thighs and rubbed his chubby, sweaty hands together. "Back in the day, we made some good press throwing the Viet Cong pot growers and the black dealers in jail when I was in the drug unit and you were the prosecutor. That's what got us where we are today. Dewar hasn't learned to identify career moves. This is a career maker for her."

"I know, I know," Scott said. "She just doesn't get it; she's funny that way."

"So you're going to talk to her?"

Scott had seen this request coming a mile away and already agreed. "I'll get her in here today and set her straight. You know, I remember that you pegged this Nastos guy as trouble when you first transferred into Sex Assault. Your instincts are as sharp as ever."

Koche never found it easy to be humble, but was too angry to bask in any praises. "Well, I don't blame Nastos for killing the guy either," he said, "but if he had been smarter about this, I wouldn't have to put him down. This mess he's in, it's his own fault. He threw himself in front of a train that can't stop — me, I can fix lots of things, but stupid isn't one of them."

Scott extended his hand. "Well, tell you what, Dave, you take off and I'll call Dewar in here right now."

"Sounds good." Koche got to his feet, shook hands with Scott and pushed his chair back to where he had got it from, then headed for the door. As it was closing, Scott spoke to him again.

"You around later? I'll let you know how it goes."

Koche checked his BlackBerry for the time, his lips pursed. "No, I have to meet a guy — just send me a text when she's sorted out. Thanks, Scott."

"Any time, Koche."

Scott tapped his intercom and dialled Dewar's extension number.

12

WITH EACH SUCCESSIVE UNAN-
swered ring, Dewar became more and more sure that Scott was
seconds away from barging in on her. *I should get my recorder
going, if I have time.* He knew when she was in—he always knew.
She thought he had a camera set up under her desk or in the ceiling
fan, but she had searched a dozen times and never found anything.

After the fourth ring, the phone went silent and the call display
screen wiped itself clean. Shortly thereafter came pounding footsteps and finally the whoosh of the door flying open.

"Oh, hi Jeff, how're you?" She tried to hold the insincere smile,
but it reluctantly faded when she saw the state he was in.

"Don't you answer your phone?" Scott pointed to accentuate his
frustration, then rested his hands on his hips. He wanted to know
what she was doing. The thought that she might actually be working must have eluded him.

"Sorry, Jeff, I was right in the middle of a thought on the Nastos
trial, so I just wanted to finish it. You stopped ringing, so I thought
you'd just leave a message."

Dewar closed off her email and started shutting down her
computer.

"Well, that's what I wanted to talk to you about. Come to my
office." He took a step back as if expecting her to race after him.
When she didn't move, he turned back to her incredulously.

"Okay, I'll be right there," she said while she reached for her purse.

"Come right now, it's important that we deal with this right away." He jabbed his left thumb in the direction of the door as if she had forgotten how to leave a room.

Despite her efforts, she found his rage a little contagious and her voice rose to meet his. "Okay, just one sec." Dewar stood up grabbing her purse. These tirades were becoming increasingly frequent. Yelling back seemed to be the only thing he understood. Until recently, she would have held back.

"No, you'll come to my office right now, Ms. Dewar — Jesus Christ!"

Dewar bolted up to her feet. With her left foot, she closed the desk drawer. Scott missed the organized collection of small audio tapes neatly inside. She reached down with her hand to tug the handle, ensuring the drawer was locked.

"Actually, Jeff," she said, "I'm menstruating this week and I want to change my plug first. Is that okay? Are you glad you asked?"

Scott recoiled, as disgusted with her words as she had hoped. Even Mrs. Black out front must have heard that one; Dewar hoped she had gotten a good chuckle.

"You can't talk to me like that," he hissed at her.

"When I say I'll be right there, I'll be right there, Jeff. I'm not always being obstinate, you know."

She walked past him, out of the office, exchanged rolled eyes with Mrs. Black, then went into the washroom. She used the mirror above the sink to place a recording device in her jacket pocket and adjusted the microphone. She washed and dried her hands and face and left for his office.

◻ ◻ ◻

"SIT DOWN THERE." SCOTT POINTED TO THE CHAIR AGAINST THE WALL and gruffly closed the door as Dewar entered.

She sat.

"Listen," Jeff began as he took his seat, "people say you are going at Nastos with a light touch. This is a career case for you; you should know that. Get a conviction and people will notice you. Be aggressive with this guy."

"I know what I'm doing here, I've been a prosecutor for —"

"I'll tell you what I've been," he interrupted. "I've been a prosecutor for fifteen years and the chief Crown attorney for another five. Don't you think I'd know when you are being too soft? People upstairs are watching you. Show them what you are made of." He held her gaze, searching for weakness.

She took a breath and replied, "Yes, you're absolutely right, Jeff."

His lips pursed, confused. "I know I'm right." He had obviously been hoping for a confrontation.

Dewar continued, "I'm sorry, sir, I'll go at him harder tomorrow."

Scott got to his feet and began pacing. "I don't know why you new breed of women need pep talks so often. I never did. Must be the estrogen."

"I guess it muddles the thinking sometimes, sir."

"Try eating more protein — apparently it helps."

"You would know, sir." While Scott's face twisted up as he considered whether he'd just been insulted, Dewar smiled broadly and made her way back to her office. She closed the door behind her and sat at the desk. Opening the bottom left drawer, she took the cassette tape out of her pocket recorder and placed it in a labelled case. She put it in the drawer with a dozen similarly labelled cassette cases and locked it up.

104

◻ ◻ ◻

CARSCADDEN SAT AT THE STAFF BOOTH IN THE BACK OF FRANKIE'S. HE had a glass of Rosemount Shiraz to one side and a calamari appetizer in front of him. He was beginning to trust himself with alcohol again. He wasn't going to let the disaster of the past repeat itself. He had only drunk that much to suppress the pain. Things were much easier away from corporate hell. One drink wouldn't hurt.

The place had a level of customer service that he was not used to and it was not uncommon for the chef to try new recipes out on frequent patrons to get their opinions. So far it was a bit salty, but the wine was compensating just fine.

"Mr. Carscadden, what a nice surprise." Viktor took a spare glass from the table and poured himself some wine from the bottle, then sat down. He was wearing a dark suit jacket with just enough stubble to show. Viktor liked the George Michael look and it apparently worked for him, considering all of the girls he had around him whenever he was here. Carscadden wondered if it would make a difference if he knew that Michael was gay. "Nice to see you again, Viktor." He waved his glass in the direction of the front of the restaurant. "Business is good." Carscadden lifted his glass and touched it to Viktor's and took a sip.

"You know, Carscadden, if you don't get the nerve soon, I'm going to have to ask your secretary out for a drink sometime." He smiled and took a bite of the calamari. "Umm. A little too salty," he said, almost to himself.

Carscadden watched Viktor's gentle mannerisms: the way he gingerly held one hand under his mouth while he tasted the food with the other. He saw nothing but kindness. Yet Viktor was a murderer. It made him doubt himself about Nastos, despite some observations he had made during the day's testimonies.

"Hopkins is out of my league. Anyways, I've had enough problems with women to last a lifetime. I just want to be left alone now, not strike out and make work life awkward." He regretted immediately that wine had caused him to loosen up about his secretary. Viktor wasn't likely to let it go now.

"Say, how's everything going with the cop case?"

"I don't really know, it's too early, but I got some information for Nastos that might help him out." Carscadden saw Nastos come in the front door and waved him down. "Here he is now."

Nastos walked up to the booth. "Well, if it isn't Viktor Kalmakov the businessman," Nastos said, reaching his hand out. Viktor took it and stood up from the booth.

Carscadden put his glass down. "Sit back down, Viktor, where you going?"

"I'm sure you have business to discuss here. I'll get out of your way. Wave down the waitress when you're ready to order." Viktor tapped the menus that were lying on the table, then excused himself.

"You got him off a few murders?" Nastos asked, taking a seat.

"No one was more surprised than me, but what the hell — I'm good at what I do. How are you holding up?"

Nastos poured the last of the wine into a water glass, leaned back into the chair and took a sip. "Drinking again, eh?"

"I'll be fine."

"How am I holding up? Let's see . . . the house bills, the stress of the trial, the Leafs can't win a game — I could use some time in jail just to get away from it all. But other than that . . ." He made a face and took a bite of the calamari. "Just enough salt. They add it to keep you drinking." He took a long slug of the wine, finishing his glass.

Carscadden was excited to tell Nastos the good news and wanted to get to it right away. "I checked into one of the dental assistants like you asked," he began.

"And?"

"And someone paid her $7,000 to sign a non-disclosure regarding the client list for the deceased Dr. Irons."

"Who?"

Carscadden rolled his eyes. "She obviously wouldn't say, Detective."

"She has to say," he replied, thumping the table. "You can't sign a contract to circumvent criminal law."

Carscadden took a big slug of his wine. *What the hell, let's both have a good time.* "Some law book say that somewhere? Great. Laws are just *words* printed on paper, Nastos. That's nothing compared to money, which is *numbers* printed on paper."

"People kill for numbers printed on paper."

"Yeah. No one gives a shit about laws, or we wouldn't have jobs. All people care about is money."

"Touché." Nastos smiled.

The waitress came over with another bottle of wine and more calamari. "From Viktor." She smiled.

Carscadden checked the bar to raise a glass to Viktor, but he was busy with a woman. Nastos was speaking and he just caught the end of it.

"Carscadden, if the time comes, she won't remember who's missing. You can't honestly expect her to remember all the names anyways."

"She must know how to get a copy," Carscadden said.

"The cops got everything when they seized the computers in the office; she doesn't have anything. It's a dead end."

Carscadden shrugged then leaned back into his chair. "We're back at the beginning."

"Unless—" Nastos said. He looked around to make sure no one was nearby.

"What?" Carscadden asked.

"The dental assistant, do you think she was a drug user?"

Carscadden thought back to the goon who answered the door, Troy, with the marks on his arm. "No, her boyfriend's the junkie. I saw the track marks on his arm."

"Didn't you say something about the drug inventory at the office?" Nastos remembered out loud. "All kinds of stuff was unaccounted for. OxyContin, right?"

Carscadden was nodding, liking where it was going.

Nastos continued. "You could've threatened to turn her in if she didn't talk," he said. "We could have worked an angle on her."

Carscadden was thinking something. "Maybe we still can."

"It's a dead end," Nastos reminded Carscadden.

"Getting the list of names might be. But if I could get her on the stand to tell the jury that she was offered cash to get rid of the list, that might be worth something when the jury is deliberating. Who knows what else we might find to stir up reasonable doubt?"

Nastos considered that. Certainly someone was protecting himself or a client. It would be nice to find out who. "Maybe it's worth a second look."

"Okay, so when do we do this?" Carscadden asked.

"Not *we*, sunshine," Nastos said. "You're a lawyer. After dinner you're going home to watch the Leafs disgrace themselves and leaving the big decisions to the grown-ups."

"Junkies are dangerous and unpredictable — you can't go alone. Besides, you have a thing called a curfew."

Nastos didn't flinch. "Well, be a good lawyer and take detailed notes on the hockey game so we both have a good alibi."

"Like your lake swim, Nastos? As I recall, you had to phone Daddy to come get you when the last party got out of control."

Nastos smiled.

"Your face has been on TV, Nastos — you try to pressure this guy and he'll rat you out."

"Who do you think is better suited to go, the young lawyer or a cop? Or failing that, an accused murderer?"

Carscadden shook his head. Allowing Nastos' breach was risky; helping wasn't such a great idea either. "I'm going with you. I can watch out or help bullshit our way out if things go bad."

Nastos grabbed the second bottle of wine and examined the label. It was two years old, Australian. He noticed Carscadden watching him — he seemed to be hoping Nastos would open it, but two bottles between the two of them was way too much when they had things to sort out. He pushed the bottle aside and smiled at Carscadden.

108

"Maybe after this mess is behind me —" Nastos tried to change the subject. " — Hopkins, that girl is nothing but trouble, I like her."

"I know Nastos, she's great." Carscadden agreed.

"So when are you to going to do the deed?"

"I don't know —" he began lamely.

"She likes you. Get her drunk and kiss her, hard. A real good one. The rest will look after itself, I'm telling you." Nastos took a sip of water. "Madeleine liked this place last time we were here."

"Bring her next time. Now let's order, I think tonight's going to be a long one and I need an hour to clear my head."

○ ○ ○

CARSCADDEN WAS GLAD NASTOS HAD PUSHED THE SECOND BOTTLE OF wine away before they left to visit Maggie and Troy. In his glory days, he'd closed multi-million-dollar deals wasted and would slam back more Scotch by nine a.m. than most Marines did all day. It was nice to have those days farther and farther behind him.

They pulled up across the street and watched the house. The fall sun was long gone but most of the streetlights were working. The neighbourhood was like post-war Europe except for the signs of electricity and newer shit-box cars in the driveways. The rows of houses were derelict — some with misshapen laundry lines, some with smashed windows and crooked wall boards. Plastic shopping bags and empty water bottles littered the streets and sidewalks, grass was over-grown. Patchy, half-hearted paint jobs were sun-bleached and peeling away from years of neglect.

There were black and East Asian kids dotted along the streets, listening to awful electronic music. Some were playing basketball; others were just standing around, maybe waiting to see a street fight. The rest were content enough to slouch against buildings and spit on the ground occasionally, trying to appear dangerous.

Carscadden had seen Vancouver city streets filled with such kids, although more violent and more drugged-up than these punks, but he found them dangerous enough just the same. When he passed by a group of five or more, he unconsciously slowed, allow- ing Nastos to walk ahead a little.

Carscadden took a position right in front of the door. Nastos shrugged and took a step off to the side, smiling and shaking his head. The doorbell rang. Carscadden saw lights on inside. The TV was loud enough to hear from outside; cycles of canned laughter, ohhhs, ahhhs, then shouts of *Jerry! Jerry! Jerry!* When the door squeaked open, he barely noticed.

"What you need?" Carscadden recognized Troy's voice from the inch-wide gap between the door and the frame. *It seems like he has a job after all.* He smiled to Nastos to say it was the guy they wanted.

"Troy, I just need to talk to you for a second."

"Oh, you again. Sure thing," Troy said.

Carscadden was smiling at Nastos like things were going smoothly when the door flew open and Troy burst out, waving a cast-iron fire poker over his head.

"Get the fuck out of here, white boy; I've got nothing to say to you." Troy poked the sharp end at Carscadden, whose arms were spinning wildly backwards as he tried to get out of range. His back slammed into the loose top edge of the wooden banister, arching him over backwards. The ragged edge scraped up his spine, peeling back a few layers of skin, while Troy continued at him and pressed the fire poker under his chin.

"Still want to talk, buddy? Still got something on your mind?"

"I don't want any trouble — keep the drugs, I just need some paperwork from Maggie." Carscadden's voice was strained and he had bent backwards too far to even see Troy, much less make a move against him.

The first bullet tore just past his left ear. Muzzle blast — the hot pressurized gases and debris from inside the gun's barrel — burned his face like acid. His heart pounded like a bird trapped in a cage, his ear ached and the blast burn felt like blood dribbling down his face.

"Oh, and it's a close shave for the white boy. I was aiming for your ear. Now stay still." The second round didn't feel as close. If Troy had wanted to shoot him, he would have. He was probably just having a bit if fun — a little show for the punks on the street. But he was on drugs, and he could get careless and put a bullet between his eyes. *Jesus Christ, Nastos, do something.*

"I'm keeping the drugs, motherfucker, you can bet on that, and as far as paperwork from Maggie goes, I'm between attorneys, so you're just going to have to fuck off for the time being. Got that, punk?" Troy pushed the poker in farther, lifting Carscadden off his feet. He considered just flipping back over the railing onto the ground behind him — it was only a five-foot drop. Only under circumstances like these would that seem like a fantastic idea.

He heard a click then a loud thump, which was followed by a scream. Then another thump and a louder scream. The poker dropped from his neck and he saw Nastos smashing a piece of the wooden banister over Troy's head. Carscadden lunged past Troy, who was splayed out on the deck, shaking his head as he tried vainly to clear out the cobwebs. Nastos grabbed Carscadden by the arm and made for the truck. He dropped the banister and matched him stride for stride.

The street kids stepped back; they had watched everything silently, enjoying the evening's main event, but now they were talking loudly.

One kid shouted, "Way to knock it out the park, Canseco," which earned him some jack-o'-lantern smiles from his half-toothed posse.

Carscadden and Nastos got in the truck and Nastos hit the gas. "What the fuck were you waiting for?" Carscadden asked.

Nastos shook his head. "I was waiting for him to *not* have the gun pointing right at your face when I whacked him." He checked the rear-view to make sure they weren't being followed. "Maybe from now on, we'll have the accused murderer deal with guys like Troy after all, eh? How's your throat?"

Carscadden flipped down the sun visor and checked his face in the mirror. "Feels like a sunburn." He rubbed and stretched his neck. "My back hurts more."

"You would have done the same for me," Nastos said, shrugging.

Carscadden pursed his lips but said nothing. For a while there he thought he was going to die, and that was with Nastos there. If he had been alone and had a gun, he would have used it on Troy out of fear for his life. *And if I had come with Hopkins, and it had been her in trouble, I would have killed Troy for sure. I would have shot at him till I ran out of bullets. Is everyone just one bad circumstance away from killing anyone else?*

As they drove out of Flemingdon, south on Don Mills, then south on the Don Valley Parkway to Eastern Avenue, pedestrians began to reappear. Carscadden watched them, wondering where they were going, the middle-aged, the elderly, the young. Streetlights strobing past the pitted windshield caught his eye, illuminating a million tiny divots. It was inevitable that over time, the glass would fracture.

13

NASTOS SAT BACK IN HIS CHAIR, surveying the jury. Trucker Billy-Jim with his Wyatt Earp moustache was ready to take on the world with his ball cap on and a coffee in his hand. The crime fiction fan couldn't have been happier if she was at a hanging. They were keen and attentive, just the way he wanted them for the next witness, his supervising jackass, David Koche. Koche didn't tolerate women in positions of authority very well. With Dewar running the court for the prosecution and asking the questions, there was a good chance there would be some fireworks.

Nastos turned away from the jury when he heard what sounded like a sigh come from Carscadden. He still seemed drained from last night. He sat like his back was stiff and he was in pain. His injuries gave him the appearance that he had butchered himself shaving, his face flushed on both cheeks, the right worse than the left, and he kept rubbing his ears. Nastos thought back to the sound of the gun's rapport and the image of Carscadden's face, illuminated in frozen horror by the brightness of the muzzle blast. *Those bullets must have been closer than I first thought. Maybe if Hopkins hears about what a hero he was last night, she'll take some pity on the poor kid and screw him half to death. Might straighten his back out and make him forget about the ears.* He glanced at Carscadden and smirked.

113

Dewar brushed her hair back, then got to her feet. "Your Honour, the prosecution calls Detective-Sergeant David Koche to the stand, please."

The judge waved a hand to the court clerk who spoke into the paging phone. "The Crown calls Detective-Sergeant Koche, to courtroom 101, please."

Koche had been sitting in the front row of the public seating in the courtroom. He stood up, trying vainly to stick his chest out farther than his stomach. His arms swayed as he held his elbows away from his body, wanting his measly shoulders to look broad. It looked more like he had picked the wrong day to try a new underarm deodorant.

Carscadden caught Nastos' look of contempt and nudged him. "Nastos, put the daggers away — the jury . . ."

"Sorry." Nastos put pen to paper on his notepad and scribbled his wish for Koche to do something to himself — something biologically impossible.

Once Koche was sworn in, Dewar glanced up from her notes at the podium and began speaking like she could not be more bored.

"Detective, I've been reading Detective Nastos' personnel file from work. He's —"

Carscadden stood to his feet quickly and interjected. "I object, Your Honour. With all due respect, I know where my colleague is going with this and I don't see how that line of questioning could be relevant unless the prosecution is planning on producing any supporting documentation that I can then essentially re-try without the jury here. Aside from that, it's all prejudicial to the accused, regardless."

The judge tapped a finger on his lips. "Would that be a touchy subject, Mr. Carscadden?"

Carscadden said, "Your Honour, for the record, I object to the presentation of my client's work record since it is brought forward to highlight aspects of his policing career unrelated to the matter at hand."

Dewar had waited; when Montgomery acknowledged her, she spoke. "It will become evident shortly, Your Honour. It relates to both motive and means, sir."

"Overruled, for now, Mr. Carscadden, but you can always appeal the decision. Happy?"

"Overjoyed, sir."

Some of the jury chuckled a little at his reply; as he took his seat, Nastos only shrugged a response.

Dewar picked up where she had left off. "Now, as I was saying, Officer Koche, Detective Nastos has been under Police Conduct Investigations four times in just the last four years."

Carscadden barely stood when he spoke out. "I'm waiting for a question, Your Honour. If Madam Dewar is just going to testify, might I suggest my mother could take the stand? She's a little older now and would love the company of such a charming woman."

Montgomery tried vainly to suppress a smile. Most of the jury were finding Mr. Carscadden amusing as well. Dewar got the message: blanket statements weren't going to get past Carscadden. She tried again. "Detective Koche, has Detective Nastos ever taken suspects to Cherry Beach for questioning?"

Koche finally got a word in. "Yes."

"Can you tell us the nature of the complaints, please?"

"Of course. Detective Nastos was accused of beating or otherwise coercing incriminating statements from suspects on all four occasions. While circumstances were nearly identical in each occurrence, there was never enough evidence for a conviction." Koche waved his hand apologetically to the jury as if to say *We tried to get him before it got this far.*

"All four of them, nearly identical?" Dewar clarified.

"Yes, and every time the charges were dropped."

Carscadden got to his feet again. "Your Honour, this was the nature of my objection. What's the point of being found not guilty if the prosecution can use it in subsequent trials in a way that implies otherwise?"

Montgomery offered some advice. "Handle it on cross, Mr. Carscadden; if you make the same objection again, it's contempt of court. Sound like a good deal?"

"You're a regular Monty Hall, sir." He sat again and grabbed the scratch pad to make a few notes.

More of the jury were laughing with Carscadden than last time, but Nastos had never heard of a single judge letting a lawyer humour themselves into the good graces of a jury.

"Mr. Carscadden, the court cautions you that your glib remarks have no place in my courtroom. If you want to practice comedy, then perhaps you should save your act for Yuk Yuk's."

Carscadden stood with his head lowered like a beaten dog. "My apologies, sir."

Dewar began again; "Officer Koche—"

"That's Detective-Sergeant Koche," he corrected her.

"Yes, Detective Koche, can you tell me the similarities between the professional misconduct circumstances and this murder in relation to Detective Nastos?"

Nastos saw the frustration in Koche building. Dewar had been a prosecutor long enough to know the police rank structure. She was mangling his precious title every chance she got and it was pissing him off.

Koche pursed his lips and mumbled something to himself before continuing. "Of course. In the Nastos complaints, various men, all later convicted of sexual crimes, were taken to Cherry Beach and beaten very close to where the dead dentist was found. Each

beating in the complaints was progressively more violent. There were certainly no witnesses and subsequently not enough evidence to link Nastos to the allegations for a conviction. All of the victims were men. They all swore under oath that Nastos did it."

Dewar asked, "What was there for physical evidence, Officer?"

Koche didn't correct her this time; he'd given up. "Well, he allegedly used phone books to prevent bruises and struck the victims in places that are hard to bruise anyway."

Trucker Billy-Jim's face squinted up. A guy his size probably caused bruises just by grabbing people. It would be perplexing to a guy that size that you could cause damage to a person without leaving marks. The elderly Agatha Christie fan must have missed the episode of *csi* that covered it, too. Confusion and raised eyebrows dotted the rest of the jury.

Nastos saw that the jury needed a better explanation by the slightly confused expressions on their faces.

Dewar asked, "Where could a person strike another person that would not leave a mark, Detective?"

"The head is tough to bruise because of the hair. A good strike with a baton shielded by a phone book would still rattle a brain without bruising. The same technique was used on the victims' testicles. They don't really bruise either. In the last occurrence, it was alleged that Nastos held the man on his back by his neck and poured a mug of lake water into his mouth. He basically water-boarded the guy. That doesn't leave marks either."

"Water-boarded?" Dewar's jaw dropped. "That's torture."

"Sure it is," Koche replied, then corrected himself. "Well, to everyone except President George Bush."

The jury snickered, as did some spectators in the gallery. Nastos noticed that James Whitmore, his friend from the other night, was only a few rows back. If there was one person in the gallery who wanted him cleared, it was that man. Or maybe he was just here to see gruesome pictures of the tortured dentist. He caught Nastos looking at him and pumped a fist in solidarity. Nastos offered a weak smile then turned back to the trial.

"Who investigated the accused in these matters, Detective?"

Koche replied confidently, "I did."

"You were in Professional Standards at that time, before becoming the accused's supervisor in Sexual Assault?"

"Yes."

Dewar flipped to the last page in her notes and took a moment, scanning the page with a pen. "That's all my questions for this witness,

Your Honour. I would ask though for permission to possibly call him again, as he may help with various timelines in this matter."

Montgomery peered over his glasses to Carscadden. "Any objections, Mr. Carscadden?"

Carscadden barely lifted himself from the seat to answer. "None, sir — whatever works."

"Then you can begin with the witness," the judge said.

"Thank you, sir."

Carscadden stood up. He took a discreet breath while flipping through at his hastily scratched notes, then approached the lectern to begin his questioning.

"Detective-Sergeant Koche, let me see if I understand this. Four allegations of severe beatings, from independent victims, over a span of four years, each more severe than the last. Each is investigated independently and my client is exonerated every time, unanimously?"

Koche obviously did not want to answer that question, but he knew it was inevitable. "There wasn't enough evidence for a conviction."

"And you were the investigator for those occurrences, right?" Carscadden asked.

"Yes, sir."

"All of them?"

"Yes, all of them."

"Then, in this case, my client is accused of killing a man who turns up in the same place, beaten to death. Again my client is accused?"

Koche answered coolly. "Yes, sir, the connection is obvious."

"With no physical evidence?"

"The testimonies were nearly identical, the only difference was that the violence increased with each incident and that the last man was not in a position to complain because he didn't survive the attack."

Nastos saw Billy-Jim turn his head to Carscadden as if wondering what he was finding so difficult to grasp. Others were nodding slightly, agreeing with Koche. Carscadden's face twisted up; he seemed to be speaking to himself as he worked through it all. "You know what, it seems to me, sir, isn't it possible . . . actually, first let's try it this way." Carscadden went back to the podium and flicked back to the first page of his notes. "I realize that in many ways you're an expert on sexual crimes and sexual criminals."

"Thank you, Mr. Carscadden." Nastos smirked when Koche's chest puffed out as best it could, like he couldn't agree with him more. Koche was much more relaxed with Carscadden than Dewar; he always got Koche's title right. *Calling him an expert was a great idea, Carscadden.*

"Is this true, then? We often hear from the media that sexual predators often communicate with each other on the internet, sharing luring secrets, pictures, pornographic literature — is that really true?"

"Yes, Mr. Carscadden," Koche straightened and turned to the jury as if he wanted to get the educational point across to them. "They often share tips with each other, helping each other become better at luring and exploiting children."

Carscadden tried again. "Then, back to the point I was going to make earlier. These alleged victims of abuse by Detective Nastos — I submit to you, sir, that their stories were entirely made up. That they came to you one at a time as they got caught with nothing more than lies of abuse, possibly using a template one of them created. And that each one was more violent because each previous allegation was not strong enough for a conviction?"

"Sorry, Mr. Carscadden, but that's preposterous."

"So, these men molest children, post it on the internet, share pictures and evade the cops for years. They destroy the lives of their nieces, nephews or strangers, but you think that they would never cross the line of lying to you to try to get off the charges?"

Koche's face flushed red and his eyes narrowed on Carscadden. "Those allegations were true, all of them. It's obvious. Especially in light of the murder."

"Well, I've got to say, *Officer* Koche, it would be a lot more obvious if my client had been convicted even once of the previous incidents.

And as far as I'm concerned, all you've told the jury is that either you're a terribly naive person, believing what you want to believe from the scum of the earth, or that you've personally tried to sandbag a good officer repeatedly and you're not very good at it."

Koche's jaw clenched tight. Nastos had never seen Koche so angry. Carscadden had just hit his first home run of the trial, assuming Koche wasn't about to jump out of the witness box and beat him to death.

"Your Honour?" Dewar asked.

Before the judge could speak, Carscadden waved him off, saying, "That's okay, Your Honour, I withdraw my last comment," then, almost indignantly, he added, "I'm done with this witness."

14

WHILE NASTOS WAS TASTING his first hint of optimism at court as his lawyer tore into Detective Koche, North was driving up St. George Street near Davenport Road to see another house with his buying agent, Madeleine Nastos. It was a perfect fall day; the cast from the sun reflected from brick-faced houses like in a travel poster. He had a green tea by his side and a cell phone up to his ear and was cruising slowly as he read the house numbers passing by.

"Yeah, Eade, I'll see you in an hour or so. I just have to pay a little visit to my next girlfriend." *Some agents put For Sale signs in the stupidest places — some sellers don't want them on the lawn at all.* He hung up and stopped his car in front of the house.

The entire street and a good portion of the neighbourhood were made up of bay-and-gables built at the turn of the century. The house for sale was Gothic revival with stained glass and bargeboards. This place could sell itself. *Welcome to the Annex, Madeleine Nastos.*

She was standing on the front step, typing into her BlackBerry. North took the stairs two at a time.

"Mr. Sitler, nice to see you again." She extended her hand and North took it.

"Yes, that's right, you too." She was as beautiful as last time. Her little pictures did her no justice. He felt a flush of heat rush through his body. Her smile was broad and genuine, and her eyes sparkled as if they were not strangers but longtime friends.

"Here, I have a key, let's get inside." She gently brushed against him as she put the key in the lock and opened the door. The innocent intrusion into his intimate space pushed his heart rate up twenty beats a minute as easily as anything. *She smells like vanilla,* he thought.

"Well, come on in. If you love Gothic, you are going to love this place." Madeleine kicked her shoes off and North did the same. He was disappointed that she didn't have to bend over a little more to get the straps, but it didn't stop him from ogling as best he could.

"I love the feel — reminds me of the old vampire movies." His eyes glimmered as he smiled. Madeleine's smile dropped ever so slightly at the edges. Her eyes went to his neck. He wondered if she might have noticed the tattoo. With his high-collared shirt, it was little more than a blue stain.

"Well, let's get through the basics. Main floor laundry, walk-out kitchen to the back deck, hardwood throughout. It's only been on the market for a week but I still thought it would be gone by now." They strode from the kitchen to the living room.

"Great atmosphere, very sensual," he said.

"They listed for 650, but they'll take 635 if it's a solid offer. I can't remember, do you have a house to sell, Mr. Sitler?"

"Umm, I see," he avoided her gaze and typed into his BlackBerry. "Shall we check out the upstairs?"

"You're going to love it; the master has a fireplace and a nice soaker tub. If you're single, this place will be perfect for you. Do you have kids?"

"Sadly, no. You?"

"One, and she gets busier every day."

North answered robotically, "Good for you. Married?" They went up the stairs; Madeleine pointed out the vaulted ceiling.

"Yes, I'm married."

"Too bad." He scanned her body up and down more obviously; he smiled, approving of what he saw.

He noted a small change in her behaviour. She had become thoughtful instead of carefree. It turned him on to watch her beginning to feel like he might be a predator and she the prey. The change in her thinking changed her manner. And now she was conflicted as she tried to suppress her natural instinct to maintain the polite façade. *Oh, Madeleine, you haven't learned to trust yourself, have you?*

"If you're trying to get a deal on the commission, it's not working." Madeleine offered a weak smile and slid her hand into her purse.

She uses humour when she's uncomfortable. How cute. "I wouldn't expect a deal; I hear you're going through hard times."

"Excuse me?" She stopped in place.

North saw that he was coming on too strong and tried to back off a little. "Sorry, I don't mean anything personal — just, you know how invasive the media is. Must be awful with everything going on, your husband going to jail."

Her voice was harsh. "It's nothing — we — can't handle. You want to see the back deck?" He had wanted to keep her off balance longer. He figured that he had pushed her too hard and too fast. He tried to pull her back in.

"Your husband is a hero for killing that fucker as far as I'm concerned. Did he tell you he was going to do it or was it just a nice surprise?"

She pulled her phone out of her pocket and examined the screen. "Listen, I have a client texting me to see if I'm going to be long. I have another appointment soon — are we done here?"

"That all depends. Don't you want to show me the master bedroom?" He walked toward her, reaching out to run his hand down the side of her body. He could feel the firm lean muscle and perfect hourglass shape.

Madeleine stepped back, breathlessly recoiling from his touch. She stared at his neck, her perfect full lips mouthing the word tattooed there: *Troublesome.*

"Admit it, you need a good fuck, you're due." North eyed her carefully, expecting her just to admit that she wanted it. He was pretty surprised when she drove her knee into his balls, dropping him immediately to his knees. She pushed past him, barging down the stairs. She fumbled for her cell phone. It slipped and danced between her fingers before she grabbed it and stuffed it in her purse.

North got to his feet angrily and focused his eyes on her fleeing form. He ran down the stairs after her, only touching the steps twice. He smashed the partially closed front door open, his eyes searching for her wildly. He saw her running up to the driver's door of her car and he locked on her like the old vampire chasing the terrified woman in a 1940s horror movie. He could smell her fear and see paralysis nearly holding her rigid.

Madeleine forced herself to turn her back on him as he charged her. She hit the wireless lock release and nearly dove into the car. She got in and locked the door, then jammed the key into the ignition. She already had the pedal to the floor when she put the car in gear, screeching away from the house as North kicked and missed at the driver's side panel.

She took the corner with her phone up to her ear. *If you're calling the office, Madeleine, it's a waste of time. I gave them a bullshit name.*

◻ ◻ ◻

DAVE KOCHE TRUDGED FORWARD, HANDS STUFFED DEEP WITHIN HIS pockets and shoulders slumped forward as he passed the darkened storefront windows on King Street West. It was a quiet and anonymous night, with only passing traffic from the occasional streetcar filled with glum, nameless faces and the red flashes of brake lights from the slowed cars.

His breath smoked behind him as if it were steam from his overheated and overactive mind. It was all about the trial. Everything rested on a conviction — it was his career and reputation on the line, diametrically opposed to that of Nastos. Koche had been the first to see that the evidence pointed to one of their own, and when he saw that it was Nastos, he couldn't resist. He essentially branded himself on the front page of the paper as the face of anti-corruption. He owned the story. This trial represented laying one of the last foundational stones for his move to lead the organization. When Prosecutor Jeff Scott and the Police Service Board chose the next chief, they would appear tough on corruption and become heroes to the left-wing fanatics who ran the city.

He loved the fact that he was getting so much mileage from the misfortunes of none other than Nastos. He thought back to when the first allegation that Nastos was smacking around his prisoners came across his desk at the Professional Standards Bureau. It had confirmed his suspicions — not that Nastos was doing anything wrong by hurting people, just that he was too sloppy. He didn't mind cops doing what they had to do, but embarrassing the service while doing it ruined it for everyone.

He had seized the opportunity to make a name for himself by burying Nastos. But when Nastos wasn't convicted, Koche's reputation took a hit. When his tenure ran up and he had to leave the Bureau, he got transferred to the Sexual Assault unit to finish what he had begun earlier. Convinced that Nastos was dirty, Koche felt that he was getting a chance for redemption.

Being Nastos' boss for the next two years only intensified his hatred. The cocky dick talked back to him, questioned every administrative decision Koche made. He had no respect for authority, was obstinate and just impossible to manage. Koche knew that Nastos' insubordination could become like a cancer in the unit and that he needed to deal with it. *Well, now the asshole is going to jail — so that'll show him and the rest of the idiots what that attitude gets you.*

125

There was only one problem, and her name was Dewar. She had gone from being the biggest shark in the prosecution office to having as much killer instinct as goldfish, and at this point it all rested on her. He never thought a prosecutor her number of years in, with her conviction rate, could be such a lightweight when it mattered most. Broads. She was cracking under the pressure. Koche thought back to how bloodthirsty Scott had been back in his day. If only he could take over the case, Nastos would be in jail by the end of the first day. But Scott had been promoted and now he was just a glorified pencil-pusher. It was up to that bitch, and Koche hated it.

A swinging metal sign above his head caught his attention and he pulled open the door to the Irish pub, the Templar. Inside, immersed in the sudden warmth and life of the vibrant place, he smelled the house stew and lukewarm dark ale, stale fumes of which seemed to radiate from the plank floorboards. Stained glass, Celtic symbols, an old mahogany bar—if the building had been a few hundred years older it would have been the real thing. Koche smiled slightly.

Koche found Scott in the corner of a private room. There were almost a dozen older men sitting around a table in their dishevelled business suits, nursing beers and talking political strategy. Scott was speaking quietly to the man to his right. Koche took a seat on the other side of Scott, reaching awkwardly around him to grab a fistful of peanuts from the communal bowl.

"I'm not going public until I get all the soft money together. I want to hit the airwaves the day I announce," Scott was saying. He turned, obviously a little perturbed by Koche's intrusive reach. "Detective Koche, nice to see you here." He forced a smile.

"I need a quick word, Jeff; we have a situation—something we need to get squared away." One of the men at the table, a white man in his fifties, turned and smiled at the expression. Koche noted the man's Masonic ring, then put together that all of the men here would be Freemasons like him and Scott. He had resented that he had had to join up for his career aspirations. But he hadn't found joining as painful as having to donate some of his drug money to the group just to make a good impression to the police chief and two of the deputies, who were also Masons. The promotion that came shortly after took some of the sting out of the financial loss.

No one runs for office in this town without their support if they want to win. Koche smiled at the man while tapping his ring on the table. All the expressions related to medieval tools. Compass, anvil, square—you met a stranger and knew he was a Mason in five seconds. Koche didn't like the chumminess per se, but it came in handy when you wanted to get somewhere. When the waitress came into the private room, he caught her attention and ordered a dark ale.

Koche wasn't too keen on the idea of going back out into the cool night to talk to Scott, so they ended up at the back of the bar by a nearly obsolete pay phone. The phone was only there as a courtesy so the married customers could call their girlfriends without fear of generating problematic billing statements on their cells. A gentle din of conversation was just loud enough for them to talk without concern of being overheard.

"Koche, I'm not really in a position to get in the courtroom and see what's going on—I'd draw too much attention. What's your concern?"

"Your pep talk with Dewar didn't work—she just doesn't have it in her. She's not emotionally involved. How can the jury be outraged and hungry for blood if she treats this like a shoplifting case?" Without waiting for Scott to answer, he continued. "They need to read her body language and see revulsion. She's not you, she's a woman. They make good nags but awful lawyers."

Scott exhaled. "Mat leave, PMS, human rights complaints, yeah, I know. I've been the chief prosecutor for years now. And for all the crap I put up with, they're just barely effective at their jobs. But Dewar actually is a good lawyer. The trial coordinator gave her the case. I could have overridden it but I didn't."

Koche lamented. "I know—in Appeals she owned the courtroom."

127

"Well, I actually thought she could do this one too. And if she looks good then it reflects positively on me for mentoring her." Scott took a slug of his beer.

Koche was silent for a moment, thinking over Scott's reasoning.

Scott started again, "I'll just have to lay out the whole thing for her. I'll have to spoon-feed her the whole trial." He nodded like he was making a mental note to himself.

Koche had a lot of respect for Scott. The prosecutor was one of the few people he considered to be as smart as himself. Scott wasn't just going to use the victory for personal advantage, but also his choice of the prosecutor, an up-and-coming female visible minority. The man could operate on several levels at once. Then Scott hit him with the type of comment that showed he was ready to get his hands dirty to win.

"It sure would be nice to see what Carscadden has in store for us," Scott said.

"It would, eh?"

"Well, it sure wouldn't hurt."

Koche tapped a finger to his lip, trying to think how he could make that happen. A name came to mind: North.

"Are you banging Dewar, Scott?" Koche asked.

Scott tightened at the bluntness of the question. "No, I'm not, sorry to say. Since she pumped out or bought that little half-breed of hers, I think she prefers to stick to her own kind."

Koche shuddered. "She only screws other Pakis?"

"She's Indian, but no, she likes the ladies, or at least that's what the rumour is, Dave."

Koche was caught off guard by that one. His eyes glazed over as if he was thinking about something that was pretty engrossing. A wicked smile crept across his lips. He shook his head. Maybe he would finish that thought off a little later. "You know Scott, about the files, I've got a guy who does —"

"I don't want to know about that," Scott said, cutting him off.

"No problem. I just have to make a phone call."

"And Dave?"

"Yeah?"

"Tell your guy to find something specific, a client list for the dentist. It was supposed to be in the case brief in the prosecution office, but it wasn't there — I've gone through it twice."

"Sure thing," Koche made a mental note. "But what's so important about it?"

"Well, everyone on the list has a motive for murdering the guy. I saw a vetted list, but we need to know everyone on the list. I don't want this Carscadden character to be in a position to distract the jury with reasonable doubt surprises right before deliberations. It's a little Perry Mason, but showy stuff like that works, and I don't want any part of it."

Koche smiled; Scott hadn't lost his touch. "I'll tell him to copy absolutely everything in the files, then to have a look around just in case."

Scott didn't want to bring up one last point but he decided that later, he would just say it had been the booze talking. "There is one more thing, Koche."

"What's that?"

"There is evidence that Nastos was in the area of the murder when it happened, but it isn't one hundred percent. I'd like one hundred percent for Ms. Dewar, something she can't stickhandle away."

Koche tried to think of something, but couldn't. "What do you suggest we do?"

"I suggest that there should be an eyewitness." Scott watched him for a reaction, for any kind of a nervous flinch. Of course, there wasn't.

"That's a good idea, Scott, a great idea." Possibilities ran through his mind. *North? No, he's too hot, maybe one of his morons.* "I think I can come up with something, someone. It'll work for a few bucks."

"Obtain a statement from the witness and get it to me. I'll see that Dewar gets the information, the statement, and that she gets the man on the stand before he gets any funny ideas, like backing out." 129

"Just like old times."

15

on the couch finishing dinner and watching the hockey game. They had the volume up but Nastos didn't have much interest in the action on-screen. "You know, Carscadden, as a guy from Kitsilano, I thought you'd be too high-brow to be a Leafs fan. I took you for a guy who'd be into culture, opera, crap like that."

"I've always been a Leafs fan — so many of the players are from a short drive from here."

"They suck, though. They're so bad it actually hurts to watch."

"True fans like the Leafs *because* they suck," Carscadden began. "They'll never win, they'll always be losers, and that's the point. They keep on fighting the good fight. It's the management team, the teacher's union that owns them and insists on a ten-percent return on money, that puts profits over the fans. They take the Leaf Nation for granted, but you can't blame the players."

Nastos went to the kitchen. "Well, while you're getting taken for granted, I'm taking the last of the chicken."

"Be my guest — you made it anyways. I haven't eaten this well in years. Hell, after this trial, you should kill my ex-wife and we can have this much fun again."

Without diverting his eyes from the screen, Carscadden answered the phone on the first ring, a flinch reaction the Leafs' goalie could have used.

"Hello? Hey, how are you? . . . Sure, he's right here." He covered the mouthpiece and turned toward Nastos. "It's your wife."

Nastos put his loaded plate down and came to get the phone. "Hey, thanks. Turn the game back up, I'll go out on the balcony."

Nastos opened the patio door and stepped outside. The air was humid and warm. This wasn't the best area of town, but at night with the city lights and clear sky, the view was beautiful. The thick oily smell of sun-heated asphalt was nearly absent. Instead, there was a mild scent of curry and coriander from a distant neighbour mixed with the smells of heated concrete and masonry from the city's walls.

Nastos took a seat in one of the folding patio chairs and put his feet up on the railing. "Hey, how's it going?"

"Fine, how's the bachelor pad?" she asked.

Great, he thought. *By the tone of her voice, she's already preoccupied.*

"I don't remember it being this lonely, to be honest. I guess back then I had you coming over as often as I could persuade you." He smiled but didn't get the response he wanted. She didn't answer.

"It'd be nice to see you in court sometime."

"I've been busy."

"I know you have."

She elaborated, "I'm trying to work more, Josie's a handful, the media are all over the trial."

"Yeah, that's fine. I understand."

Her voice was hushed. Maybe she didn't want Josie to hear. "Nastos, what the hell have you done to us?"

He took a moment to figure out how best to play this one. She was a tough girl, but things were obviously getting to her more than he thought they would. He was a little disappointed, but not surprised. "They're trying to screw me over, plain and simple."

"*Trying* to screw you over? No, they *have* screwed you over. You're going to jail, Steve, take a good look around." He could imagine her sitting up in bed, under the covers. There'd be a box of

Kleenex not far away. She only called him by his first name when she was pissed.

"Listen, Madeleine, it's —"

"Josie is really confused about all of this," she cut him off. "She thinks you're convicted already and that she'll never see her father again." He heard her blow her nose.

"I didn't ask for this, but it could have been worse. If I was denied bail I would have lost my job automatically. It's a condition of my employment not to go to jail. This bail, being away from you and Josie, it's just going to justify a larger financial settlement when I get exonerated. I'm not going to go to jail for this. Milgaard, Truscott, Driskell. Those are just the wrongly convicted we know about. How many more were wrongly prosecuted but were exonerated at trial? I'm going to be cleared, then the lawsuit will be our early retirement. Freedom Forty-Five."

She wasn't convinced. "That's comforting, thanks for that. I tried to show a house yesterday and the buyer turned out to be a pervert who works for the local news — this is getting ridiculous."

"What happened?"

"Nothing I couldn't handle, don't worry about it."

And with that he knew why she had really called. Someone had gotten to her and he was powerless to help her. "I'm sorry you have to go through this. I wish there was something I could do."

"And there isn't a person out there who doesn't think you did it, you know. Everyone just assumes you beat this guy to death because of Josie. And now she's going to be visiting Daddy in jail until she's thirty."

Nastos took a breath, trying to slow things down. "Listen, I don't really know what to say here, but I need you to stay positive. I'm coming home — no jail, not even for one day. I'll be on bail until I get cleared, then I'm going to sue their asses off. After this trial is done, I'm going to retire and take a job with your uncle at the insurance bureau. I'll be on the pension and making a good income and —"

"What the hell are you saying, Nastos?" she interrupted. She was practically shouting now. "You're on trial for murder, for fuck's sake." She started again, this time trying to hush herself. "You're going to rot in a jail cell until you're sixty-five. You need to think about today, right now—this isn't the time for daydreaming. You've got to be thinking about Josie and me so we don't have to go through the rest of our lives without you. You have to snap out of this.

"You've been a bitter, tired man for the last few years, then you get charged with murder, and now it's all ponies and rainbows. How about a reality check?"

She only got sarcastic when she was really pissed. There was no arguing with her when she was wrong; there was certainly no point in trying when she was right. "How's Josie?"

"She sleeps with me every night. She usually comes in after the first round of night terrors, when she wakes up screaming. Her grades are a mess, and she's peeing the bed for the first time in years."

His eyes welled up and his voice betrayed his emotions. "Our little baby."

"She knows we love her, Nastos. She's going to get better. It would just be a lot faster if you were here with us. Sometimes a little girl just needs her daddy."

"Sometimes a daddy just needs his little girl."

◘ ◘ ◘

CHAMBER MUSIC FROM A QUARTET WAS THE ONLY SOUND THAT COULD be heard as the car came to a stop on the darkened and desolate street. He opened the glove box, moved the nine-millimetre Glock pistol out of the way and pulled out a small leather pouch. With a twist of the key, both the car and the music died and he stepped out onto the roadway. North was dressed in a black suit and overcoat. After reaching back into the car, he put the small leather pouch in a lawyer's satchel, gently closed the car door and began walking to Carscadden's office.

He passed businesses that were closed for the night, a dry cleaning store and a hair salon that was actually an after-hours booze can that hadn't opened yet, using the angled glass to make sure no one was behind him. No traffic, no people, no stray dogs, nothing. He walked up the steps to the front door of Carscadden's office.

Inside the small leather pouch were lock-picking tools. The deadbolt was installed well, which actually made it easier to pick. Getting a lock open is all about control of the cylinder. The torque wrench goes in at the bottom of the lock, the circle-like portion. Shaped like an exaggerated hockey stick, the longer portion sticks out sideways. North pressed down gently with a finger while he inserted the pick over it and into the pins. He pushed them up from front to back to front again till they all came clear of the cylinder. Like magic the cylinder spun and the lock was open. Had the lock been poorly installed or just old, he would have had to stop it from jiggling around to control it better. The ace who installed this lock made picking it a ten-second job.

There was no tone from a security system, so North placed his satchel on the floor inside the door and got to work. He methodically ransacked the office, prying open the desk drawers, going through the cabinets, slowly destroying the place. He found the Nastos file he was looking for and put it down on Carscadden's desk. He took out a portable scanner no larger than a pen, with a roller wheel on each end. He flicked a switch and one side came alive in a bright green light. As he rolled it down the pages, it was scanning everything on the paper.

He went through the folder page by page, copying everything. Once all of Carscadden's notes were copied, he put the file back where he had found it. The work portion of his visit finished, North began working for himself and searched the less obvious places this time: the freezer in the kitchenette, the back of the toilet, the pockets of the jackets hanging in the closets. He peeked under the desks, sofa, searched absolutely everywhere.

North was driven by more than a work ethic. Everyone has secrets, large and small, habits or needs from time to time, that are best kept to oneself. How many lawyers had been known to smoke a bit of weed or snort the odd line? How many judges or cops too, for that matter? Everyone had something going on. A little rush of excitement from shoplifting some petty trinkets, maybe just a propensity for visiting the occasional body-rub parlour or picking up a working girl. Everyone had something that gave them a bit of a rush. North found it very exciting to learn what someone's curiosity was. Not only was it thrilling for its own sake, but if you found the right person, with the right soft spot, you could even make yourself a bit of extra spending money. And that would be just fine for North, because the soft spot *he* had — cocaine — was getting pricey these days.

Before leaving for his next appointment, North took the time to smash in a few drywall panels and topple several pieces of furniture. The only thing he didn't do was smash any window glass; the last thing he needed was to attract the public when he had one more stop to make.

◙ ◙ ◙

NORTH SAT IN HIS CAR AS THE LAST OF THE COCAINE WORKED ITS WAY through his body. The sun had left the sky for the first of the evening stars to mark some of the universe's constellations. Streetlights sparked to life. North saw things differently while on coke. He watched the imperfect surface of roadway glisten from his angle of observation. She walked out of the house. Between the slowly lightening universe and the road's refraction of the offset lighting, Angela Dewar appeared in front of him. She drew from him conflicting emotions, lust and loathing. She had everything of value in this world, while circumstance had taken everything from him. And there she was, with her perfect life.

Her long legs, in two-inch heels, strode adeptly down the stone steps of her porch to her car. She had her back to North, which suited him just fine when she leaned forward to put her gym bag deep in the car's trunk.

He watched her get in the car, start it and pull out of the driveway. After a few minutes, North got out of his car and walked across the street carrying his briefcase. Cool air entered his lungs with a menthol-like bite that he found invigorating. Or maybe what he found invigorating was excitement from what he was about to do.

He stopped at her front door and put his suitcase down. It was a standard deadbolt, so again he pulled out the medium torque wrench and a pick with a large hook. It took all of thirty seconds for him to push the pins out of the way and twist open the cylinder.

A tone sounded when the front door opened and, courtesy of the lines of coke North had done just an hour ago, he set to work calmly and efficiently with no monkey on his back to make him fidgety.

He closed the door behind him and opened the suitcase on the floor. He pulled out a small device and with a quick series of motions he ripped the alarm box out from the wall leaving the wires connected, attached alligator clips to the exposed wires and turned the device on. Within five seconds it had communicated with the alarm box and deactivated the alarm, silencing the tone.

He had never been tempted to sell his electronic items to fuel his recreational drug use. He knew them to be the tools of his trade and to hock them would be a short-term fix for a long-term amount of pain. Also North was not an out-of-control addict. He would never choose drugs over food; he never let himself go too far. He needed little more than six hundred a week for his modest habit, which he could handle with his current income level and modest lifestyle. A few days without using wasn't a big deal either, but after a week he'd become anxious for a hit.

North found the home office. He barely noticed the girl's doll house and stable of toy horses on the floor behind the door and opposite the computer. He turned on the desktop computer and while it fired up he had a brief snoop in the living room, examining the ser-

136

ies of pictures on the mantel. One showed Dewar and a young girl hugging in a park. Another showed Dewar graduating from law school, a third with Dewar hugging her girlfriend. She certainly had good taste in women. *A doctor, very impressive.*

The computer was ready and North began searching for files. *R vs. Nastos.* He clicked Print All. The printing would take a while so he decided to complete a more detailed search. Koche might consider it a little off script, but North began installing audio bugs and two small video cameras. The first camera contained the master bedroom and ensuite bathroom doorway in its field of view. The second captured the shower and the area in front of the bathroom's vanity. The positioning likely had little to do with the Nastos trial. A small micro-cam can go anywhere, but North felt light fixtures and smoke detectors were the best places.

He searched everything, including her underwear drawer and night table. He had been expecting some private sexual items, but was rather disappointed. However, what he found in her jewellery box moments later nearly stopped his heart in place. Under the white gold bracelet and matching diamond earrings was a photo. And in the photo was Angela Dewar hugging and kissing Detective Nastos, the man she was prosecuting for murder.

North stood still, considering what to do, then remembered his pocket scanner. He took a copy of the picture and returned to the computer. It had finished printing the Nastos file, so he logged on to the net, accessed his home computer remotely and checked the video feeds. Both his cameras were placed perfectly. He could already imagine seeing her glistening, naked, wet body after she stepped out of the shower.

"This one is free of charge, Detective Koche."

16

WHEN HIS CELL PHONE RANG, Nastos had to remind himself of where he was. Carscadden's place. It was dark and the bed was cold without his wife next to him. *Madeleine?* His hand banged into the bedside table as he grabbed his phone. He flipped it open and the screen was too bright to read the time or the name of the caller, but it was early — he had been in a deep sleep and it was still black outside.

"Madeleine?"

Silence.

"Madeleine? Who is this?"

"I'll tell you one thing, sport: I bet she's a real fun ride."

Nastos sat up in bed and turned on the dim light at his side. He checked the display screen, but all it said was Unknown Caller. "Who the fuck is this?"

"I had the pleasure of your wife's company earlier this evening. Tall, blond, nice ass . . ."

He pulled the phone away from his ear and stared at it. "You just signed your own death warrant, asshole. When I —"

"I'm right outside." The man interrupted. "Look out your window."

Nastos got to his feet and threw the curtain back. He had to go back to turn off the bedside light to cut out the glare, then he scanned the street below. A man stepped from the shadows of an alley and walked under a streetlight. He waved slowly.

"I'm right here, tough guy. You want to come talk, here I am."

Nastos never had the chance to kill Irons before someone had done it for him. In part, he felt that even the chance to kill the man, the opportunity to fantasize about it, had been robbed from him. This was like Christmas.

He eyed the phone again. *Set-up written all over this. That voice — the homeless guy?* It was another line of bait to lure him out past curfew so he could go to jail.

"You haven't been out with my wife — you're full of shit."

The man allowed himself a small chuckle. "Maybe you two aren't on speaking terms. You should call her and ask."

Nastos thought back to the conversation he had had with her earlier in the evening. *The buyer turned out to be a pervert who works for the local news.* "I've had enough people fucking with my family to last a lifetime."

"Then come out and we can talk about it."

"Not a chance, you want to breach me." Nastos said. "Pretty cowardly, if you ask me. You come up here, it's nice and private."

The man on the other end of the phone was silent. Nastos watched out the window, studying him, trying to memorize his mannerisms, but he was barely moving, giving him nothing.

He repeated, "You're a coward, whoever you are."

"Nice try, Detective, but I'm the one driving this train."

This guy feels protected. Someone has got his back . . . Koche. Who would Koche get to do this? Not a cop, it would be too big of a risk. A shit-rat, or a retired guy, one of the two. It could be anyone.

There was a stalemate between the two men, but then the stranger broke the silence. "Well, maybe I can come up for a second or two. Buzz me in."

Nastos stared in disbelief as the man began walking toward the building. He crossed the street, but kept the phone line active. Nastos studied his movement, the sound of his breath. Not a wheeze, not even a change in the cadence as he became active. He was fit.

Nastos turned the hall light on to find the door-release buzzer and pressed it right away. He held it for ten seconds, then waited by the door. He figured he was legally fine to step into the hallway, but he didn't want to reveal himself too early. He considered waking Carscadden, but before he could finish the thought he heard the elevator chime. His heart was racing; he felt light-headed and had to take some deep breaths.

A man emerged from the elevator wearing a Halloween mask: a red devil with yellow teeth and long black lips wisping up the sides of the face in a gruesome smile.

Nastos stepped into the hallway, allowing the door to close under its own weight. It might have locked — he didn't care. Nastos dropped his phone to the ground and the fight was on.

Nastos swung hard with his right fist, but the man stepped in close, allowing Nastos' arm to wrap around him. Nastos took two hard strikes to his stomach and stepped backward and looked down, then the devil shot his head up, shoving Nastos' jaw back into his head. Nastos fell back into the condo door with the devil on top of him. They exchanged punches and kicks, but the devil was slowly out-manoeuvring him. He was a skilled fighter. Nastos protected his face — hell, with the mask on the stranger was basically fighting blind — but it made no difference. Nastos started taking shot after shot to the face, ears and jaw. The guy was going for a knockout.

Nastos tried everything — kicking, rolling, punching — but he couldn't land a solid hit; it was like fighting air. A hand closed around his throat, warm and sweaty; it didn't so much squeeze as slowly begin to press down into his neck, suffocating him. He grabbed hold of the mask and tried to use it as leverage to shift the man off of him, but it was useless. The best he could do was lift a side to reveal something of a neck tattoo, some lettering. With the pressure on his neck, he couldn't suck in any air, not even through his nose. Panic washed over him as he began to see stars, followed by the beginnings of blackness.

The condo door bucked violently into both Nastos and the assailant, once and then twice. Nastos had long given up on getting the hand off his neck and dreamily grabbed at the devil's head with both hands. He managed to gouge an eye. The third strike from the condo door was full force and connected directly with the devil's head. The man careened into the far wall and got to his feet, trying to shake out the cobwebs. Nastos rolled onto his side and was sucking in air when Carscadden burst into the hallway. He took a swing at the devil who avoided it easily and ran down to the far staircase. He disappeared, leaving only a closing door. Click.

"What the fuck was that?" Carscadden asked.

"That's what a corpse looks like when it doesn't know it's dead yet."

17

CARSCADDEN AND HOPKINS SAT in the ransacked office. They had balanced a twelve-inch TV monitor in some law text books that were propped up on his smashed desk. Carscadden sat on what was left of an end table while Hopkins sat in the swivel chair, the sole survivor amongst the furniture. Pictures were tilted on kicked-in walls and the cheap panel door to the closet was missing completely. Carscadden and Hopkins speculated for a moment about where an entire door would wander off to, before deciding to drop search-and-rescue operations for the time being.

Their priority was to watch the video that Ms. Hopkins was starting. It had been her idea to have an internal video camera system installed after Carscadden's work began with his previous client, Mr. Kalmakov. She figured that it was only a matter of time before both she and Carscadden were murdered by the man's goons upon his conviction and she wanted there to be some kind of record. Carscadden had thought it was a brilliant idea. He didn't blame her for banking that he would lose — anyone with a brain had thought the same thing.

The cameras were small pin-hole lenses stationed throughout their office space hooked into a digital recorder hidden in the ceiling. It recorded seventy-two hours continuously before recording over itself. Since its hard drive was no larger than an iPod, someone would have to look for it specifically to find it — and they obviously hadn't.

142

They watched a man pick the front door lock and get right to work. He photocopied files, trashed the place, then searched again in finer detail. Near the end, Carscadden felt he had seen enough and he stopped the video with a freeze-frame of the suspect's face. "Recognize him?"

"Not the maid," she replied. "You like 'em bustier."

He smiled. "Not the appliance guy either — you like them shirtless."

"He's a pro, nonetheless."

Carscadden pointed to the screen. "What's that on his neck?"

She moved toward the screen, and incidentally closer to Carscadden, peering in for a closer look. "Dunno, shadow?" Hopkins squinted as she traced the image with her finger and paused.

"Umm, a tattoo." She turned to Carscadden.

Carscadden scoffed. "What kind of a winner has his neck tattooed?"

"Well, the Russian mafia and Mexican street gangs both used to, then they figured out it made them too easy to identify. This is English, though. T-R-O-"

"Well, it's a place to start. I see it now, T-R-O, then it goes under his shirt. I bet a cop could run a tattoo search and find out if he has a record." She pressed Print Screen on the keyboard, turned off the monitor and disconnected the small drive. They both leaned back a little and turned to face each other as the image came out of the printer in a glossy 8×10.

Their age difference didn't stop him from noticing the ever so faint lines around her eyes, her full, strong lips.

Carscadden ran his fingers through his hair, then began tapping the table. "Listen, something happened at the apartment last night."

Hopkins leaned back in the chair. "Was she pretty? You could have called me over."

He shook his head, blushing. "Some guy came over — he and Nastos got into a fight. He was wearing a devil mask. I thought they were going to kill each other."

"What brought that on?"

"Nastos said the guy was following his wife around and wanted to lure Nastos out of the apartment. If he'd been caught on video, he would have been breached and sent to jail."

"Obviously that didn't happen?"

"No, but the guy came to the door instead. Sounds like a psychopath." He examined the picture that they had printed out. "Must be the same guy."

"Well, don't tell Nastos you have his picture — he'll go crazy and do something like kill him on national TV."

Carscadden nodded in agreement. "That he would. It has to be the guys at his work, they hate him." He pushed away from the table, turning to face her. "What exactly do they have against the guy, anyway?"

"When you were in trial a few days ago I dropped by and got talking to one of the detectives who was at court for something else."

Carscadden leaned in. "Oh, yeah?"

"He wasn't my type, don't worry." She patted his hand in mock reassurance. "Apparently Nastos got kicked out of Homicide years ago and got himself a chip on his shoulder. No one wanted to work with Nastos; he was a lawsuit waiting to happen. Being anti-authoritarian doesn't work well in a rank structure. If Nastos ever felt he was getting pushed around, he always pushed back. He obviously pissed off someone who holds grudges. One day, an opportunity came up to teach him a lesson."

Carscadden got to his feet and turned off the TV. "That's what buddy said?"

"Yup."

"Maybe they also think he did it."

"So, they think you might win and need to make sure that doesn't happen? Is that it?" She handed the hard drive over to Carscadden. He noticed her fingers touch his.

"That's all just speculation, but we can agree that there is another investigation going on here."

"Want me to call the cops, have the room printed?"

"Not a chance. It's just a break-in. It'd be twenty-four hours before they'd show up — waste of time. Besides, I wouldn't trust them in here with the files, for Nastos or anyone else."

Hopkins stood close to Carscadden, then leaned forward slightly to adjust her pants. "We could just take the files out."

"We've seen the video; he used gloves. All we have is the picture, and I'd rather not involve the police when it's fifty-fifty that it was one of them who did it. We can try to work with this ourselves, find the tattoo guy."

Carscadden was a little startled when the front door chimed and they shared expressions of surprise when they heard someone walk into the lobby area. They both smiled, relieved when they heard a woman's voice.

"Hello?"

Carscadden stood up, straightening his pants. *Of all of the days to finally get walk-in business, it has to be right after the office gets trashed by a psycho. She'll be walking out faster than she walked in.* Carscadden took a quick scan around and saw it was hopeless to hide what had happened here. His desk was smashed in two and one of the chairs was missing.

Hopkins went out to greet the visitor. He heard her speaking and the other woman's voice growing louder. His receptionist led the woman into his office. She was tall with blond hair, older than he was, maybe forty-five. Tall, thin, blond — she was pretty much every guy's type.

"Mrs. Madeleine Nastos to see you, Mr. Carscadden." Hopkins smiled at him, then shrugged to Mrs. Nastos, apologetically. "We had a break-in." She mustn't have felt that was adequate so she added, "On top of that, the maid quit, the masseuse is on holiday, the armoured car is late with our paycheques — really, I could go on."

Madeleine Nastos replied, "I'm in real estate, if you're thinking of a different neighbourhood?"

Carscadden moved a chair out his way, which caused a book-shelf to topple to the ground. "I appreciate the offer, Mrs. Nastos, but there is no way I'm giving up the excitement of living in the Garden District. Why don't we go out to the lobby and chat there? There's less splinters and busted glass." Carscadden tried to make going to the lobby sound like it was something reserved for dignitaries. He offered his arm and she took it.

"Mr. Carscadden?" Hopkins began. "I'm going to Starbucks, can I get you two anything?"

"I'll take whatever you're getting. You, Mrs. Nastos?"

"No thanks, I'm good."

Hopkins grabbed her purse and left the two of them to talk in privacy. She would return in about twenty minutes empty-handed, since neither she nor Carscadden drank coffee. Carscadden smiled to himself, thinking about how they were becoming quite the team. He flipped the lobby's leather futon right side up and took a seat. Madeleine took a seat next to him and turned to face him.

"So, what can I help you with, Mrs. Nastos? How's your daughter doing?"

"Poorly, Mr. Carscadden, she's not doing very well." Madeleine smiled her response, then blinked away the water that began to well up on the inside edge of her lower lids.

"I'm sorry to hear that."

"Josie's in counselling, she's having nightmares, she's wetting the bed at seven years old."

"I can't even imagine . . ." Carscadden saw the hurt behind her green eyes, the gold and black flecks trapped in orbit around the infinity of her pupils. He realized that his outer thigh was touching hers on the small couch and moved away slightly. Her anguish could not have been more evident — her child hurting, her husband soon to be gone forever. *It's a loser case, Kevin, you've got to prepare her for what's coming. This is going to get messy.*

She spoke again, pulling him out of his digression. "Reporters are interfering with my life. I tried to show a house yesterday and the guy turned out to be a real creep. It was a little unnerving."

Any delay in the legal forecast he had to give her was a good thing. "Really? What happened?"

"He wanted to know if Nastos told me in advance that he was going to kill Dr. Irons. Then he started asking personal questions, like if I was getting lonely."

Carscadden's face twisted up a little as he thought that one over. "That doesn't sound like a reporter."

"I don't care who he was, I don't ever want to see him again."

"What did he look like?"

"Tall, thin, grey hair. Like a creepy funeral director."

Carscadden considered her description, then began nodding his head gravely. "The guy I have decorating the office here for me —" Carscadden got up went into the office, then returned holding out a photograph for her to see. "I don't suppose . . ."

She studied the picture, the overhead shot which captured the man's profile. There were dark shadows in his sunken cheeks, that creepy smile on his face. She waited to see if Carscadden was going to tell her more about the man's identity but he didn't. "Yes, that's him."

"You know, Mrs. Nastos, your husband can be very complex and difficult to read. I can't help but think that if he was a little more open with me, I would be able to represent him better."

She smirked and shook her head. "You know, when I first met Nastos I was dating another guy at the time. This guy was a project manager for the city. He made good money and was dependable. He seemed like an athlete, but the sports he played were things like racquetball and tennis. He wasn't very decisive, always asking me what I wanted. He was nice to a fault. One night I was out with friends and some guy was coming on to me too strongly at a bar. Nastos came over and got right in his face. When the guy tried to push Nastos aside, he ended up with black eyes and a few loose teeth."

"How did that make you feel?"

"Well, I was brought up by a single mom. She dated a few abusive creeps and no one did anything about it. One day we got a new neighbour, Dave. Not too long after, one of Mom's exes came over drunk and he and my mom got into it. There was a big fight over nothing, with this guy throwing stuff around and screaming his head off. Without saying a word, Dave walked right into the house, bounced the guy off every surface in the place, then busted his nose. He dragged him to the end of the driveway like it was garbage night."

Carscadden winced. "Holy shit."

"Tell me about it. The house became quiet. It felt like it was the first time it was ever quiet. I remember just watching that creep from my bedroom window, no longer a menace, completely silenced. Dave was a good man, handsome, hardworking, and he knew how to treat a woman. When he married my mom two years later, I cried because I was so happy. Dave and Mom were together from that night on. I'll never forget what I learned that night."

"What was that?"

Madeleine took a breath. "As a woman in this world, no matter how nice your man is, if he isn't ready to fight to protect you and your family, he isn't worth much. That project manager I was dating was no Dave. And he was no Nastos. That creep that hurt Josie will never hurt another child. It'll never happen again. That's why I know Nastos did it and that's why he'll go to jail. He knew it was a risk, but he figured it was worth it to make Josie feel safe."

Carscadden took a moment to consider her words. It didn't seem like the best timing to say what he felt he had to say. Instead, he thought he could play it another way. "Let's fight the good fight and not give up yet."

"You actually have hope?"

"I'm a Leafs fan — you can't get the hope out of us. I've learned there's nothing wrong with having hope, even when things are hopeless. In fact, that's when you need it most." He placed his hand on hers and gave her a squeeze. "Do you have a place you can go, a friend's house?"

"No, Josie needs stability; we need to be home together. I won't be caught off guard next time. Anyway, I've taken enough of your time."

"Is this what you came here to tell me?"

"Actually, I brought a bag for Nastos—clothes, the book he was reading. When I saw your office in shambles with everything tossed upside down, in a weird way I think I just felt at home. I guess I just needed to talk. I would appreciate it if you didn't tell Steve anything about that creep bothering me. He has enough to worry about."

Almost dismissively, Carscadden said, "Well, I appreciate your company, and I won't say anything to Steve." He saw the Kalmakov file folder sprawled out on the floor, then heard a voice in his head— one that spoke with a Russian accent. He added, "And I might have a plan for that friend of yours. I'm going to have someone talk to him."

"You think that's a good idea?"

"Oh, the more I think of it, the more I think it's going to be a great idea. You know, you can drop by my place. Steve can't leave but I can go out to a movie or come to the office to do some work. Maybe you two need to spend some time together." Carscadden surveyed the damage in the room. "I suppose I could even tidy up a little."

"I'm working extra to stay above water and I need to focus on Josie. Steve knows that, she's all that's important. She's what this drama's all about. You don't need me to chat anyways, you must get all the company you need from your secretary. She's very pretty."

"I'm too young for her, she probably sees working here as baby-sitting," he said, shaking his head.

"She doesn't think that." Madeleine smiled.

"What?"

"Why are the good-looking men always complete idiots?"

18

AS DOORBELLS CHIMED ON Madeleine's departure from the office, Carscadden rummaged through debris searching for the telephone that used to reside on Hopkins' desk. He found the base easily enough since the phone cord was still plugged in, but the cordless handset was AWOL. He pushed the Page button on the base unit and heard the phone beeping its mayday message from under a heap of files.

When he took the cell phone from out of his pocket to retrieve the number he needed, he began to shake his head at how stupid he had been for even bothering to look for the office phone when he had his cell safe and sound. *It's not like it's a sign of psychosis,* he told himself. *There are mistakes surgeons make and people die. Accountants make mistakes and people get audited. Lawyers whose offices have been burglarized and client's wives harassed get a little confused. No biggie.*

He scrolled through the address book on his BlackBerry and dialled the number. Kalmakov answered on the second ring. By the din of voices, it sounded like a busy time at the restaurant.

"Mr. Carscadden, how are you, sir?"

"Good, thanks, Viktor. I need a favour." Carscadden winced to himself after he said the words. *No going back now.*

"I'll tell you now the answer is yes."

"You remember that cop who killed the child molester?"

"Yes, my kind of man."

"Well, I think what's happened is related to that — some guy broke into my office and smashed everything to pieces."

"Tell you what; I'll kill this fucking piece of shit."

"Jesus Christ!" Carscadden cringed, half-expecting the cops to bust the missing door down and take him down.

Viktor laughed. "You need a sense of humour, Mr. Carscadden, you're turning into a stress case."

"Viktor, can you just get this guy's name and make him back off?"

"Did he take anything of, umm, ours?"

"It's too early to tell — looks like a bomb went off in here."

"Do you think there's a chance that this was about me?"

Carscadden had never even considered that, but then realized that there was no way it could be true. "No, no, it can't be about you, because on top of trashing my place, this guy I'm defending, his wife, she is being bothered by the same guy. Came right up to her being a creep. I caught him on video. She said it was the same guy. Can you make sure he doesn't bother her anymore, either?"

"I'll deal with it, sir. Email me her address and this guy's picture. I'll have one of my friends manage him as discreetly as possible. How's that?"

"Thanks, Viktor," Carscadden said.

"Don't worry about it, helping the —" Viktor might have been about to say *cop*, but chose his words in relation to the company he had. He instead finished, " — helping this client of yours, it's basically community service."

◌　◌　◌

NASTOS SAT ON CARSCADDEN'S OUTSIDE PATIO, LEANING BACK INTO the chair with his feet up on the railing. The second beer was going down better than the first, but he was going to have to stop there for what he had in mind. He took out his pay-as-you-go phone and dialled the number to his work, the Sexual Assault office. When the voicemail came on, he pressed his partner Jacques' extension.

"Sexual Assault Unit."

He sucked in a breath. "Jacques, it's Nastos."

There wasn't the slightest pause. "Mom? I can barely hear you."

Nastos smiled. "I need a favour."

"Listen, Ma, your cordless phone's horrible. Give me a sec, I'll move somewhere quieter." The phone clicked. He'd been put on hold. Soon enough, Jacques came back. "Hey bud, nice to hear from you. What do you need?"

"I need a name. Some asshole's been bothering Madeleine."

"What can you tell me about him?"

Nastos took a gulp of beer. "Try a local search for tattoos, on his neck."

"Of what?" Jacques asked.

"It's a word, on the side of his neck. Starts T-R-O. Is that enough?"

He heard Jacques typing. "One sec. I don't do this search parameter too often. I got to find where to put the text. How's the trial going?"

"Bad."

"Just say the word, and you can hide out at my mom's in Quebec—she declared sovereignty years ago and there's no extradition treaty." Nastos was going to smile, but Jacques became serious. "How old is he?"

Nastos dropped his feet, sitting up straight. "Maybe fortyish."

"Hair colour?"

He tried to recall. "Dunno."

"Height?"

"Five-ten? I'm guessing." Jacques would be scrolling through dozens of nearly identical faces. *This is a waste of time.*

"Holy shit, that's James North."

"Who?" Nastos asked.

"He used to be a cop, he got busted in that drug unit thing. The one Koche managed to avoid."

Nastos put his beer on the deck and stood up. "You're fucking kidding me. How can you be sure?"

"He matches the description. He used to be a hell of a fighter too. Extradition — yeah, that was bullshit. Not this."

◻ ◻ ◻

NORTH'S CONDO WAS TIDY AND SPARSELY FURNISHED WITH A MODERN minimalist feel, inside a building in East York's Crescent Town. Both the stove and fridge were stainless steel; the countertop was granite and the kitchen floors tiled. The rest of the space — 1400 square feet — featured bamboo flooring and was decorated with oil paintings, all acquired before he left the employ of the police service. While no police officer's base salary could afford this place, the various forms of graft money he had "earned" from his days in the drug unit had made this and much more possible.

He had this condo on the side. His wife had never known anything about it, which was a good thing since she would either have gotten it in the divorce or told the fine lads at Internal Affairs, who would have probably taken it, sent him to jail or told the Revenue Agency about his untaxed income — whereupon he would never have been able to earn an honest income again. At least now he could earn income from both streams: his private investigations business, which generally catered to crime organizations, and the under-the-table piece work he did for previous co-workers who had matters that they wished to be dealt with unofficially.

Now, with the glory days of ripping off drug dealers gone, so were his early retirement plans.

His condo's patio faced southwest, with a view of the city lights, and he could see just enough of the lake to advertise a lake view should he ever want to sell. Even better though was the vacant construction lot straight down from his apartment. It was an acre of fenced-in gravel and abandoned construction scraps. There was supposed to be a strip mall going in, but it was held up in the zoning. It was perfect for North.

The doorbell rang and he got up. Checking the peephole to ensure there was just one man he opened the door. A middle-aged working-class black man handed North two hundred in cash. North took the money, flipped through the bills, and as the man left North turned back into his condo and closed the door. After fifteen minutes of working on the paper's Sudoku puzzle and checking his BlackBerry for text messages, he promptly took an empty can of Coke Zero out of his recycling box, put in a baggie containing a few grams of cocaine from the freezer and went out to his balcony. He aimed and tossed the can to the same place as always, near a garbage Dumpster, then went back inside, back to the Sudoku. This was a frequent process for North, who did not even drink Coke — but at seventy-five profit a can, the investment was worth it.

He'd learned this trick while on the drug unit. They had arrested a man for trafficking cocaine and other drugs out of his house. Once the house had been identified, they watched discreetly as customers went to the door, made the buy then left. They would arrest and search the customers down the street, then release them without charges if they agreed to be a witness. After enough evidence was obtained, they raided the dealer's place. Most of the cash and drugs were submitted as evidence, with the modest remainder split between the officers. Eventually the man was convicted and sentenced to home arrest, whereupon he went right back to business — only this time the man had started employing the Coke Can Method. This time, if police hassled the customers leaving, they would be left empty-handed. A reasonable time later, the buyer would return, look around the vacant lot — or in that case, neighbour's backyard, find the lucky can of Coke and go on his way. North went straight to this advanced technique and even his friends who were still cops had no idea what he was up to.

154

His phone rang. "North."

Koche asked delicately, "Did you get everything sorted out?"

North checked his watch for the time, then turned on his TV. "Yeah, I have the copies; I've had things to do here at the house this morning and didn't want to email you anything or call you at work."

"You could have sent a text." Koche was pissed, but did not want to push too hard.

Using his TV remote, North switched the video feed to his computer instead of the cable. On screen was the live video coming from Dewar's bathroom. The glass shower door was steamed up. Forgetting about Koche, he jacked up the volume and listened to the jet of water and splashing sounds. "I just have to look after something, then I can meet you anytime you want, okay?"

"And I need one more thing, something extra and easy."

"Fire away."

"We need a testimony job for the trial. The cleanest guy you can get who'll be solid."

"Five grand." North winced a little when he said it, thinking he had gone too high.

"Deal."

I love the private sector. "What's he have to say?"

"Just that he saw Nastos leaving the park that night."

"That's it?" North asked.

"That's it."

North shrugged. "Sure."

"I'll send the witness statement over, I want your guy to memorize it cold. Send a text when you're good to meet."

"Okay, bye." North said.

"Bye."

The image on the TV changed when the glass door opened and Dewar stepped from the shower naked. North took a seat on the couch, leaning back to enjoy the view. He was in no rush; it was all being recorded. She reached for a towel, bending forward and wrapping it around her long, black hair. She grabbed another towel, putting it around her waist, and stood in front of the mirror. North's BlackBerry buzzed with a text that he didn't even hear. As Dewar braced one arm on the vanity, she began plucking her eyebrows in the mirror. When the towel around her waist fell off and to the floor, she just left it there and went back to plucking.

"You're my kind of girl, Madam Prosecutor."

◊ ◊ ◊

NASTOS SAT OUTSIDE NORTH'S CONDO BUILDING IN CARSCADDEN'S pickup truck, holding a pair of binoculars. He'd seen three dirtbags go in and out. So far two Coke cans had come flying out the window he'd learned was North's.

A picture of the man was beginning to form in Nastos' mind: a marginalized, forgotten soldier who had been scapegoated and wanted a way back into the good graces of the establishment. North would know all of the tricks Nastos did, maybe even more. And he didn't have bail or cops to worry about. He was anonymous and had little to lose. He wanted to go in there right now and deal with him, but that likely wasn't a good idea. He put the truck in gear and drove back to Carscadden's. He was going to have to plan this one properly. North was too dangerous; Nastos couldn't do a half-assed job.

19

KOCHE SAT WITH SCOTT IN THE office space, a large square room with pre-fabricated, taupe-coloured fabric cubicles in the centre and shoebox-sized offices around the perimeter. Scott's office was in the back corner of the building, away from the main entrance and reception area. Dewar's office was down a back hallway from there. Her own receptionist, like most of the others, was gone for lunch, leaving a skeleton crew to ignore the phones as best they could.

Koche and Scott had the door propped open so they could see her when she came in. Koche had his feet up on his desk; he was scanning through the copied Nastos files and already he didn't like what he saw. When a person was arrested, a court package was made up by the investigators. Everything remotely related to the case was supposed to be in there: documentation, forensic reports, witness statements, the synopsis of video interviews — everything.

Not all of the reports themselves were always present because some forensics or other evidence could still be getting worked on. But the lead investigator needed to have things referenced and organized so that everyone knew what was going on and what future evidence was in the process.

The court package had gone to the prosecution's office; it had been signed off. An intake attorney had gone through it and made sure the basic information was there and even made a few requests

157

to the lead investigator, Clancy Brown, for Google Earth pictures, overviews and street-level shots. Eventually, the case had been assigned to Dewar and she had had carriage of the case from then on. Dewar sent a disclosure package over to Carscadden, but the two files weren't a perfect match.

What annoyed Koche and stopped him in his tracks was the murdered dentist's patient list. Every name on that list was a possible suspect, a person with just as much of a motive to kill the dentist as Nastos. Yet four of the names were blacked out on her list. Carscadden's list was a typed version that didn't show the redacted names. That was a big omission. Dewar knew of four other people with a potential motive to kill Dr. Irons whose names were missing. That was four people who didn't have to provide alibis or even be interviewed. The defense was entitled to their names, but they weren't being provided with them.

For the first time in thirty minutes, Koche spoke to Scott. "I see what you mean about the names. If Carscadden notices the glitch, he'll get a long delay. He gets a long enough delay, it could cause problems."

Scott agreed. "You watch. It'll be some stupid thing like disclosure delays or omissions that get the fucking case tossed out."

But it also piqued his interest. "Who do you think these people are, Scott?"

"Not a clue. I have no idea what shit Dewar is trying to pull. On one hand it's like she's trying to toss the case, on the other she's playing hardball."

Koche mused, "Maybe she's actually bisexual."

Scott's face squinted up. "I don't get it."

Koche smiled. "Seems to me like she's fucking everyone." He laughed at his own joke, then laughed some more at Scott's disgust.

◊　◊　◊

DEWAR CAME IN THE FRONT DOORS PAST THE RECEPTIONIST AREA, always staffed during business hours. They called it the bubble since no one there had any privacy and they took turns working it throughout the day. The woman currently staffing the bubble was in her fifties and overweight. She dressed like it was the 1980s, wearing a poorly fitting grey business suit. She had been there for years and had proudly hated Scott longer than anyone.

"Hello, Ms. Dewar," she said as Angela walked past.

"The name is Ang, Janice."

"I think Jeff wants to see you, Ms. Dewar."

Dewar smiled and walked by. "Thanks for the warning." Rather than follow the common walkway, she took the long way around the cubicles to the back wall. There was a janitor walking toward the back room. She thought that seemed a little unusual since the janitorial staff normally didn't start until five p.m. The janitor was wearing a blue one-piece overall and a baseball cap. He seemed to have something smudged on his neck. *No*, she corrected herself, *it's a tattoo. Where the heck did they get these guys, at their parole board hearings?* She opened a door to the more private area and tried to sneak past Scott's office on the left.

"Ms. Dewar, in my office, please." Scott poked his head out of his door, staring at her as she walked past without slowing.

She spoke over her shoulder. "I'll just drop my bag off first, be right back." She felt Scott's eyes running up and down her body; it was nothing new. It was more the relentless abuse that made her want to just shoot him dead. There was no mood that would make a person interested in talking to that man.

"No, right now!"

She turned and saw that he had stood up from his wheeled office chair. His blood pressure was up, his face flushed. *Why does everything have to be a pissing contest?* "I'll be just a sec, what's the big deal?" Scott's tirades were common gossip in the department. He was always yelling at somebody. Dewar knew she was the only one who ever gave it back, usually because she was recording it. This time she didn't have her recorder going and there was no chance that she could get it. She was going to have to handle him differently.

"Jesus Christ, Dewar, in my office." Scott pushed his chair back behind his desk and pointed to the chair near the door. Without looking away from the folder on his lap, he said, "Sit down there."

Dewar observed Koche there. He resembled the wolf who wanted Little Red Riding Hood.

"No, thanks, I'll stand." She came into the room, but left the door open, hoping the receptionists could hear or would maybe even come over to eavesdrop on yet another Dewar/Scott yelling match. *This should get him up to full volume.* Quietly, at almost a whisper, just under her breath, she said, "Just say what you have to say, asshole."

His eyes narrowed, his lips curled up like he had just bitten into something sour.

"What the fuck?" he hissed at her. "What the fuck did you just say?"

"What?"

"Who the fuck do you think you're talking to?"

"Hey, if you're going to swear and shout, then I really don't have time for this." On her way out of the office, Dewar made eye contact with Janice, who acknowledged with a sad smile that she had heard it. *And if Janice heard from the front, everyone heard.* She headed for her office and her recording device.

"Get back in here!" Scott shouted to an empty doorway.

She shouted back over her shoulder, "I'll wait till you cool down a little," and just kept on going. She passed the door to the women's washroom, where another receptionist, Penny, had been listening in, afraid to even walk past the office.

Penny whispered to Dewar, "Sooner or later we have to do something about him. What a misogynist." She was only twenty-two, but didn't seem the type to want to take shit from Scott her entire working life.

Dewar agreed. "Tell me about it." Looking toward her office, she saw the janitor come out through her door and walk away from her. Blue overalls, tattoos and an expensive black leather briefcase. *What's a janitor doing with — hey, that's mine!* He glanced back over his shoulder, turned away and began moving faster to the staircase and exit ahead.

She asked, "Hey, can I help you?"

The man broke off into a full sprint. Dewar took off after him, leaving Penny in the dust. Without slowing his stride, North kicked the exit door open and thundered down the stairs as fast as he could go. Dewar tried to keep up, but the man spiralled down the stairs effortlessly. He found the main floor fire doors that opened with an access card, which he lacked. When the doors didn't yield, he went immediately through the first-floor office space, occupied by a private company. A woman shrieked in surprise, curling her arms over her head as North plowed into her, knocking her to the ground, and kept rolling.

A man who had heard the ruckus came out of his office. "What the fuck?" He fared no better than the secretary, getting launched back into a wall before sliding to the floor. North made it to the main doors and left through the front of the building. By the time Dewar got to the man in the hallway, the janitor was long gone.

"Damn it!" She pounded her fist into the wall.

"Who the hell was that?" The man got to his feet slowly. He was in his thirties, fit and wearing an expensive suit.

"I don't know — did he touch anything we can fingerprint?"

"Just my face." The man stepped past Dewar and helped the secretary to her feet.

"You okay, Beth?"

The woman smoothed out her outfit and brushed her short brown hair back from her face. "Oh yeah, I do Pilates, a lot of treadmill work — that was nothing."

Dewar handed the man her business card. "There's my card and my email. When you get the video from your IT department, print off a still shot of that guy and send it to me, okay? He stole things from my office upstairs. I'm one of the prosecutors."

"Hey, sure thing." He read the card, front and back. "Hey, you might want to write down your home phone number in case we need to talk later." He smiled coyly.

The secretary shook her heard, saying, "Nice, Romeo, guess we can't blame you for trying."

Dewar returned to her office to find that it appeared untouched. The computer was off, her pen and message pad were still in the centre of her desk. She took a seat in her chair and checked her desk drawers. They were all closed, but when she pulled them one by one, they were all unlocked. She pulled out the bottom drawer all the way and saw that her audio tapes of Scott were all missing. Even the recorder was gone.

"Oh, great." She had a sick feeling run through her body. It felt like a trap door had just opened under her feet. "So he's got the list too. It was in the case." She put her hands over her face and rested her elbows on the desk. Her phone rang, but she did not even flinch at the sound. After five rings, it stopped on its own, probably going to voicemail. She leaned back in her chair, pulled out her cell phone and dialled a number.

"I just chased some guy out of my office — he got the list. . . . No, I have no idea who, but I'm working on it. I think we're going to have to bring Carscadden in on this one."

20

NORTH STOOD SLOUCHED, HIS
back against the building across the street, reading the newspaper, watching them. With another day of trial behind them, Nastos and Carscadden walked together out of the court building and down the stairs and then turned north on the sidewalk. The office was still a mess from the break-in and Carscadden had no intention of letting Nastos see it that way. While they bounced around ideas such as Thai, Indian, steak or pasta, they were both oblivious to North.

When the two got in front of him, North put his paper in a recycling receptacle and began to follow. North was excited to be so close to them without their noticing. He was becoming so deeply involved with the intimate details of their lives, but even if they were to look right at him, they would have no idea who he was.

With his short hair, but not a crew cut, and an expensive business suit, he had the perfect urban camouflage. When Carscadden and Nastos turned toward the parking lot, he began dialling his phone.

"Hello?" the man's voice said.

"Yeah, this is North. You got them?"

"Yeah, they're the two right in front of you, we got them." The men were in a SUV parked across the street. One had binoculars and was holding a cell phone up to his ear. North had used Shawn

163

Eade and Michael McCort before, and they had proved themselves to be reliable. As the Old Boys' Club expanded, he planned on using them more. North had seen first-hand that it was an apt moniker from their debt recovery services.

"Is the secretary still out of the office?" North asked.

"They have a sign up saying it's closed for the day," Eade replied.

"Okay, I'm going to search the place again and set up the bugs; once you're sure Carscadden and Nastos are in for the night, come back to the office and look out for me."

"Sure thing, North."

North hung up the phone and turned back toward Carscadden's office.

◻ ◻ ◻

CARSCADDEN AND NASTOS GOT IN THE TRUCK AND STARTED OFF FOR home. The traffic was still light because it had been an early adjournment. Dewar had asked for a longer afternoon recess since the jurors had taken in a lot of technical information and Montgomery thought it was such a good idea he just adjourned at four p.m. for an early weekend. Nastos was relieved when Carscadden choose not to argue the early break in front of the exhausted jury; it had been getting hot in the courtroom and he thought the break was a great idea. They took a few moments to chat after the courtroom was clear and were on the street by four-thirty and in the truck by a quarter to five.

Nastos saw that Carscadden was chewing on his bottom lip. He was pensive about something.

"It's Friday, what could be bothering you?"

For a lawyer, Carscadden wasn't too good at giving bad news. It was painfully obvious that he was psyching himself up. "Dewar says that Josie might have to testify Monday. She'll be in a separate room with me, her, the judge and your wife. The jury and you will watch it on TV from the courtroom."

"I'd rather her not to have to go through that."

Carscadden checked his blind spot and changed lanes around a stopped TTC bus. "Steve, after she testifies, I'll make a motion for you to go back home. You get your life back."

"At her expense?"

"Listen to me. A few more days and the three of you will be together again."

Nastos shook his head. "You think a guy like Montgomery — the hanging judge — will go for that?"

"I can play him both ways, Nastos. If he thinks you're innocent then he'll think you've been through enough already. If he thinks you're going to get convicted, I say that it's the last time you can spend time together as a family for a long time. Honestly. I think tomorrow, you should be ready for a good day."

"Then why were you reluctant to bring it up, Carscadden?"

"Because I take no comfort in the questions that your little girl is going to have to answer. At least Dewar is a mom. It won't be as bad as you think it will."

Nastos considered that.

Carscadden tried to change the subject. "So, Nastos, what's your feeling on the juror with the big tits?" Nastos smiled, shaking his head. He wasn't used to lawyers with a sense of humour. He was happy to play along.

"Two things: one, they have to be fake; two, I think she wants to see me rot in hell." Then he lobbed one back to Carscadden. "What do you think about the steroid freak with the tattoos?"

Carscadden smiled. "His tits are likely real, and if you two were in jail at the same time, I think the daddy role would be spoken for."

"You just had to go there." Nastos leaned his head back, twisting his head from side to side, stretching. "Hey, why don't we go to the office? You can chat with Hopkins while I run across the street and get roti for dinner tonight."

Carscadden winced and shook his head. "Hopkins is redecorating; I thought it best to stay out of her way," Carscadden said.

"Why aren't you dating her, anyways? Women don't get a lot better looking than her, she's smart, nice . . . What gives, she shoot you down?"

When Carscadden didn't answer, it occurred to Nastos that Carscadden had been asked that question too many times.

"Listen, Nastos, I just got out of a marital jackpot that cost me everything I owned — I'm a little gun-shy. Second, I'm her boss and I just don't want to be that washed-up has-been who hits on his secretary when I'm barely thirty-five. Third, she's like ten years older than me so she would probably think I'm just some love-struck pest. I can't imagine she would want anything to do with me anyways."

"Sounds like you've thought about this a lot." Nastos smiled.

Carscadden said nothing.

Nastos continued, "I think she likes you, I'm just saying. You'd be a good fit."

Carscadden checked the rear-view mirror, then glanced at Nastos.

Nastos asked, "Finally notice the suv following us?"

"Yes, I guess I'm not good at this."

"Have some fun, lose him."

"You think I should?" Carscadden asked.

"Holy shit, man, live a little. It's almost five. We've got an hour to get home."

"Okay, what the hell." Carscadden hit the gas and veered off through a corner lot gas station. Sure enough, the suv followed, driving much more smoothly. There were two occupants, two fat guys stuffed into suits.

Carscadden just barely made it through a red light, but the suv following wasn't so lucky. The two men in the suv were entering the second lane of through traffic when they rammed into a Dodge Caravan, striking the driver's door. A loud crash accompanied the bursting glass as the van skidded sideways, gouging the roadway, bursting the tires and careening into the curb on the other side. Early afternoon pedestrians turned, frozen in place watching helplessly until the vehicles came to rest.

The skidding tires and broken glass were so loud, Nastos immediately turned his head to see while Carscadden hit the brakes, watching through the rear-view mirror.

❧ ❧ ❧

INSIDE THE SUV, IT WAS SMOKY AND CRAMPED. THE IMPACT OF HITTING the minivan had pushed the dashboard back six inches or more toward the occupants, the airbags had gone off, shattering the windshield, spraying expansion powder everywhere and deflating over them, blinding their attempts to unbuckle their seatbelts.

"You okay?" the passenger shouted.

"We're fucked!" the driver replied. "It's dead." He was trying to start the engine, but it wouldn't turn over.

"Open the glove box!"

"We don't —"

The passenger pushed the airbag back out and through where the windshield was supposed to be and twisted the glove box door open.

Inside was a thirteen-ounce bottle of Scotch. As he stared at it dumbly, his companion grabbed it, cracked it open and started dumping it all over the inside of the SUV, even on himself.

"This thing traceable?" the driver asked.

"The VIN is a clone from Detroit, it's clean," the passenger assured him. North had connections everywhere and knew as well as anyone to use clean vehicles.

"We split up. I'll take a cab from the bus station," the passenger said. He frantically got his seatbelt off, grabbed his briefcase from the back seat and started crawling through the windshield.

The driver started slamming his body weight against his door, trying to muscle it open. "I'll put on a bit of a show and take off to the subway." He eventually got the door to open as he staggered to the ground. He got to his feet and dusted himself off before heading to the closest subway entrance.

Nastos and Carscadden parked at the side of the road and began running back to the scene of the accident. The driver of the Caravan was a woman, maybe thirty years old, but it was tough to tell with all of the blood on her face. There was a young child crying inside the vehicle. Pedestrians had begun to accumulate around the Caravan. The driver's door and the post behind it were caved in and crimped; it was going to take the jaws of life to get it open.

Nastos noticed that there was no glass anywhere on the driver's side of the vehicle and ran right to the driver's door, Carscadden following.

The driver's left leg appeared mashed and swollen and she was bleeding from the head, but it wasn't a fatal injury. The woman was frantically asking about her baby. Carscadden followed the sound of the screaming child and saw her in the back seat. She was about two years old with red curly hair.

"Nastos, check out the little girl," he shouted, but Nastos was already on his way over.

Maybe happy wasn't the right word, but Nastos wasn't saddened to see the girl. Her car seat was on the opposite side from the impact and she was buckled in properly. She seemed totally fine, just scared. He began trying to soothe her, still a little reluctant to take her out of the car seat without the say-so from a medic or doctor. He considered it for a moment and checked out the integrity of the car seat. It was intact, so he unbuckled it, and took it from the back seat and brought it around to the driver's side.

Carscadden spoke to no one in particular. "Anyone call this in yet? She's hurt!"

"I'm calling now," a woman said.

Carscadden wanted to identify the suv driver while holding the driver's head still to stabilize her neck. He didn't see the drunk disappearing into the crowd.

Nastos spoke to the girl, "Can you hear me, little girl? Can you settle down? You and your mommy are both going to be okay."

Nastos saw Carscadden standing with blood all over his hands and suit from the woman's head.

An ambulance wailed away from the accident with both mom and child. Nastos and Carscadden provided statements to police and answered what seemed like hundreds of questions. The investigating officer thanked them for their assistance, taking down their names and contact information and was about to send them on their way when his police radio squawked in his ear. He excused himself and stepped away for a moment.

Carscadden asked Nastos, "On TV this stuff takes five minutes — what the hell time is it?"

"Jesus, it's got to be after six — so much for an early night."

"Tell me about it. And I could eat the armpits out of a dead rhinoceros."

The officer came back over. "No word on the extent of injuries. It'll be a long time before she's even seen by anyone. But thanks for helping, guys."

Carscadden could read Nastos' face. He was obviously concerned about the time. "Excuse me, officer, can I just mention something?"

"Sure. What's up?"

"Well, my client here is out past his bail curfew. We had to be in by six p.m. But we felt we had to help out here." Nastos and Carscadden observed the officer, but he barely flinched at the news.

"I would have to be a real jackass to breach a guy for helping a scared young girl. I knew about the curfew — I recognized you, Nastos — but I don't imagine the average cop gives two shits."

Carscadden was visibly relieved. "Thanks. I'm just glad we were there to do what we could. Just do me and my client a favour and get the asshole who did this, would you?"

"All we can do is try," the cop replied. "There's no shortage of assholes."

Nastos and Carscadden began walking back to their truck. Nastos said, "Sorry I told you to live a little. We caused this."

Carscadden shook his head. "All we did was hit the gas — those guys shouldn't have followed us through a red light."

"That nuance escapes me."

21

DEWAR SAT IN THE PRIVATE mediation room outside court with the Nastos brief lying on the table between her and Jeff Scott. It was eight forty-five and the trial was to begin in just fifteen minutes.

Scott took two handwritten pages out of his satchel and slid them across the table to Dewar. She took the pages, turned them around and saw that they were on the Attorney General's letterhead for witness statement forms. She began reading. The handwriting was not perfect; the grammar was maybe at a grade ten level. She stopped halfway down the second page and flipped back to the top of the first page. *Shawn Eade — who the hell is that? Last Friday at five p.m.? He did this at five on a Friday?*

"What is it now?" Scott asked.

Dewar realized that she must have had a perplexed expression on her face. "Where'd this guy come from?" She flipped back to the second page and read the last of the statement.

"Who the hell cares? He puts Nastos at the park that night." Scott's mouth hung open and he flipped his hands palm side up, shaking his head as if to say, *Aren't you going to thank me?*

"Mr. Scott, what did you have for breakfast August fourteenth?"

"Probably oatmeal, Dewar."

"Probably oatmeal. At what time exactly, Jeff?"

"Depends on if it was a weekend or a weekday."

"So, you don't really know when and you're not entirely sure if it was oatmeal in the first place. And this guy Eade comes out of nowhere and is certain beyond any doubt that he was at the park on August fourteenth and that he's a hundred percent positive that he saw this total stranger, Detective Nastos, leaving at this time." She slid the statement back over to Scott. "Total bullshit."

She caught something out of the corner of her eye. It was a tall native man peeking in the window. "Is that him?"

Scott shrugged. "Yeah, I think that's him, big native fellow. The man must be anxious for his chance to tell the truth."

"He keeps peeking in the window."

Scott shrugged. "Dewar, like I said, he's probably anxious."

Dewar checked her watch again and slowly got to her feet. She pulled the case file over, then closed it up. Scott handed her the witness statement and she took it reluctantly. "This is a bit of a sandbag manoeuvre, Jeff. Carscadden will shut it down."

"Then let him try. This guy is basically a witness to a murder. You're going to have him testify right away, when the jury are the most receptive."

Dewar blinked and tried to stall. "Actually I was going to recall Clancy Brown to get the last of the forensics covered off." She lied.

"That's redundant. This testimony will put an end to the whole thing and you're going to do it, Dewar. Jesus, what's wrong with you?"

Where's my tape recorder when I need it? "You really think starting with him is the best move?"

"Yeah, I do. Now get in there and do it."   171

Scott needs a motto for his office. Abandon hope all ye who enter here is already used at the gates of Hell. Maybe something simple like 'I'm not happy till you're not happy.'

Then he got to what he probably really wanted to say. "And the breach, when are you dropping that bomb? Today?"

"Pardon?" Her eyes nearly bugged out of her head and her mouth hung open in surprise.

Scott smiled; he kept getting happier. "Nastos breached last night, out past curfew. If I know it, surely you know all about it."

"How'd you hear?"

Scott ignored the question. "After you get Mr. Eade off the stand, you're going to bring up the breach. I want Nastos in jail this afternoon, sooner if you can. Do it right away."

"I'll . . ." She just couldn't agree. "I'll . . ." she repeated herself.

"I'll be watching, Dewar. Don't disappoint me."

◘　◘　◘

THE COURTROOM BEGAN TO FILL ONCE THE STENOGRAPHER HAD unlocked the main doors. Dewar took her seat, as did Carscadden and Nastos. Glancing back into the gallery, Dewar saw Eade sitting down. He was tough to miss, due to his large size and poorly fitting suit with the avant-garde leather tie, circa 1985.

She glanced at Nastos. His eyes were on his wife and daughter in the first row. Josie wanted to climb over the gate to get closer to him. Madeleine had to stop her by wrapping her hands tightly around Josie's. Dewar wished she could put him on alert that something was wrong, but he was preoccupied. She felt a burning in the back of her head and knew Scott would be there, beaming.

Judge Montgomery came into the room and everyone stood. Court began and Dewar walked toward to the podium with no idea what she was going to say.

"Your Honour," she brushed her hair back and wobbled on her heels then put a hand out to the lectern for balance. Feigning sickness wasn't difficult under the circumstances.

Montgomery crouched over the bench, asking, "Ang — Ms. Dewar? Are you okay?"

She motioned for him to take his seat and Montgomery did, reluctantly. "Your Honour, I'm very sorry. I'm not feeling very well today, as you've apparently noticed. I thought I could get through to lunch, but now I'm not thinking so optimistically. I'm very sorry for everyone's time, but I humbly request that we adjourn till tomorrow."

She turned to the defense table. "Sorry, Mr. Carscadden, I should have contacted your office this morning." She took a seat, shaking her head.

Carscadden got to his feet, an expression of concern on his face. "Your Honour, I respect Madam Prosecutor's attempt not to inconvenience any of us, but—"

A voice from the gallery spoke. "Your Honour?"

Dewar turned to see Scott standing behind her. *Damn—he's going to wreck it.* She tried again to catch Nastos' eye to give him a signal. All it seemed to do was make the man more nervous.

Montgomery waved to Scott who approached the bench.

"Your Honour, if I may. I'm Chief Prosecutor Scott, initial J for the record, as you know, sir. In light of my colleague not feeling well, I'm available to step in very briefly, just to sort out some minor administrative issues so that the day is not a total waste."

Montgomery could tell Dewar was obviously not keen on the idea. She subtly shook her head no.

Carscadden interjected. "Your Honour, a change in prosecution counsel at this point of the trial—"

Montgomery spoke. "I'm inclined to agree, Mr. Carscadden. A one-day delay isn't the end of the world. I doubt the jury would mind having the rest of the day off." The jury foremen nodded yes.

Scott took a position next to Dewar. "Like I said, sir, it's only for a couple of administrative issues—won't take long."

Montgomery took a breath and produced what Dewar recognized as a fake smile. "That would be great, Mr. Scott. Ms. Dewar, you're excused. If you need more time, call my office as soon as you can." He paused. "Actually, Ms. Dewar"—he waved a hand to indicate the jury—"for the benefit of the jury, we're going to assume that there is no trial tomorrow either unless you call me yourself and advise that you are ready to go; that way the jury only have to go through the hassle of coming in if they get a personal call from my office."

"Thank you, Your Honour." Dewar rose, shaking her head at Carscadden. She tapped her cell phone and he nodded his understanding.

He shrugged, there was nothing that could be done, whatever was coming. She went straight for the closest washroom. She sat in a stall and began typing a message into her BlackBerry.

◻ ◻ ◻

CARSCADDEN WATCHED AS SCOTT SLIMED HIS WAY TO THE PODIUM. "Yes, Your Honour. Now, the first thing I'd like to do is call a witness, a Mr. Shawn Eade."

Carscadden flipped through a few pages, then got to his feet. "Sorry, Your Honour, I just don't see that name listed here."

"Scott?" Montgomery asked.

"Yes, sir, our office just became aware of this witness recently and did not have time to arrange disclosure. However, with the court's indulgence, it won't take more than ten minutes." He smiled like a lizard.

Montgomery tapped his fingers on his bench as he waited for Carscadden, who was whispering back and forth with Nastos.

"Your Honour," Carscadden began, "court procedures were created by better men than I. I don't concede this privilege to my friend, Mr. Scott, and I hope you don't either."

Eade stood up, ready to take the stand. His was a smug, used-car-salesman smile. Montgomery appeared to read something on his desk then turned his attention back to Mr. Scott.

"Not this time, Mr. Scott. Mr. Carscadden requires disclosure and proper notice. This is out of left field."

"Your Honour," Scott whined.

"Move on, Mr. Scott." Then he pointed to Eade. "And you can turn around and sit down, sir, I never said you could approach."

Eade's broadening smile dropped flat. He turned and began walking out of court. When he was nearly out the door, he gave Montgomery the finger without turning back.

"Anything else, Mr. Scott, or was that it?"

Scott smiled confidently. "One more thing, sir."

"Let's hear it," Montgomery said.

"A matter of a breach, sir. Mr. Nastos was out past his curfew last Friday night."

"He was?" Surprised, Montgomery turned to Carscadden and Nastos. "Can you repeat that, Mr. Scott?"

Scott handed a sheaf of papers to Carscadden, another to the court clerk then a third, for her to pass to the judge. "A car accident after court, sir. As you can see, Nastos, who wasn't even involved, filled out an accident statement. It seems he just can't let go of the power of the badge and had to get involved in something that had nothing to do with him."

Montgomery studied the paper.

Carscadden read the accident report in his hands, the very one he and Nastos had filled out. *How the hell did he get it over a week-end? How on earth did he even find out?* "Sir, it was after court. We stopped to help the mother of a young girl who had been injured in a car accident. To leave her bleeding in the street would have been reprehensible."

Scott was ready for the comment. "Everyone gets first aid training these days, Your Honour. Anyone could have helped at the scene and Mr. Nastos has a responsibility to the court to abide by his bail conditions." Scott turned to Carscadden. "It's a breach in a murder trial, sir. You were there with him, you should be sanctioned—"

Montgomery chided Scott, "Make sure you address the court, sir."

Carscadden interjected. "I was right there with him, Your Honour, it was with the best of intentions."

Montgomery flipped through the pages, but was going too fast to actually be reading anything. He checked his cell phone, reading its screen, then put it down. He was flustered. "Well, I must say I'm a little surprised by your cavalier response, Mr. Carscadden."

"Thank you, sir." Scott smiled.

"Yes. This is very serious indeed. Mr. Nastos is on trial for murder, for heaven's sakes. I'm—" He stopped as if considering something. "I'm ordering Mr. Nastos to be incarcerated until I feel it is no longer necessary. Now, that will be protective custody, and we'll revisit the issue each week for the rest of the trial."

Carscadden felt his knees go weak. His stomach felt like it was ready to drop to the floor. "Your Honour, this is unwarranted and repugnant and—"

"Spare me the hyperbole," Montgomery said. "He breached; he's going to jail."

Carscadden scowled at Scott. If he had been any closer to the smug son of a bitch, he would have decked him.

"Anything else, Mr. Scott?" Montgomery asked.

"No, thank you, sir, that's it for the day," Scott replied.

"Bailiff, please take the defendant."

◊　◊　◊

A FEMALE OFFICER IMMEDIATELY GRABBED NASTOS BY HIS WRISTS; she brought his hands together behind his back. Nastos kept his shoulders rigid trying to display stoicism. Carscadden saw past the veneer. For Nastos, the only tell was his head tilted back to plead to the fluorescent lights where God should have been.

Carscadden felt just as helpless. A woman shouted, "No!" It was probably Madeleine but Carscadden didn't look back. He was too distracted by little Josie's sudden leap, her arms wrapping around her father's waist.

"It's going to be okay, Jo. Don't worry." He couldn't move his hands and was unable to comfort her.

Carscadden couldn't tell if she was trying to climb up his body or pull him down. Either way, it wasn't going to be easy to get her off him. "I don't want you to go, Daddy. Don't go."

Carscadden felt himself reaching out for Josie and gently pulling her little arms away. He felt sick inside, prying her off him, but someone had to do it.

Nastos crouched to whisper to her. "Jo, this is Kevin, he's my friend. He's going to fix everything. Let him take you back to Mommy, okay, sweetheart?"

The bailiff ratcheted the cuffs around Nastos' wrists. She grabbed him by the elbow, pointed to the side door and shoved him forward to get him going.

Scott was beaming—Carscadden knew he'd never forget that as long as he lived.

Montgomery barely acknowledged Josie's breach of court protocol; instead he just waited patiently until Nastos was out of sight. It left Carscadden alone, feeling like the world was falling apart around him. *Staved off that Eade fucker, but that breach was total bullshit. This is a fuck-show.*

Carscadden stole another glance at Scott and didn't like the expression on his face. Scott had something more planned. Slowly, Scott turned to the Judge.

"Judge Montgomery?"

"Yes, Mr. Scott?"

"I see here that my colleague anticipated calling Josie Nastos to testify here today. I was under the impression she was calling Officer Clancy Brown. I don't see why we should inconvenience the Nastos family any further by asking them back another day."

The judge seemed impressed with Scott's gall. "Mr. Scott, are you suggesting that we continue with the witness deposition on camera?"

"It won't take more than an hour."

Montgomery turned to Carscadden, who rose to his feet.

"Your Honour, I'd much rather Ms. Dewar ask the questions. She knows the story here a lot better and she's a compassionate person who prepped the witness. Frankly, I don't think Mr. Scott is the best person for the job."

Scott was obviously excited at the opportunity to make Carscadden appear unprofessional, but Montgomery stopped him. "I'm not going to say I disagree with you, Mr. Carscadden, but Mr. Scott knows what he's doing."

Carscadden wasn't convinced. "Thank you, Your Honour." He appraised Madeleine Nastos. Josie was in her arms crying silently and Madeleine wasn't holding up so well herself. The one time she came to court and it had been a disaster.

◦ ◦ ◦

WITH COURT DISMISSED, CARSCADDEN BARGED INTO THE HALLWAY wanting to find Dewar. He saw her sneaking out of the woman's washroom. He grabbed her arm, turning her around to face him. "Ms. Dewar, a moment, please?"

She pulled her arm away and searched the area for spectators, there were none. Carscadden was perplexed that she seemed more concerned with being seen with Carscadden than the fact that he was being rough with her. "Not here."

Carscadden barked, "My office — I'm going there right now." He thought about the break-in and it just didn't feel one hundred percent safe. "No, Frankie's Restaurant. I have a table in the back."

Her face wrinkled up. "The mob place?"

"Best pasta in town, no cops, no surprises."

Dewar brushed her hair back. Scott had appeared, watching her from the end of the hall. "Okay. There's Scott. I'm going to have a talk with him. Send me a text when you're ready."

Carscadden fantasized about punching Scott's face in. He could nearly feel his knuckles aching from the man's jaw, and it felt awesome.

◦ ◦ ◦

AS DEWAR DREW CLOSER TO SCOTT, SHE SAW THAT KOCHE WAS THERE too. "Mr. Scott, can I have a moment of your time, please?"

He shared a smile with Koche. "I thought you were sick — go home."

Dewar began, "That was insulting to me, the way you did that."

"What's insulting is that I had to do it for you. You're an embarrassment."

Dewar spoke through gritted teeth. "That breach — he was helping a scared little girl."

Koche stepped up to Dewar, speaking right in her face. "What's the big deal, you dating her mom or something?"

"Shove it up your ass, Koche," she replied.

Scott tried to pull in his dog. That last thing he wanted was a public spectacle. "Easy, easy. Koche, give us a few minutes."

Koche slunk back to the desk behind him, where two court officers were sitting. He didn't notice them leave like he had the plague when he had his back to them. "Okay, okay. I'll be right over here."

Dewar took a moment and began a new attack on Scott. "The public perception of breaching Nastos on this matter will backfire. It makes us appear inhuman. The jury will consider that and—"

"Look, it was a freebie. In this business, you take them for all they're worth. It was an opportunistic tactical edge. Now he's in jail. He might be more inclined to make a deal. That's what we want: a confession. It's better for the police service and our department if he owns up to this. We don't want John Q. Public thinking that he's just the guy who got caught. They have to know that this is aberrant behaviour of a rogue cop, not a systemic use of violence to get street justice."

"It'll backfire. I'm in the trenches reading this jury every day. What seems good from the outside where you were is not the reality of the twelve people who are not convinced that the guy who murdered a child molester needs to be punished for it. You assigned me, you should trust—"

"I assigned you, but you obviously still need guidance. Now, be a big girl, take your lumps and get back at it Monday morning. I'm sure if you think it over you'll see that it was the right thing to do. Anything else?"

She said "no" like she was saying "screw you."

"Good."

Koche saw that the conversation was wrapping up and came back over to gloat some more. "You done, Jeff? Let's go grab a bite. I could use a tuna sandwich." He turned to Dewar. "I hear that's your favourite."

"Enjoy it, it's probably the closest a guy like you can get to the real thing." She sneered at him.

"What did you just say?"

"Face it, Dave. I can get girls a guy like you could only dream about."

Koche's face flushed red, but Dewar stood her ground.

Scott conceded. "There's no denying that one, Dave. She's probably converted more women than we could count. But on the bright side— maybe while Nastos is in jail he'll have a conversion of his own."

Koche smiled. "Yeah, whether he wants to or not. I can't wait to hear how that plays out."

22

HIS WRISTS AND ANKLES WERE cuffed with the links fed through a long floor chain, which in turn linked him to half a dozen other prisoners. Nastos walked in small, measured paces toward the paddy wagon. They were in a large garage, dark from a lack of windows with guards by the doors. He could smell sweet, poisonous diesel exhaust from the armoured vehicle; it was thick in the air, along with an odour of stale tobacco.

It was a surreal moment in his life, almost like an out-of-body experience. He was going to go to jail, possibly for the next twenty years. It was not part of any plan; he had rarely even allowed himself to make contingencies for such a thing. It just wasn't supposed to happen like this at all. He was supposed to get off the charges and go home with his family, lawsuit and financial settlement pending, pension intact, integrity restored. This, though, was a nightmare. If there was a demographic that had a rougher time in jail than pedophiles, it was cops — even if they had murdered pedophiles. Jail was not a place of fine distinctions or cleverly parsed legal arguments; it was a place where you were beaten down emotionally and every so often, physically.

He followed the chain to the back of the vehicle, then, as the prisoner in front of him did, he stepped up on a precarious narrow step and ducked to enter the small caged place.

A guard shoved him forward at that moment, cordially inviting him to "try not to bump your head," as he landed face first on the metal seat inside. Nastos untangled himself from the chain and crawled up to the bench seat.

A second guard shouted to the first. "Hey, easy, he's the guy that killed the molester."

"Oh, really?" the first guard replied. "Hey, sorry, pal, keep up the good work, there's lots more where you're going."

Other prisoners piled into the back next to Nastos. Black, Hispanic, white, all of them much younger, many covered in tattoos. The heavy, armoured door was heaved shut, casting them all in total darkness, until the fluorescents slowly flickered to life.

"You killed the molester?" the Hispanic next to him asked.

Nastos didn't want to answer, but he didn't want to *not* answer either. "Me? I'm here for unpaid parking tickets. Lawyer fucked me." He tried to reveal no emotion when he spoke.

The Hispanic made sure he had everyone's attention before speaking again, louder, spitting the words out. "I heard that the guy who killed the molester was a cop."

"Yeah, that's right," a second prisoner said, and then a third agreed.

Nastos was all too aware that he was alone and outnumbered. *If I can make it to jail, I'll actually be safer.* "Well, that's not me." He tried to be confident, to have a steady voice, but his throat was suddenly dry. His hands were sweaty and cold.

"Bullshit, it ain't you," the second prisoner replied coolly.

The mob of prisoners was on him immediately. He had been punched in the face half a dozen times before he could even get his hands up, but by then he was already on the floor, more worried about getting stomped to death. He was taking most of the impact on his flanks and neck. The wind was kicked out of him by a devastating hit to his stomach. When he was eventually able to suck in air, it was scented with a combination of vomit, pine cleaner and feces. There was no thinking anymore. The conscious analytical part of his brain left him and all he could do was writhe on the floor, trying to breathe in and out and protect his face and balls while they tried to kill him.

He became conscious that the truck was moving, then it stopped abruptly, sending the attackers careening and him rolling forward into the wall separating the prisoners from the cab. In police jargon, it was called the Screen Test or Black Dog. Cops used it to settle down unruly passengers. It was called the Screen Test for the waffle pattern it often left on one's face or Black Dog for the alleged fully legitimate reason why the officer had to take such evasive action in the first place. It was a much lazier approach than having to stop, get out of the truck, go to the back and hose everyone down with pepper spray, which of course would be the next step if they didn't settle down. Like all of the oldest tricks in the book, Black Dog worked and the other prisoners left Nastos to bleed and suck air in peace.

The guard in the passenger seat leaned foot his feet up on the dashboards and leaned his head back. "Sounds like Dorothy isn't enjoying the tornado ride out of Kansas."

"Dorothy?!" The driver snorted. "Not exactly the nickname a guy wants to have where that poor fucker's going." The two of them laughed heartily and the truck began to move again. The passenger turned on the radio to cover over the noise from the back; though the melee from before had stopped, now Nastos got the occasional kick or punch to make sure he stayed on the floor. FM 97.3 played Steppenwolf's "Magic Carpet Ride."

◘ ◘ ◘

NASTOS LIMPED INTO THE OPEN CELL AND COLLAPSED ON THE VACANT lower bunk. The guard behind him tossed a pillow and blanket onto the floor near him, saying, "There's your shit. Try to play nice from now on." With a hand wave Nastos acknowledged his appreciated of this sage advice, then lay back on the bed. It was barely six feet long, maybe twenty inches wide, on a tightly wound metal frame, and it felt like heaven. Nothing was broken, surprisingly enough; it was impressive how much pain a person could feel without actually breaking anything. But his body hurt with every creak of his ribs, whether he breathed or not. His back muscles were locked solid in a contorted position that made it impossible to lie flat, so he stayed in a semi-sideways heap. Most of the bleeding from his face and arms had clotted to a stop and the gouges in his wrists from the handcuffs were already turning purple.

"You been in before?" a voice asked from the top bunk.

"No, but I know the rules." He had to clear his throat twice to get the reply out.

"Humour me," the voice said.

"Go fuck yourself." Nastos tried to roll onto his back, but winced and thought better of it.

"I don't think you're in much of a position to talk to me like that." Nastos heard the voice get louder. The top bunk creaked and two big, hairy legs swung over the edge.

"Listen, I'm on trial for murder and I've been around the block a few times. When a guy is in jail for murder, especially if it's his first time in jail, cops often put an undercover in the jail cell with the guy to befriend him and see if he brags or cries about what he's done. Either I'm right and you're not going to do anything, or I'm wrong, in which case yours is just one more ass I'm going to have to kick today. Either way, I don't give a shit."

"Why don't you sleep this one off? Consider it a freebie. But tomorrow is a new day. And I've already got all the friends I need in here, asshole."

184

◻ ◻ ◻

JAMES NORTH SAT NEXT TO SHAWN EADE OF THE INHUMANE SOCIETY. Michael McCort was a little too drunk for the operation, which suited North just fine since he had something special in mind for Madeleine Nastos. They were in Shawn's car, a tinted down Royal Taxi with an expired licence plate and two bald tires. Both North and Eade were enjoying the solitude to relax and dreamily spend their money in advance.

North found Eade to be highly reliable. At six-two, two-forty, Eade enjoyed handling the requisite violence involved in gangsterism. Everything from beating the hell out of people to extortion and robbery were in many ways the most exciting parts of the job, and it was work that could never be replaced by machines or be outsourced to India. It was all about up close and personal customer satisfaction.

McCort, smaller at five-ten and one-eighty, usually took the thefts and frauds, but was also not shy about permanently disfiguring people, maiming or scarring for life as per instructions from the paying client. As a team, they covered all the bases.

Money was money and North knew Eade to be a man worth his weight in gold when your back was against a wall. North paid well and left them to do their work without providing tiresome details or any rules of engagement that could make the beatings or torture too much like actual work. When you have good people working for you, micro-managing only stifles creativity. No, all North had to do was hand over the cash and the picture of the target and wait for the result.

When Madeleine stepped out onto her porch and turned, locking the door behind her, the two men sat up abruptly. North checked the time on the car's radio — six thirty-five. The sun was nearly down and she was taking the family retriever for a walk. How cute.

Eade asked, "Would ya?"

North smirked. "I'd throw her over the hood of the car, fuck her brains out. Classy bitch, she'd be screaming for it." North was practically salivating as he watched her long legs striding down the steps. "You?"

Eade wiggled in his seat for a moment and pursed his lips as he gave it serious consideration. "I'd strangle her while I drilled her. Just as she started to come, I'd spit in her face." They laughed at each other's humour, shaking their heads. North sometimes thought Eade wasn't joking when he said such things. He seemed more to be laughing at the fact that North *thought* he was kidding, and it was a little creepy, even for North.

Madeleine turned left when she hit the sidewalk, slinging her purse over her shoulder. And the two men got back to business.

"What are you waiting for Eade? Follow her."

"She'd notice a slow drive-by. Hey, I'll just get out. When she gets around the corner you can come do your shit and ransack the place."

"Okay, let's go."

They got out of the car, staying on their side of the street, and began walking after her. She had long strides and they had to walk quickly to keep up with her, but found the shape and movement of her body to be a good motivator. Eade closed in until he was only twenty feet behind her, then crossed the street.

When she made it to the corner, North made his move for the front door. It was locked, but he picked it quickly, closing it behind him. He smelled something cooking. *She must have put something in the oven to warm while she's out, so she won't be too long.* He left his shoes on as he raced up the stairs and into her bedroom. He turned on the light and took a moment to see where she slept. She hadn't made the bed and he admitted to himself that he was just a little disappointed. It seemed that with hubby gone, she was letting things slip a little. *What a shame, Madeleine, I'll have to sort you out.*

He opened her dresser and found her underwear drawer. He took a few thongs to remember her by and stuffed them in his pocket. He opened his coat and took out a picture he had made up especially for her. It was a copy of the one he had obtained at Dewar's place, featuring Steve Nastos kissing that beautiful prosecutor, Ms. Dewar, on a fall day. It was a nice picture. He took a moment to admire it, propped it up on her dresser in a nice frame he had picked out at a dollar store. It was a self-snap. Dewar's hand reaching out of frame, an offset angle, tree branches in the background and the beautiful smile of a woman truly in love. North knew it was going to be a real hit with Madeleine. *If there's one thing a beautiful woman can't stand, it's a more beautiful woman, and with her man too.* He came back down the stairs and went to the kitchen. He needed a good drink, but resisted. Saliva was too good a source of DNA; he had to be careful. Instead, he went into the living room and found the wine cabinet. The selection of reds was a little disappointing, but not as much as the messy bed. He took an Australian red, leaving the whites completely.

North could have used the picks to re-lock the door, but that was the last thing he wanted to do. It would be much more thrilling to see the obtuse expression on her face when she came home found the door unlocked. He could practically envision it in his mind. *She'll begin to doubt herself and get concerned. Then, because she's a stupid woman, like they all are, she'll ignore her intuition and go in anyways, risking her life — or at the least, her sexual integrity.*

North smiled to himself as he left the house. He got back to the car and took the driver's seat. With his quick text message sent, North knew that Eade would be on his way back in no time, mission complete. All he had to do was wait for the fireworks to start.

○   ○   ○

CARSCADDEN SAT AT THE BACK TABLE AT FRANKIE'S RESTAURANT. IT was secluded, lit only by dim candles on a white tablecloth. He was drinking Perrier and dipping bread into a plate of oil and balsamic vinegar. What a Russian mobster was doing owning an Italian restaurant, Carscadden had no idea, but it was the best food in town, bar none. Even better was that he never had to pay. He was beginning to accept Victor's generosity more easily. The open invitation was greatly appreciated. A one-hundred-dollar-a-plate meal, not including drinks, was a luxury he couldn't afford and he didn't want to overstay his welcome. Viktor insisted on the perk though; he was a very gracious man and seemed disappointed that Carscadden often came by himself. *Well, you won't be disappointed tonight, Viktor.*

He was distracted from his bread and oil doodling by the front door chime and saw Angela Dewar approaching. She slid into the bench seat across from Carscadden, not saying a word.

"Glad you could make it." The honeyed, rich mahogany behind her brought out the gold flecks and creamy undertone of her skin.

"What do you plan to do about Steve going to jail?" she said, staring at him, almost angry.

"Your boss sent him there, it's going to take time to get him out. And what do you care, anyway?" He couldn't eat the last of the bread and dropped it to his plate.

Dewar took a sip of water. "That was a travesty of justice."

"So you honestly didn't want him to go to jail?"

"Well, you should know by now that he didn't kill the dentist." Dewar cocked her head to a slight angle, the way a Jack Russell looks at you when it thinks you're missing the obvious.

"I should? I'm not so convinced — how can you be?"

Carscadden's phone rang. He checked the call display — it was Madeleine Nastos.

"Hello?" He had to hold the phone away when she started shouting in his ear. "Easy, easy, easy. When? When was he in the house?" He saw that Dewar was concerned by his half of the conversation, held up a finger to stop her from interrupting. "Then, what the hell are you even doing there? Where's your mom live, can you stay with her? Picture? How the hell should I know? What does she look like?" Madeleine gave him the description of the person sitting across the table from him.

Carscadden shook his head, his mouth dropping open. "Yes, I'd feel better, and I know your husband would feel better, if you left and stayed with family. I know I said that. I'll deal with that one right now. Sorry, Madeleine. Call me when you're okay. No, anytime, I'm not going to sleep tonight unless you call. Okay, bye."

Dewar sat waiting till he hung up the phone and put it on the table. She started slowly. "Nastos' wife, I take it?"

"Yes. Nastos goes to jail, the deposition of Josie was a nightmare, and then this."

An expression of dread washed over Dewar. "What did Scott do?"

"It started off pretty rocky, Ang," Carscadden said, and gave her a sour smile. "But at least Montgomery kept him on a tight leash. Scott basically wanted Josie to go through every single detail of the assault — the more disgusting and agonizing for her, the more motive for her dad. Accusing a seven-year-old of avoiding the details of what happened to her didn't make Scott any friends with anyone in the room. I got it back on track, then Montgomery stopped it after fifteen minutes, mostly because of Josie crying and Madeleine glaring at Scott like she was going to kill him. My read on Montgomery was that he would have liked to punch him himself."

Dewar said, "Montgomery was born a few hundred years too late. He should have been a judge in the wild west — a bible in one hand and a length of rope in the other."

Carscadden thought, *Scott might even have gone too far anyway, teetering on the justifiable homicide angle. This case cuts both ways so fast, it's a razor's edge.*

"And Madeleine's been harassed too?"

Carscadden took a sip of water. "Yeah, someone's been following her. He broke into her house and left a little present." He was still staring at Dewar, shaking his head. Viktor wasn't far away. He noticed Carscadden dining with a woman and came over.

The Russian had a robust smile and an extended hand. "Mr. Carscadden, I hope everything meets your satisfaction tonight?"

"Best food in town, Viktor — it's not that, it's —"

Viktor grabbed a chair from an empty table nearby and brought it over. He smiled to Dewar and turned his gaze back to Carscadden. "Go on?"

"I asked if you could help watch a friend of mine, Mrs. Madeleine Nastos. You remember that?"

Some colour left Viktor's face and a slight expression of dread disturbed his features. "Oh my god, did something happen?"

"No big deal, just someone got a little too close again. She's pretty scared, Viktor."

"Damn it, I'm sorry, Kevin. I'm so sorry. I swear to god I told my guy. I spelled it out pretty clear." He slammed his dishtowel on the table hard and his fists clenched up.

Carscadden felt a little sorry for Viktor. He was obviously upset, but Madeleine was terrified, very deservedly. "Listen, Viktor, don't beat yourself up over it, but I'd appreciate —"

"Name it, I'll get a car out front of her house right now."

"Actually, Viktor, don't bother. She's leaving town to stay with family. It's for the best till things blow over."

He ran his fingers through his hair. He stole a glance at Dewar and Carscadden thought that maybe he was becoming a little embarrassed. Maybe he shouldn't have brought it up in front of a woman; Viktor was so concerned about his image with the ladies. Carscadden tried to minimize the damage.

"You know, Viktor, you're just a restaurant guy, you can only do so much."

"True, very true," he agreed. "Listen, I should go. Try to have a good night. I'll have to deal with my associate."

"Thanks, Viktor."

He left the table and began dialing a number in his BlackBerry.

Carscadden took a sip of his water, his eyes fixed on Dewar.

"What?" she asked, turning to meet his gaze.

"There was a framed picture placed in Madeleine's bedroom of Nastos kissing a beautiful Indian woman. Long, hair, perfect smile — you don't know anyone like that, do you?"

Dewar didn't speak; she took a gulp of wine.

Carscadden offered, "I take it that it's from a long time ago."

"Years ago, before Madeleine."

Carscadden knew that Dewar was holding back information and he had to admit that he didn't trust her much. He decided she didn't need to know about North, at least until he had a chance to talk with Nastos and to run it by him first.

"This man, whoever he is, got into her house. Was Nastos with you the night of the murder? Is that why he won't give an alibi?" Carscadden's mind was reeling; he had fifty questions to ask, but didn't know where to start. He found himself staring at her, mouth agape, like an idiot. "You'll be disbarred—there'll be a mistrial—holy shit."

"Listen, he didn't kill the guy."

"Then withdraw the prosecution's case tomorrow morning and end this."

When she looked down at the table and began fidgeting with her hands, he knew she wasn't going to be doing that anytime soon.

"I know he didn't do it, so I took the case. He should know I have his back, but I'm getting direction from upstairs, like the meddling you saw in court today. I can only do so much."

"That explains his secrecy with me. He thinks you've got him covered, so he doesn't have to co-operate much with me." Carscadden began running through past conversations in his head. *Should I have seen this coming somehow? What else am I missing? Why do I think she is still not telling me everything?*

"Listen, I didn't know I was going to have this kind of pressure from Scott. He was reading my notes every night when I left the office. I started taking everything home, but I think he got in there too—as crazy as that sounds. Now, he's taken me off the case and is going to finish it himself."

"Yeah—if he gets a conviction, your career is done and he's a hero," Carscadden observed.

"I even caught some guy stealing things from my office. I chased him, but he got away with something very important."

Carscadden seemed not to have heard the last thing. "If anyone finds out about you and Nastos, you'll be fired and charged with accessory after the fact, breach of trust—"

"Listen to what I'm saying. They're getting into my house—people want to string him up from the rafters."

"They think he murdered someone—what do you want them to do, bake him a cake?"

Dewar took a breath. "In my office, there was exculpatory evidence. It's gone missing. They got it. You were losing the trial when

I was prosecuting and I wasn't trying. With Scott running the show, you don't stand a chance."

Carscadden reluctantly suggested, "We should go to the police."

"You're crazy if you think that's a good idea."

"Why's that?" he asked.

"I'd need a lot more evidence before I could get the police to investigate Jeff Scott."

"What did you just say?" Carscadden asked.

Dewar spoke slowly, spelling it out for him. "Whoever got into my office is who we have to deal with. If Scott or Koche get any hint that we're coming after them, that evidence will disappear. Nastos goes to jail for good and my tapes disappear."

Carscadden found himself agreeing that Scott, Koche and now North were seemingly working toward a common purpose. Scott and Koche wanted the conviction, North was trying to breach Nastos. North was definitely working for them.

And he had to agree that going to the police with such a convoluted story during a murder trial would seem contrived and desperate. They were going to need more proof.

And he had already lost the jury. "Ang," he said, "if I find any way to clear him, even if it means you go down, I'm taking it. He's my client here, not you."

Dewar pleaded. "Just give me a bit of time before you tell them about me and Nastos. I think we can still save everyone's asses." She didn't sound convincing enough for Carscadden. He hung his head, pondering, then leaned forward to say something to Dewar, but stayed silent. She reached for his hand and he allowed her to take it.

A shadow appeared across the table that drew their attention. Ms. Hopkins was standing there; she had an uncomfortable smile and had noticed their hands touching in the centre of the table. Dewar tightened up, sensing that things had just gotten awkward. Hopkins appeared confused and disappointed.

She's going think I'm such an asshole. Just when I was ready to go for her, I screw it up.

Dewar saved him. She pulled her hands away and stood up.

"Hello. My name is Angela, call me Ang. I'm trying the case against Carscadden, I'm winning, actually." Hopkins took her hand.

"Tara Hopkins; I'm Mr. Carscadden's personal assistant."

"I think you caught your boss trying to console me on a personal issue. I just don't want you to get the wrong idea. Actually, I date women — and that shirt is great on you."

She was doing so well, then she flirted with my secretary. Oy vey. "Can you sit down, Ms. Hopkins? This is getting awkward," Carscadden suggested.

She smiled at Carscadden, then took a seat next to Dewar. "You don't mind, do you?"

"Fine with me." Dewar smiled at Carscadden before breaking into laughter, obviously enjoying his reaction.

Carscadden could feel his face flush hot. Trying to get back to business, he racked his brain for a way to get Nastos out of jail. With Scott prosecuting, it seemed hopeless.

"So, did Scott officially take you off the case — like in writing or anything?"

Dewar was confused. "Not really."

"So if you show up for court tomorrow morning and Scott doesn't, it's you again?"

Dewar nodded like she saw where he was going. "Yeah, I guess it would be me again."

"Good. I think I have a way to make sure that happens."

October 4, 2011

NASTOS TOOK EACH STEP FROM the basement holding cell carefully, up the stairs to the court's side entrance and took his seat next to Carscadden. He was bruised, with partially healed lacerations on his face and hands — the rest of his injuries, bruised ribs, other lacerations were hidden under clothing. By the shocked expression on Carscadden's face, Nastos figured that he must have looked even worse than he felt.

Court was full of well-dressed, sweaty human meat of various shapes and sizes. Reporters took up the entire front and back rows on both sides of the aisles. Nastos saw that there were some of the dentist's other patients, whose children had been molested, as well as a few police service officials and union members. Only the parents of the other victims seemed to have any sympathy for him.

Dewar sat at her table alone, stoic but tired, leaning over some notes that had been handed to her by the bailiff. She set them aside and began sending a text message on her BlackBerry. Carscadden interrupted his appraisal of her.

"You look like crap, Nastos," he said.

Nastos cleared his throat. "Yeah, well, the welcome wagon offered a courtesy seminar in mixed martial arts."

"Lucky bastard. You never know when that'll come in handy."

Nastos offered a weak smile. The bailiff interrupted the murmur in the court by asking everyone to rise for the Honourable Judge

Montgomery. The courtroom rose in near unison and Montgomery walked in. Nastos took the longest to get to his feet. Montgomery took his seat. The bailiff then announced, "Please be seated."

Nastos whispered to Carscadden, "I thought Scott was prosecuting from here on out?"

"He had car trouble this morning." Carscadden smiled. He was proud of himself for making Nastos shake his head.

"What'd you do?"

"I punctured two of his tires. Coincidentally, a taxi went by his place, but the driver was some Russian guy who doesn't know the city very well."

"Nice one," Nastos rubbed his hands together. "So, what's the plan now?"

"Watch and learn, Nastos."

Dewar took her position at the podium and waited for Montgomery to acknowledge her with a smile before she began. "Your Honour."

"Glad you're feeling better, Ms. Dewar. I thought that Mr. Scott was taking carriage of the prosecution."

"He's not here this morning, Your Honour. I haven't heard anything from him."

Nastos saw that Montgomery didn't seem to take the news very well. "He knows the start time — maybe this trial isn't very important to him, but it's important to me, the jurors and the people of this city. Ms. Dewar, I'd like you to continue the trial and to begin immediately."

"Yes, Your Honour. I believe Mr. Scott had planned on calling a Mr. Shawn Eade. Could his name be paged, please?"

The stenographer picked up the phone and dialled a few numbers. "Shawn Eade to Courtroom 101, Mr. Shawn Eade to Courtroom 101."

Nastos turned back to the galley. No one stepped forward. Montgomery seemed to be becoming more angry. "Ms. Dewar, would you like to try your next witness?"

"Yes. Dr. Michael Hall of the Centre of Forensic Sciences." Nastos noticed a man getting up from the back of the courtroom. He was wearing a black suit. He was tall, roundish and sweating profusely. The bailiff swore him in and he took a seat.

Over the next two hours, Dewar asked Dr. Hall four or five questions about his work in blood analysis. Dr. Hall spoke his answers in a steady breathless monotone. After the first half-hour, four members of the jury were asleep. After the next half-hour, two more. Even the elderly crime fiction fan was ready to pack it in. Nastos appreciated that Carscadden never objected once for reasons of relevance to the case. He just let the horror continue. The slideshow, examples, minutia of irrelevant detail bogged the trial down. Montgomery even sent a few text messages of his own; Nastos noticed it before he himself dozed off.

When his head snapped back, Nastos woke. He gulped a small cup of water and checked out the galley of the court. Half of the people were gone — not asleep, but gone.

Eventually, Dewar called a stop to the abuse. "Your Honour?"

"Yes, Ms. Dewar?"

"I feel we've covered a good amount of ground today. Any chance of a break?"

Montgomery wasn't happy. "A break? You mean Dr. Hall has more testimony?"

"Just another few hours, Your Honour."

Montgomery shifted in his seat and glanced at the jury apologetically. "I'm sorry, Ms. Dewar, but this testimony is a little on the dry and theoretical side. If there is going to be much more, might I suggest that we break for the day and revisit this tomorrow?"

Nastos checked the reaction in the courtroom. As Dewar paused to ponder the request, more and more heads began to nod, encouraging, even imploring her to agree.

"Well, I suppose, Your Honour, but if we're breaking for the day I just have one brief request."

Montgomery turned to the witness. "You're excused for the time being, Dr. Hall, and thank you so kindly for your informative and thorough testimony."

"Thank you, sir." Dr. Hall smiled, leaving the stand.

Then to Dewar, Montgomery asked, "What's your last issue before we break for the day?"

Carscadden kicked Nastos under the table and smiled to Dewar.

"Yes, Your Honour," she began, "I'd like to revisit the issue of court-ordered detention for Mr. Nastos. I think he's learned a lesson to take his bail conditions more seriously and I don't think it serves the public to house and feed him at the government's expense when there are alternatives."

Carscadden rose to his feet.

Montgomery asked, "Going to object, Mr. Carscadden?"

"No, Your Honour, no objection here."

"Granted, for now, Ms. Dewar, but Mr. Carscadden, if your client is careless again, he's going to regret it."

"Agreed, Your Honour."

◌ ◌ ◌

THEY MET AT FRANKIE'S RESTAURANT: NASTOS, CARSCADDEN, DEWAR and Hopkins. Instead of the usual staff table, the waitress moved them to a private room in the back.

Carscadden slid a digital print across the table for Dewar to examine.

"The guy in my office," she said.

Carscadden said, "The guy in my office too. Barely left an intact piece of drywall. James North."

Nastos flipped the picture around and appraised the man. "He's ex–Metro Drug Squad. He worked with Koche. He got his hands caught in the cookie jar and was fired five years ago. Back then, he was taking steroids and beating the hell out of people, when he wasn't stealing their money and drugs."

Hopkins asked, "Is he single?"

Carscadden was encouraging, "Single and looking."

Nastos slid the picture back to Carscadden. "That's my friend from the hallway. And Carscadden, why didn't you tell me your office was trashed?"

Carscadden couldn't hide his indignation. "Because I felt the need to tell you everything about as much as you felt the need to tell me everything." Before Nastos could say anything, Carscadden added, "Did I know about you and Dewar? No. Have you ever told me where you were that night? No. Why do most people at your work hate you? I've got no friggin' idea. You're more questions than answers, Nastos."

Nastos disputed nothing. "I trust you now, Carscadden. It takes a while to tell how dirty other people are willing to get to do the right thing. Most don't have a stomach for it, and we all have lines that we won't cross. I was trying to protect you, as cheesy as it sounds."

Carscadden shook his head. "Yeah, that's a debate we'll have to finish later, when we get this mess sorted out. Let's get back to North — he's the real problem here. We all have a reason to want to teach him a lesson and in Dewar's case, to get her stuff back."

Dewar added, "And while you were in jail, he broke into your house and left a picture on your wife's dresser of us together from years ago."

Nastos saw that Dewar took some enjoyment out of pushing that button herself. She wanted to make sure he was going to be in on whatever was going to happen with North. Still, it felt like an emotional betrayal on Dewar's part to wedge herself between him and his wife. He breathed and tried not to show the degree of hurt he felt. Through gritted teeth he said, "Trust me, Ang, I don't need any encouragement. This guy's going to wish he'd never been born."

Nastos clenched his fists, feeling the rage build up inside; it was a warm sensation and provided a singularity of purpose.

A waitress came over to take drink orders. She smiled at Carscadden. "Viktor is going to be happy when he hears you were here. And with two such beautiful women." She smiled at Dewar and Hopkins. "What can I get you to drink? Everything's on the house for Mr. Carscadden and his guests, so don't be shy, ladies." The woman had a mild Russian accent. Tall, brunette, a little on the thin side.

Dewar ordered an Australian Shiraz; Hopkins said that she might as well bring the bottle. The waitress left and soon enough came back with two bottles and more bread and vinegar along with a shrimp platter. She passed out the menus, saying "Just let me know when you're ready—"

Nastos interjected. "I'll take the sixteen-ounce rib steak, medium well, the baked potato and house salad, some garlic bread, and I'll start with some calamari."

She asked, "Anyone else ready?"

Carscadden said, "No, give us five minutes." She left with the one order.

Carscadden asked, "Little hungry, Nastos?"

He smiled. "Yeah, well, jail food isn't as good as they make it look on TV."

Dewar asked Nastos, "So, what's the plan? How do we get my stuff back?"

Carscadden pulled out his cell. "Here, I'll just phone buddy up and ask."

Dewar added, "I want them back before he listens to them — or worse, gives them to anyone." Dewar poured some wine and started on the shrimp.

Nastos took a sip of wine. "We're going to have to be up close and personal for what I have in mind. Dewar, call him up, make a date."

Dewar took out her phone but stalled. "Are you up to this, Nastos? I heard the hallway didn't go so well."

Nastos exhaled, his impatience growing by the minute, "This guy's a loser, he's not Genghis Khan. Call him up and arrange a meeting. Tell him whatever he wants to hear; when we get there, he's going to get a surprise."

She dialled.

Ms. Hopkins asked. "What are you going to offer him, Dewar?"

"I speak the international language." She flipped the picture side back up, appraising the man.

Nastos watched her take a breath and prepare.

NORTH WAS IN THE SPARE BEDROOM THAT HE HAD SET UP FOR WORKING out. One wall was all mirror, another had a TV mounted in the corner on a swivel in front of a treadmill. He was sitting at the bench press, shirtless, in jeans with a towel around his neck. When his cell rang, he answered it.

"North," he said. ·

"Yes, you seem to know a lot about me, but I don't know much about you. You were in my office?"

He paused. "Ms. Dewar, how can I help you?"

"You have my tapes and I'm willing to pay you to get them back."

"I don't think you have more money than my client. You can't afford me." He twisted the phone in his hand to access the end button with his thumb, but paused when she said, "How about fifty thousand dollars?"

He listened intently for the answer. "You don't have it."

"I do, Mr. North, and that is what those tapes are worth to me."

He began wondering if this was a stall, a way to trace him. But she had his name and number — she must already have his address. She could write a warrant herself for the cops to just break the door down. *She doesn't want the cops involved or else they would be here already.* "Why don't you come over and we can see if we can work something out? There're more valuable things in this world than money. For example, the patient list from the dead dentist. I saw the names, Dewar. I know what you've kept hidden and I know why. You're in this deeper —"

"Okay, okay," she said.

North enjoyed the silence from the other end of the phone. He had struck a nerve. He could ask for anything he wanted. He had total control over her.

"Seems like you've been keeping secrets, Madam Prosecutor. If you'll pay fifty grand for the tapes, surely the list is worth an evening of your life." North thought about her delicious body and what he was going to do to it. "Drop by tonight at ten," he continued. "Come alone and be ready for a good time."

There was the slightest hesitation in her reply. "You'll have everything ready for me?"

"If I get what I want, you'll get what you want."

"Well, Mr. North, sounds like you're going to get the rodeo ride of your life."

"I'll see you soon."

They both hung up.

Her last sentence rang through his mind again and again. He couldn't believe he had heard it. The bitch was going to give it up. Moving to his bedroom closet, he opened a tiny hidden door he had installed on the side wall. A small panel almost resembling a breaker panel was mounted there. He flipped a few switches and returned to the workout room, turning on the TV and DVD player. The screen warmed and came to life, showing a split screen with multiple angles from the master bedroom. He slid a blank DVD into the player/recorder and set the timer to start at ten p.m., just in case he forgot to set it later.

24

NASTOS GOT OUT OF THE BACK
seat, aching and sore. They had parked down the street from North's
condo building, away from the vacant lot so there was no chance he
could see them. Carscadden put his truck in park and turned off
the engine. Dewar got out on the passenger side and closed the
door. He didn't know how much he could count on them to keep
their cool. North was a dangerous man and they were about to hit
him where he lived.

Nastos stretched, making sounds like a tired dog. "I should
have drunk less wine."

"I should have drunk more wine," Dewar replied. She smiled but
still seemed scared as she walked around the truck. He shook his
head, knowing what she was talking about. Hopkins had reluctantly
agreed that someone should stay at the office in case they got into
trouble. If no one called her in one hour, she'd call Nastos' ex-partner
Jacques and tell him everything.

It was a cool night, the kind that held the faintest scent of winter
with calm winds and a sky full of constellations.

Carscadden rolled down his window. "This is stupid. Sorry. We
should just forget it."

Nastos said, "We have no choice, Carscadden. We're just going
to talk to him all nice and see where it goes." Carscadden began
drumming his fingers on the steering wheel. He was antsy.

Nastos grabbed Dewar's hand and tugged her toward North's apartment. "Okay. No screwing around, let's just do what we need to do and get the hell out of here."

He scanned the condo building, recalling which windows were North's. He would have felt a lot better if he had a gun.

"Ready?" Dewar asked.

Carscadden called out to Nastos, "When we're in jail, I'm calling the top bunk."

NORTH WAS IN HIS BEDROOM, FINISHING THE FINAL TOUCHES BY POSI-tioning his video cameras throughout the room. He had the ceiling covered with one in the ceiling fan and had every corner covered with a cell phone camera, an iPod for audio and two other cameras he had bought from the spy store downtown on Yonge Street. He wasn't going to be able to zoom in for anything, so he wanted wide coverage from all angles for future editing.

After he was done with the cameras, he lit a few candles and pulled some incense out of a drawer where he kept a variety of lubricants, vibrators, feathers and restraints — first date stuff. After one last look around, he figured that he had everything covered. For a pre-game warm-up, he grabbed a Scotch and sat down across from the TV in the living room to review the previous footage he had obtained of Dewar in her bathroom, half-naked, plucking her eyebrows. He tried to relax, but his heart was racing. He had had a shower earlier, but he could smell the nervous sweat from his armpits. He checked his watch; he didn't think he had time for another shower. He sure as hell was not going to miss it when Angela Dewar came calling to give up her body to get her stupid tapes back. No sir, he was going to answer the door on the first knock before she got cold feet. *She'll just have to shower with me when she gets here. I don't have any video in there, but I won't be long.*

There was a tap at the door; North's heart skipped a beat. He was giddy with excitement. He was going to do her every way he could possibly think of. He peeked out the eyehole and saw her standing there. She was wearing her black hair down past her shoulders and had on a business suit. *You're about to become a part of movie magic, Ms. Dewar.* He craned his view to the far left and right; he could see no one with her. She had come alone. He opened the door. "Right this way, Ms. Dewar." He waved his arm into the apartment.

"Thanks." She gave him a seductive smile and let her eyes run down his body. She put her purse on the kitchen counter, then she turned to watch his face as it flushed. His eyes fixed on her waist when she hung her jacket on a hook by the door and started unbuttoning her shirt.

She paused. "You better be serious — I need my tapes. If I do this and you don't deliver . . ."

She had nothing to threaten and they both knew it. He let her squirm for a moment. "Don't worry, they're here. You'll leave with them." North still wasn't sure that was the case, but she seemed to believe him. She left the shirt hanging open. He could see the white lace bra against her brown skin. *No,* he corrected himself, *not brown skin, chocolate. It's a flavour, not a colour.* He stopped breathing when she approached him slowly, meeting his gaze. He watched in near rapture as a wicked smile crept across her lips and she reached down and gently squeezed his crotch with one hand.

"Hope you don't go off too fast on me; you should at least show a lady a good time."

His throat felt dry. With her so close, he found himself observing the part in her hairline. He began to wonder what she'd look like just a little further down when she squeezed his shoulders and spun him around so that his back was toward the front door and he was leaning against the kitchen counter. "Why don't you just lean back here for a second and let me take care of the developing situation you've got going on here." He vaguely remembered that he hadn't locked the front door yet and that there wasn't a camera capturing anything in this room. *Who cares?*

North didn't hear Nastos come around the corner and by the time he saw movement out of the corner of his eye, it was too late. Nastos pounded him in the neck as hard as he could with a hammer fist. North's knees buckled and he dropped, his head smacking the ground. The next thing he knew, his eyes were fluttering open. It took him a minute to realize where the hell he was—lying on the floor of his apartment—and that the voice in his ear was real, not a dream.

"I have a silencer," the guy said. "No one will notice a thing until your brains start leaking through buddy's ceiling below us. Should take a few days."

"Gotcha, thanks," he said.

North certainly felt something pressed against the back of his head that could be the silencer on a gun. He stayed frozen, still trying to take deep slow breaths. He realized that his hands had been bound at his lower back with duct tape and there was a throbbing ache spreading over his right temple, but he forgot all about it when he tried to lick his lips and exquisite pain shot through his jaw. He began to figure out that this man must have hit him while he had been busy checking out Dewar and then he or both of them made a quick job of restraining him. He wanted to put together a plan to get out of this, but he knew for the time being that it was best to stay still and learn as much as he could about the people in his condo before trying to do anything.

"Where is it?"

"What?"

"You know," Nastos said.

"Find it yourself." He could hear another person in one of the back rooms, likely Dewar, ransacking the place to get her stuff back. It was just a matter of time; he had to think fast. He snuck a quick peek over his shoulder and recognized the man on top of him: Nastos.

Nastos was pressing him down with a left knee on the back of his neck and his right foot planted on the ground. He saw that Nastos was twisted around and had noticed the TV and the image on it.

"Nice TV show, North. Ang, check it out!" North heard the person in the back room come out to the living room. Courtesy of Nastos, he now knew it to be Dewar. He would not do well fighting two rounders, but a woman and pussy Nastos from the other night was a different story.

Dewar saw the image of herself on the TV, naked and bending over with her bum to the camera as she plucked her eyebrows. She found the DVD player and ripped the disk from it. North heard a lamp being toppled, the corner of the room got a little darker, then heavy footsteps come his way. The first lamp strike to the back of his head hurt much worse than the second, mostly because it was just a glancing blow. His scalp opened up, and thick, dark red blood oozed down the back of his neck and welled onto the tile floor.

His world began to spin and he was glad that he had not been standing or he might have lost a few teeth in the fall. He wanted to have his arms free to give her a taste of the rough stuff, to see how she liked it, but the duct tape was impossible to remove without a knife.

"Well, you do have nice legs, Angela." She hit him again, this time in the back.

His shoulders and upper back flexed him up into a convex posture, then he twisted and dropped back down to the floor.

He waited; he couldn't do anything else. Dewar dropped the lamp to the ground in front of North's face, then went back to trashing the place.

"We know what we're doing, North. We can clean this place up in a way that will never be traced to us. The cops will think it was a drug deal gone bad, a homosexual domestic, who knows what, but they sure as hell won't be asking me about it. Hell, I'm on bail. I can't leave the house."

"If you know what's good for you, you'll kill me right now. I'll hunt you down, that's a promise."

"I don't think you've really thought this through. My lawyer has defended the Crips, the Bloods, Asian gangs, the mob. All self-admitted murderers, any of whom would be more than happy to show some appreciation for getting them off multiple murders by dismembering you while you're still alive. How long do you think you'd last?"

North shrugged, "Oh, not long I guess." He wanted to keep Nastos talking. *If these gangs owed Carscadden so much, they'd be in here right now. You're full of shit, Nastos.* North was beginning to get less nervous. They weren't going to kill him and that meant that sooner or later he'd be loose. It would be their turn to be tied up and he planned to have much less mercy.

"You're going to put this one down as a loss and move on, Jimmy-boy. Now, where is it?"

"Bedroom closet, false wall," he said. *The sooner they're out of here, the sooner I'm free and hunting these walking dead.*

"Bedroom closet, Ang!" Nastos shouted.

"On my way." North heard her in the closet tossing his clothes out onto the bed. Blood was slowly beginning to congeal, gluing his face to the tiles. He could smell its coppery salt odor; the taste made him want to puke.

Dewar came back over with the box of tapes. She cracked it open and saw that the list was in there too. She showed it to Nastos, who let out a deep breath, relaxing the hand with which he was holding the point of a curling iron against North's head. North detected the movement of the object against his head and pressed back a little, testing Nastos and the object. *It feels more like plastic,* North considered. He became a little angry with himself realizing that he had been held at bay by nothing. *It wasn't a silencer, so it wasn't a gun either.* North tested the duct tape. All he needed was a paring knife — and he had one in the second drawer down, next to the fridge.

Dewar closed the box and hugged it close to her. "Time to go." She left through the door as quickly as she could, taking the case and grabbing her purse from the kitchen counter. Nastos waited till she was out of view, then got up himself.

"Good night, North."

"Till next time, Nastos."

Nastos backed out the door. "Just let this one slide."

"Sure thing."

◻ ◻ ◻

CARSCADDEN SAW NASTOS AND DEWAR RUNNING FOR THE CAR, SO HE hit the unlock button and moved to the back seat. Nastos got into the driver's seat. Dewar took shotgun as Nastos put his hand on the key and started the engine, locking the doors and turning the lights on.

"You know, Dewar, that went pretty—" The back window of the car exploded as a bullet burst through it. Carscadden shrieked covering his head with his arms as fragments of pulverized glass sprayed past them. Through the side mirror, Nastos saw a figure charging toward them. The figure raised his right arm, then the side-view mirror shattered as another bullet ripped through it. There was barely any sound from the gun. *He must have a silencer, a real one.* Nastos floored the gas pedal and the truck lurched forward as he pulled out into the middle of the road. "You okay back there?" He shouted more loudly than he had intended.

"Does every road trip we go on have to involve gunfire?" Carscadden asked.

"Me? I thought it was you!"

Dewar peeked back between the front seats. "He's calling your bluff, Nastos, now what?"

"We go to the cops—what else can we do?" Tears ran down Dewar's face; she pursed her lips but said nothing.

"I'm sorry," he said, and he was. Once they were at the police station everything would come out—those names on the patient list that she wanted to keep private, the fact that she had a relationship with Nastos. How would she explain that she knew him to be innocent, but was running a show trial at his expense because she had been bullied into it by Scott and Detective Koche? As far-fetched as it seemed, they were being shot at and she was more scared of the police.

Nastos sped around a corner, east on the Danforth, at first unsure where he was driving to. He considered getting on the 404 north-bound but disregarded the idea. Highways were fatal funnels and North would only have to catch up to find them. No, he preferred to keep to the surface streets, where he could drive in every direction, maybe even find a place to duck in and hide. It occurred to him that they could go to the warehouses on Eastern Avenue at the south end of town, near the lake and the beaches. Too bad he'd turned the wrong way. Eastern was an industrial area, with dealer-ships and junky plazas. He could try to lose North in there. He had only been there a couple of times, but he was sure he knew it better than North. And for whatever reason, the name Viktor Kalmakov came to mind. "Hey, Carscadden?"

"What?"

"Does Viktor still have a warehouse on Eastern?" Nastos looked back through the spider-webbed remnants of the back window. He saw a dark sedan come around the last corner sideways with the hub-caps all but flying off. It recovered from the driver's over-correction of the wheel and accelerated smoothly toward them, getting within a hundred metres. There was muzzle fire from the driver's window but only the third bullet thumped into the back of the car. "Never a traffic cop when you want one." Nastos smiled at Dewar, but she didn't smile back; instead she started to cry.

"We're going to die," Dewar said, "I can't believe this."

Glass on all sides of the car began to explode as more bullets ripped through the car.

"What are we going to do?" Carscadden asked.

Nastos spun his head to the left and caught a glimpse of North's position. "Lean back!" he shouted. With his right hand, he pushed Dewar's chest back into her seat as he floored the brake pedal. The truck screeched and slid uncontrollably at first and he had to put both hands on the wheel. Through the sedan's window, Nastos saw North's eyes shoot wide open as he narrowly avoided hitting the car by swerving to the left.

Dewar and Carscadden flew forward. Dewar was held back by the seat belt. Carscadden, who wasn't wearing one, landed between the front seats and would have impaled himself had there been a floor shifter. Nastos threw the truck into reverse and floored the gas pedal, backing into a closed gas station, smashing over several garbage bins, then hit the gas to go back the way they had come. North saw the impending collision and hit the brakes, careening right. When he over-corrected the wheel, he sideswiped two parked cars, coming to an abrupt stop.

Nastos never looked back, but if he had, he would have been disappointed. North rocked his car forward and back, flooring the gas to break free of the twisted metal, then took a wide lazy turn to the left, running up the curb on the far side of the street and speeding after the two lawyers and Nastos once again.

Nastos saw that Carscadden had taken out his cell phone and was dialling.

The shards of glass remaining in the side-view mirror showed more muzzle flashes. "It's ringing," said Carscadden tersely.

"Here," Nastos said, reaching back. "Pass me the phone."

Viktor answered. "And Mr. Carscadden, how are you?"

"Viktor, this is Steve Nastos — you busy?"

"Nastos, nice to here from you, actually I'm just out of town right now, why?"

Nastos took a corner fast and gunned the engine on the straightaway. He zig-zagged to avoid being shot, but found it slowed him down, so he went straight up the centre of the road. "I'm driving like a maniac with some asshole shooting at me. I'm driving to Eastern Avenue, to your warehouse."

"Is this guy North also the driver?" Kalmakov asked impassively.

"Yeah." A bullet whistled between Nastos and Dewar, striking the windshield. Fragmented glass burst into the air like fine powder, leaving a finger-sized circle between them.

Dewar shrieked, "Hang up and drive, Nastos!" and tried to crouch in the front foot-well on the passenger side.

"Well, don't believe that junk on TV, there's actually quite a knack to shooting from a car, especially for a driver. I wish I were better at it."

"Jesus Christ, Viktor, can you help or not?"

"I'm way up in the north end of town; I had a meeting with my accountant. I'm thirty minutes away, which might as well be an eternity, but I'll start down right now, okay?"

"Okay, I'm going to your warehouse."

"And Nastos, if this guy hurts you, I'll send him to hell one piece at a time."

"Great, thanks."

Nastos tossed the phone into the back seat. With something of a plan thrown together, he felt that he had more time to think. He considered the neighbourhood; no one was going to be calling the cops. Madeleine must have been scared when North was following her — he thought of how violated she must have felt when he came into the house. What would North do to her if Nastos wasn't around to protect her? He shook his head. He wasn't going to jail with this asshole on the loose. That wasn't going to happen.

An observer might have noted a stoic calm washing over his face. Relaxed, he felt his shoulders drop and he took a deep breath. He turned around so they could both hear. "I have an idea," he said. "I'm going to do something here. But Ang, you have to promise me something first."

"What?" Dewar shouted.

"Ang, if I take care of this guy, will you drop the charges?"

"Of course I will."

"What are you doing?" Carscadden asked, totally confused.

Nastos ignored the question. "Carscadden, how much did you pay for this piece of shit truck?"

"Two grand, why?"

ⓒ ⓒ ⓒ

NORTH RIPPED THE MAGAZINE OUT OF HIS GLOCK AND REPLACED IT with a full one. *You have to love this city. There are so many gang shootings, domestics and shit like that — as long as we stay away from the nice parts of town, we can go like this all night.* He found that Nastos was not such a bad driver under the circumstances, but he was done fooling around. He seemed to be leading him to the industrial district by the lake, which suited North just fine. He used to work patrol down there; he knew the area well.

The terrain rolled up and down, like a saw's teeth, eventually working its way down to the lake. They crossed over the last of the railway tracks, until there were just one or two little hills to go — then he'd be able to shoot again. He felt a buzz in his chest pocket and realized that his phone was ringing. *Oh, what the hell,* he thought and put the gun down to check it. The call display said *Nastos,* so he answered it.

"Tired of getting shot at, Nastos?"

"You could say that," Nastos said, sounding exasperated. "I give up — just promise you won't shoot us. What do you want?"

A smug smile slid across North's face. "You're going to jail, so there's nothing I want from you. Put Dewar on the phone — she's got money."

"What the hell makes you think you can get away with this? She's a goddamned prosecutor. Don't make me have to call the cops, North — I'm trying to avoid that, but it's my only option."

"I'll tell you why I can get away with this. Because I know her name is on the list. She's the one that killed the child molester, or at least she was involved. I know all of her little secrets, so I know she won't go to the police." North paused a moment. *Why is this guy asking such stupid questions? Unless he doesn't know,* he mused. *She hasn't told him.* There was silence on the other end of the phone. Poor Nastos finally figured out that Dewar has been playing him the whole time. He realized that he was in a position to get everything he wanted. Nastos would go to jail, for Koche and Scott; he would blackmail Dewar to put Nastos away and take some cash just for the hell of it, or else he would take what he knew to the police and she'd be the one in jail. It was going to be perfect.

North eased off the gas a little, but kept close enough to them that they couldn't slip away. He saw that they were driving more predictably. If he decided to shoot again, he'd have a much better chance of hitting. He sped up, just a little bit. They were nearly over the crest of the last hill before the topography flattened out.

◖ ◖ ◖

NASTOS THREW THE PHONE BACKWARD TO CARSCADDEN AND STOLE A glance at Dewar. "North told me the names on the list — two of the four, anyways: you and your daughter Abby. I can guess the other two."

Dewar said nothing. Carscadden leaned between the two of them. "You killed Irons?" he asked.

"No," she said. Her response was weak. Nastos took her reply to mean that she hadn't swung the bat or that she didn't feel guilty about it. He couldn't just give up and leave her fate in North's hands. North would take her for all she was worth, then turn her in, or worse, let Koche do it and turn himself into a hero. No. North had messed with his wife one time too many and there was no way Nastos wanted anyone punished for killing the monster who had hurt Josie.

Nastos took a deep breath and committed himself. Once he was over the last hill, out of North's view, he locked up the brakes, coming to a stop as fast as he could. He reached across and opened Dewar's door. "Run, go there!" He pointed to a loading bay in one of the industrial buildings. Before she could say anything, he unclipped her seat belt and shoved her out on to the road. She landed on her knees, scraping them. Carscadden piled out on top of her. They could only sit dumbfounded as they watched what he did next.

213

◖ ◖ ◖

WHEN NORTH CAME OVER THE HILL, HE DIDN'T STAND A CHANCE. OF all the things he expected to see, the lawyer's truck racing up the hill backwards right at him was not even on the radar. He had slowed a bit, anticipating the corner at the bottom of the hill, but the closing speed between the two vehicles was still close to a hundred kilometres an hour. With a deafening crash, Carscadden's truck rammed right into North's, hitting dead on. The front end of North's car and the rear of Carscadden's truck were flung up into the air from the momentum, both vehicles seemingly disintegrating. There was the hissing of hoses, mechanical death rattles.

The front third of North's car disappeared, and so did the pickup truck as far as the rear axle. The airbags burst open. Their powdery film-like talcum powder that allowed for a smooth deployment covered everything in a small radius around both vehicles. North's engine dropped from his car as soon as the motor mounts fractured from the impact, cratering into the asphalt. There were no flames, but fragmentation from glass and plastic had exploded in all directions. The sound was like a plane crash-landing. The vehicles lurched back to the ground, the springs creaking to a stop, and it became eerily quiet.

Carscadden got to his feet, his knees feeling loose and rubbery as he ran over to what was left of his truck. "Steve! Steve, what the hell did you do?" The back half of his truck was demolished almost up to the back of the driver's seat, where the remnants of North's car began. Broken glass was everywhere and he could smell the thick, sickly odour of radiator fluid. And blood. He could smell blood.

He must be dead. That was an awful impact. He heard a cough, then a second, and then a bloodied hand grasped the edge of the door frame where the glass used to be. He ran up to find Nastos, slumped over to the passenger side, trying to pull himself up. Nastos unclasped the seat belt and began thrusting himself against the door to get it open. He didn't even seem to notice that Carscadden was standing right next to him.

"Nastos, what the hell were you thinking?" Carscadden asked. He tried pulling on the door, but the mangled frame had bent the door shut.

"I'm okay, just help me get out of here." Nastos' clothes were covered in blood and broken glass. There was powder from the airbag on his chest. Dewar came over and the two of them helped Nastos climb out the window. He was warm and slippery with blood, but Carscadden hardly noticed. It wasn't until Nastos was out that he even thought about North and his gun.

The three of them walked back to the other car and peered inside. North had smashed his face off the door post to his left. His neck was broken, his head hanging at an impossible angle. His eyes bulged, staring blankly into nothing; blood trickled out of the sockets and from his ears. Congealing blood trailed down from both corners of his open mouth.

They silently evaluated the dead man.

"Whoops." Carscadden said.

Nastos rubbed his chin slowly. "Whoops."

"Now what?" Dewar asked.

Nastos shrugged his shoulders. "Ang, Viktor won't be long. Is there anyone you think you need to call about this?"

She thought for a moment. "I have everything we should need."

25

A REPORTER STOOD ON THE wooden footbridge in the Cherry Beach Park, the lake behind her, the sun casting a warm, honeyed light on her beautiful but tired features. She spoke to the camera confidently, as if she knew all there was to know about what she was reporting for the city news.

"An elderly couple taking their golden retriever for a walk this sunny Sunday morning found something that is becoming far too common in Cherry Beach these days — another dead man. They found him floating in the lake, face down, the victim of multiple and severe traumas. Disgraced detective Steve Nastos is currently on trial for a previous murder in the area, but investigators on this case say it's too early to determine if the deaths are connected . . ."

The camera panned out to show cops near the lake taking pictures and measuring things. Other officers were trying, and failing, to loop a rope around the body to pull it to shore. A fireman, a twenty-five-year vet with a smoke in his mouth speared the corpse's thigh with his pike pole and beached the body with a good pull as the horrified couple looked on. Kojak, the retriever, on the other hand, with his broad, toothy Hollywood smile, didn't seem terribly shaken up by the experience.

THEY SAT. MONTGOMERY WAVED TO DEWAR, THEN SPOKE. "PLEASE, carry on where you left off, Ms. Dewar."

She stood and walked to the lectern with the new file in her hand. She separated a copy from the paperclip, giving one to Carscadden and one to the bailiff to pass to the judge. Montgomery began flipping through the pages.

"Your Honour, I have just received this file this morning. It's in relation to a dead man found at Cherry Beach earlier today; did you hear about the death on the news?"

"No, Ms. Dewar, I did not," the judge replied. He seemed thoughtful, wondering where she was going with the information.

"Well, sir, the body of a man was recovered — a white man, approximately forty years old. He had apparently been beaten to death, rather severe injuries. He was found floating not twenty meters from where our victim — or rather the victim in this case — was found. The lead investigator for this occurrence, Detective Clancy Brown, who testified before us just a few days ago, had the preliminary file sent to me."

"And . . . Ms. Dewar?" He leaned forward.

"In light of the need for a review of all of the facts and circumstances, Your Honour, the prosecution seeks to have all of the charges against Detective Nastos stayed for the foreseeable future."

"Are you telling me I can retire a few months early, Ms. Dewar?"

"Yes, sir."

Montgomery was not yet convinced. "What kind of linking circumstances were there for the record, Ms. Dewar, if this is the last time we may speak to this case in open court?"

"Your Honour, police identified the dead man and conducted a search of his apartment, a search that is apparently still underway. They have found property belonging to Dr. Irons."

"His business card, Ms. Dewar?"

"Quite a lot of pain medication, OxyContin and the like." She held up a picture. "They were found in a false panel in his closet. Looks like he kept some mementos for personal use."

Montgomery still didn't seem convinced. Nastos started to get the feeling that to Montgomery, the news was too good to be true. "What's the theory on that, Ms. Dewar?"

"This man ran a private investigation business; he's run loan sharks and enforcers. Possibly, Dr. Irons was a murder for hire. It's too early to say, but certainly on the surface it appears like a much stronger case than the one against Detective Nastos."

Montgomery adjusted his glasses. "Mr. Carscadden, any comments?"

Carscadden rose to his feet like he was pulling two sandbags up with him. "No, sir. The defense is content with my client being released with a stay in proceedings so we can begin the civil case against the police service and the crown attorney's office."

"Good answer," Montgomery replied. "I hereby order the immediate release of Detective Nastos and order that all charges be stayed for one year. In that time, if the prosecution does not restart its case, all the charges will be irrevocably withdrawn."

The gavel struck the block and with that, Nastos was a free man.

Judge Montgomery stood up and the bailiff took his cue. "All rise," he said, and the judge disappeared behind the door to his chambers.

They walked outside the courtroom, joining the masses in the hallway, then down to the main doors where they exited the building. A scrum of reporters surrounded them. Carscadden winced in pain whenever his arm was jostled. Nastos wore a tired expression of disdain for the camera lights and microphones being thrust in his face. Carscadden stopped Nastos when they reached the top of the steps and they waited for reporters to take up positions with their cameras.

One of the reporters, an ancient man who probably could have retired ten years ago, had the official first question when everyone was set. "Another dead body found in Cherry Beach, a dramatic turn of events — how much of that was a factor in charges against your client being dropped?"

"First," Carscadden replied, "I knew and stated for the record that Detective Nastos was innocent, right from the start. What we have here is a culture in policing where it's sometimes advantageous to turn on each other for personal gain, playing to the prejudices in the community, rather than doing the right thing, the thing the police are sworn to do, to properly investigate crimes. The fact that police turned on one of their own, an officer with such a stellar reputation, and attempted to sandbag him for personal gain only shows that none of us is safe. If it can happen to a detective, it can certainly happen to disadvantaged youth, the economically marginalized. I invite you all to follow the lawsuits that will be filed soon and I would be happy to discuss it further with you all at a future date in my office. For now, I ask for a little time for myself and my client. Detective Nastos would like to have some time with his daughter, one of the real victims in all of this."

"What kind of settlement are you looking for?" a second reporter asked.

"One with a lot of pretty zeros. This circus cost Detective Nastos his job and his reputation, not to mention the emotional and physical scars from prison. He was not afforded protective custody, which is essentially mandatory in such cases. Be reminded that all of this tore him away from his daughter when she needed him most. Heads will roll. I can't wait."

Carscadden and Nastos got into the waiting taxi and drove off.   219

26

opposite each other, with his desk between them. Koche had been a cop for nearly twenty years, had seen dozens of guilty men avoid a conviction for murder, but they had all had dream team lawyers, deep pockets and political connections. Koche couldn't believe that Nastos had done it with none of those. *That Paki bitch let this guy go. For whatever reason, she let him get away with murder.* He and Koche had handed her a career-maker — all she had to do was be able to read and speak, the case file spoke for itself. He knew first-hand that Scott had obtained convictions with evidence far more tenuous. "Where do you think it all went wrong, Jeff?"

"You had everything all planned out, Koche. You tell me?"

"Dewar," he said. "She was driving the train when it went off the tracks. My guy North should look into the story. I'll tell him to go all the way back to when she was born in Calcutta, or wherever the hell she came from."

220

Koche went to the window and pulled the cord to open the wooden slats. The sidewalks were nearly barren; the morning commuters were already at work and the first blustery winds had sent the rest to the underground transit, away from the first below-freezing day. The sun had little interest in making an appearance. Instead it only cast the meagre, greyed overcast light that a godless underworld might deserve. He knew that at best, this Nastos mess would put him in career purgatory.

"But I've been trying to reach my guy — I even went to his apartment. I must have called him twenty times, he's not answering. It's like he fell off the face of the earth." Koche pulled out his BlackBerry; there were no new messages.

Scott turned from the window. He crossed then uncrossed his arms, eventually sliding his hands into the back pockets of his pants. "I don't like this, Koche. The list is out there, the tapes are out there and your guy is gone. He flipped, he must have. We're fucked."

"No, he's a druggie. He's wasted someplace, spending his new-found wealth in advance is all."

Koche's heart skipped a beat when Scott's secretary, Janice, walked right into his office without knocking.

"Mr. Scott?" she said.

Scott was incensed. "What the fuck did you just do, Janice? You can't just come in here —"

Behind Janice, two men in dark business suits entered, strangers to Scott, who with their alien presence had obviously committed an even worse infraction in his eyes. Janice left, sharing a mischievous grin with one of the two men.

"Mr. Scott?" one of the men said. "I'm a process server. You're getting sued, buddy."

Koche grinned, enjoying watching the guy call Scott *buddy*; Scott's skin visibly crawled. "Sued? For what?" Scott asked.

"I guess the malicious and wrongful prosecution of Detective Steve Nastos." He tried to hand Scott a manila envelope with his name typed on the front, but Scott wouldn't touch it, so he threw it on the desk in front of Scott instead. "Oh, and here's another one. This is for Human Rights violations in the workplace."

Scott stared at the envelopes, then at Koche, who could only shrug a response. Scott eyed the process server, his jaw clenched as he thought of what to say. There was a knock at the office door.

Koche vaguely recognized the two plainclothes detectives standing by the door. They were dressed in matching black suits and by their crew cuts and rigid stances, they looked like prototypical secret service agents. Koche recognized the shorter man, Owen, from Internal Affairs.

"I don't know who the hell you two are, but I'm in the middle of something. Come back in ten minutes," Scott demanded.

The process servers smiled to the cops, then back at Scott, then excused themselves. Squeezing past the cops, they disappeared down the hallway. Owen stepped forward.

"Yes, Mr. Scott, we're with Professional Standards. It seems those men have finished with you, so we'd like you to pack your things and vacate the premises immediately. I've got two officers coming over to make sure you leave in a timely manner."

"All this for a petty lawsuit? We get sued all the time — lawsuits mean we're doing our job." Scott was incredulous.

"We heard the audio tape recordings, Mr. Scott," the officer began. "The way you have been treating your subordinates . . . the Attorney General himself called us and asked that we advise you that you're suspended."

"This is an overreaction, it's —"

"It's about time is what it is, Mr. Scott," the man said.

"Pardon me?"

The officer only answered by way of a full smile. Koche knew what the cops were thinking. The only thing better than a pay raise to a cop was screwing over a weaselling lawyer. Koche had to admit that Scott was as slippery as they came, but he had always fought on the cops' side. Koche stood back, choosing to remain silent and impartial. He tried to squeeze past Owen and the other officer.

Owen asked. "Where do you think you're going?"

"This is getting a little awkward. I'm out of here." He turned back to Scott. "Give me a call when you get this sorted out, Jeff. I'm here for you, buddy." Then left, walking down the hallway to the main doors. He didn't like watching the world crash down all around Scott. It was ugly the way they were all ganging up on the man.

Andrews' voice called from behind him. "Koche?"

"Not now, I'm in the middle of something." *The last thing I need is to be dragged into that mess. I'll get back to the office and see what I can do to sort this thing out with North.* He got to the double glass doors, opening one and stepping out into the cold grey air. There, Koche found Detectives Weiss and Crockford standing waiting for him. Weiss grabbed his elbow as he tried to walk past, but he brushed it off and tried to keep going.

"Hey, get your hands off me, Weiss."

Crockford grabbed his arm and squeezed harder; this time, Koche stopped. "Excuse me, Detective-Sergeant Koche, I'm Detective Crockford and this is Detective Weiss. We're with Homicide."

"Good for you, goofs. Now get out of my way." Koche tried to walk, but Crockford squeezed tighter, holding him still. "You're not going anywhere until we talk."

"I outrank you, Crockford, so watch yourself. And you can let me the fuck go." Koche tried to push past them, but they shoved him back into the doors.

"What the fuck do you guys want?" He was mad enough to start swinging, but thought better of it. *Homicide? Who the hell's dead?* Koche, as it turned out, wasn't going to be too happy with the answer.

"Your buddy North's been found dead in Cherry Beach."

Oh. "I'm not sure I know who you're talking about."

"Maybe you would like to explain how and why you two have been exchanging phone calls and text messages for the last month. Where were you last night around midnight? Why were you the last person he called?"

An awful sinking feeling came over him — no, it was more of a drowning feeling. The sounds of city traffic, horns, accelerating engines, disappeared and there was a heavy, claustrophobic feeling in their place. The two men seemed to surround him and the air grew too thick to speak.

"I don't know what game you guys are playing—"

"Listen, just relax and come with us, Dave. Answer a few questions and we can all sort this mess out." Crockford obviously saw the life-flashing-before-his-eyes expression on Koche's face. "Don't go acting all suspicious—unless, of course, you killed this guy, in which case we can call you a lawyer."

Koche felt the double doors push him forward as they opened behind him and he was swept to the side. Scott walked past him carrying a banker's box full of citations and plaques, leaving his office for the last time. Scott didn't acknowledge him. His shoulders were slumped forward making him appear scared and defeated, with a police officer on either side of him. Scott followed the officers' lead.

◻ ◻ ◻

DEWAR AND NASTOS SAT IN THE BACK BOOTH OF FRANKIE'S Restaurant. It was eleven p.m. and the place was closing for the night. The bartender was ringing out the cash register and counting through the float; the kitchen staff were mopping up and stocking shelves with clean dishes.

"After all we've been through, you can trust me. And I deserve to know what secrets you're keeping." Nastos took a sip of his water and took a piece of shrimp from the plate they were sharing.

Dewar shrugged and slid the patient list across the table. "When something happens to you or to your family, the rules go out the window. We see it every day: child molesters getting away with their crimes because the traumatized children aren't as articulate as they need to be to convict these guys. Very few judges will send someone to jail on the say-so of a five-year-old—they're perfect victims."

Nastos was barely listening as he read through the names, wanting to see the ones that had been blocked out. He already knew what the missing two names were; he just needed to read it for himself. Dewar was still talking, rationalizing.

"And it's not like there's some magic therapy for these guys. How long would someone have to talk to you to make you change your sexuality? Honestly, how much would I have to talk to you to convince you that you should be gay for the rest of your life? It's impossible. There is no cure for pedophilia." Dewar took a sip of her wine.

"So we kill them," Nastos deadpanned. "We round them all up and kill them. That's the only solution here: the death penalty on the say-so of a five-year-old."

Nastos noted that she couldn't look him in the eye.

"I watched the video of what happened to my Abby—not all of it, just enough to know that I couldn't deny it."

"Where's the video now?"

"Burned. But I had videos of the other kids. Someone has them in a safe place. I was going to produce it in the trial if I needed to."

Nastos saw why. She'd sabotage the trial.

"I planned to do it in a way that would backfire on the case. The jury would be so disgusted and angry that there'd be no way they could convict you. They would've agreed with the crime of passion argument that you would no doubt have made upon seeing the video yourself."

"Why did it even go to trial? If you knew I didn't do it, why take such risks?"

Dewar leaned back in her chair. "Once Scott and Koche had you charged, we had to do some quick thinking."

"We?" Nastos asked.

"We," Dewar confirmed. "When did you figure out who it was?"

Nastos smiled. "Who killed Irons? During the trial. Couldn't miss it—all those text messages. The ones you sent, the ones he checked from time to time."

Dewar pondered, probably wondering if she was too obvious. "You think Carscadden put it together?" Nastos saw that she was a little nervous, and he enjoyed that. It so different from what he had been through. "When Carscadden left the morally ambiguous world of corporate law for criminal law, he thought he'd find a better defining line between right and wrong, but he found this world to be even murkier and messier. Like poor Macbeth, he was mired so deep in a river of blood that turning back was just as messy as crossing over to the other side. Carscadden got a small taste of that."

"So did the rest of us," Dewar said. She was thinking again, probably wondering which shore in the river of blood she had finally washed up on. "If he puts it together, what do you think he'll do?"

Nastos didn't answer; he had no answer. Anything he said would just be a guess. For him it was over. He'd get a settlement, a pension and his daughter back. He'd walk her to school every day and pick her up. He'd make her lunch and go on class trips. He'd be over-protective until he felt that she was going to be okay enough to trust the world again.

He also had work to do on his marriage with Madeleine, who had her own trust and security concerns. And he'd never work as a cop again. He didn't know how he felt about that. "Whatever Carscadden does, I'll support him."

27

A MUSTY, RED CORDUROY LANE wound between the orange and yellow–tinged fall leaves of the maples and mixed deciduous trees. Pulling his car up to the lake house, Carscadden saw the man pushing a wheelbarrow full of raked leaves to a smouldering fire pit in front of the house. The man was wearing khaki cargo pants and a red plaid shirt with the sleeves rolled up to his elbows. He turned at the sound of Carscadden's beamer, his eyes squinting in a vain attempt to see past the windshield's glare.

Carscadden parked next to a Land Rover. He got out of his car, leaving the other man inside. He smiled to retired Judge Montgomery and took a moment to look around the property appraisingly, stalling. There was a bite in the air, and grey, heavy clouds above, a sure sign of the changing of the seasons. The still, black waters of Pine Lake were motionless behind the house; songbirds twittered from their branches. With the carnivorous insects long gone, the place was a Canadian paradise.

Montgomery walked over with a warm smile and, after dusting his hands off on his pant legs, offered a firm handshake. Carscadden accepted his hand, but was unable to smile back.

"Nice surprise, Mr. Carscadden. Just in the neighbourhood, were you?"

"Not exactly, Judge."

227

Montgomery glanced at the car and his eyes squinted again. He could just make out the shape of a man in the passenger seat. He turned back to Carscadden. "Been two weeks since the trial — you want to raise a few more objections?" Montgomery studied Carscadden's face, trying to read him. He found the dark circles under the eyes trapped in the web of wrinkles so out of place for a man his age.

"I know everything, Your Honour, I know the whole story. What you did —"

"What I did? No, what he did, it's about what *he* did."

Montgomery was like a bird trapped in a cage. He appeared out of breath, like he needed to sit down. Carscadden could only imagine the fear going through his mind. Maybe something like what went through Dr. Irons' mind when he saw the judge approaching with the bat in his hands.

Montgomery glanced at the woods. Sounds of birds, creaking trees and swaying grass surrounding them. There were noises from everywhere. They appraised each other. Montgomery pointed and Carscadden followed as the old man walked to a porch step and sat down. Carscadden took a seat next to him, watching the slow burning fire Montgomery had been feeding. The heat from below dried the wet leaves on top. The smoke and steam rising from the top were indistinguishable from one another and were both going to the same place — disappearing into the wind.

"How's your grandson, Judge?"

"Listen, Carscadden," Montgomery said as he smiled. He shook his head, not where to begin. "My only regret is that that monster didn't get what he had coming to him thirty years earlier. I don't even want to think about how many victims are out there who could have been saved lifetimes of anguish and suffering."

"It doesn't sit right with me, to say the least. You must have known that I might figure it all out. Did you plan to kill me too, to cover it all up? Did you somehow think I could just keep it all secret and become an accessory after the fact?"

A new sound, barely perceptible, emanated through the still air. Carscadden heard it, cocking his ear to the sky. Montgomery heard it too, but Carscadden wasn't sure the old man could distinguish that it was a siren; it was too elusive just yet.

Montgomery continued. "We knew you were smart and hungry. You made some waves when you got the Russian clear on his charge, the no-winner. It was Dewar who wanted you; she was adamant right from the beginning."

Carscadden rubbed his hands together. "Who decided to kill Irons, to murder him? That was the biggest risk of all." He turned to Montgomery, wanting to see the expression on his face, to see if he was being honest or not. Instead, Carscadden saw remorse which turned to fear when it became clear that the sound in the distance was a siren approaching.

The sound came from all directions, echoing from each of the trees and from over the lake. It even seemed like it was coming from the sky. Montgomery's posture slumped and withered. Carscadden saw a man lumbering under a heavy burden.

"That was my call," Montgomery said, taking the blame with his few words. "Dewar wanted it, of course — the rage was eating her alive — but I told her it had to be me. I was beyond reproach."

◻ ◻ ◻

CARSCADDEN SAT BACK, REVEALING NO EMOTION AS MONTGOMERY stopped and examined him. Montgomery was probably wondering if he was wearing a wire.

"Was it easy getting on the trial?" asked Carscadden.

"No one wanted it — it was a political tightrope. Getting the case was the easy part. It was like offering to take out a bag of used diapers." Montgomery glanced back at him, appearing beaten, lost. "You know, Carscadden, you seem to be struggling with something. What's troubling you? Have *you* done something you regret?"

A mild, then grotesque expression of fear appeared on Montgomery's face as the siren grew very loud. It was painful to see the distinguished Judge, the well-respected pillar of community, diminished so much. Like a rabbit caught in a trap — a frightened animal frozen in panic. A thump at the end of the driveway drew their attention as the police car came into view. It was a black-and-white with the roof lights flashing blue and red. Carscadden watched it lurch over a hump in the driveway. The siren stopped and the cruiser came up the rest of the way silently. Every second seemed an eternity. He felt the hairs on his arms rise as the cold sweat began. Montgomery might have wanted to run, but his jogging legs must have been forty years behind him.

Of course, Montgomery should have known this to be a distinct possibility. You can't conspire to kill someone and leave the corpse on a city beach without considering that it could all lead back to you, especially with your co-conspirators still out there. With a little something called forensics, you can't even count on dead men to keep your secrets for you.

The squad car pulled up and as the driver's window opened, Montgomery somehow managed to get to his feet. Carscadden led the way to the driver's door.

The officer was a man was in his early thirties with a standard country-issue cop moustache and shaggier hair than you could get away with in a city force. He might as well have been working a gob of chewing tobacco or spinning a toothpick in his mouth from the local grease-hole diner. The officer grabbed something from the seat next to him and got out of the car.

"Morning gentleman, can either of you give me some help real quick?" His voice was deep and smooth like a late-night talk-radio man. Before either one could answer, he slapped a map book on the hood of the cruiser and waved them over. Carscadden saw it was a local map; he'd be of no help.

"I'm looking for 3345, but half the houses don't have numbers — any guesses?"

When Montgomery spoke, his voice sounded dry and sore like he had walked through a desert for forty years, but he forced his way through. "You know the name, Officer, or get any landmarks?"

"Dan Phillips. He's supposed to be retired real estate, but I'm new here and—"

Montgomery exhaled. "He's about four houses down on the left. You'll see a mailbox made out of a wooden toy farm tractor—his is the next place on the left. It's a long driveway. You'll see the blue-stained house." The cop was obviously relieved, but nowhere near as much so as the good judge, who didn't know whether to shit or go blind.

He closed up the map book saying, "Thanks," and made to get back in the car.

"Hey, Officer," Carscadden asked, "what's going on down there?"

The cop sat down, closing the door then turned the ignition, starting the engine.

"A couple bears in his back garden. He's the only guy up here without a gun to shoo them away."

Montgomery's voice was stronger now. "Hey, before you go, tell him Judge Montgomery is up for the month and to give me a call— I'll lend him my shotgun for the winter while I'm in Florida."

"Much appreciated, I'm sure. I'll tell him. Totally illegal, mind you, without a permit, but I doubt dead bears fill out many police reports."

Montgomery agreed. "People in the country like to solve their own problems."

"Fine with me, saves me driving forty-five minutes each way for bullshit."

As the cruiser backed down the driveway, the two men returned to the steps. Montgomery sighed as if he had been holding his breath for an hour.

"How's that for timing?"

"Nearly killed me," Montgomery said.

"Well, at least I know where you can get a good lawyer." Carscadden smiled, but he didn't think Montgomery had heard him.

He was staring at his hands, trying to wring them dry from either the cold sweats or the blood he saw from behind his haunted mind.

Despite the weeks since the trial and the long drive up, Carscadden still didn't have it straight with himself about how the whole mess made him feel. He just found himself talking. "You know, I never had children, but I guess I'm not too old to rule it out. As an only child, the closest I ever got to something I had to look after was a puppy my parents got me when I was twelve. We lived in the country and that little escape artist — Hartley was his name — got to following me to school every day. We lived in a quiet subdivision and back then kids were allowed to walk to school instead of being encased in bubble wrap and chauffeured there and back in armoured suvs.

"Anyway, I tried to get Hartley to stay home, but he got more and more comfortable with the idea of following me and I got more and more comfortable too. Sure enough, one day I came out of school and there he was, waiting for me across the road. He ran over to me and was hit by a truck, right in front of me. There he was, eighteen months old, sixty-five pounds of blond, wavy, fur looking up at me, unable to move. I could tell by his breathing and the blood all over him that he was as good as dead, and he knew it too." Carscadden was the one now wringing his hands while Montgomery watched silently, letting him speak.

"He had this expression on his face, like he wanted me to help him — me, a twelve-year-old boy. He wasn't ready to die. There was nothing anybody could do, especially me. So, I rubbed his fur and told him that he was the best dog there ever was and after he died I swore I'd never have another dog and I haven't. I can only imagine the hell you, Dewar and Nastos have gone through after you unknowingly took your kids to that pervert.

"I never felt any animosity toward the truck driver since it was my fault for letting Hartley decide the safety rules. In college, my girlfriend Beth died in a swimming accident, then years later after I got married there was all this pressure to have kids. I started working overtime and, when that wasn't enough, I started drinking.

I drove Emily away just like everyone after Beth who had the same plans for me.

"Like I said, I can't imagine what you went through — I don't ever want to know. But considering how hard I have been on myself for the last dozen and a half years over a host of bullshit — even aside from the dog — I guess I can say that I understand. I can't imagine a parent out there having their child hurt so much and not doing something about it."

"It was your and Dewar's names on that list that were blacked out — I saw them and no one else alive did. Let's hope it stays that way. I'll take it to my grave, Judge — I guess maybe that's what I came here to say." Carscadden wiped the tears from his face with the sleeve from his coat, avoiding eye contact with Montgomery.

"I'm sorry it had to go the way it did, Carscadden. I'm sorry that man had to die, that Mr. North — I'm just glad it didn't spin as far out of control as it could have."

"How's your boy doing, Judge?"

"Good. He's in town at a friend's house tonight. He's looking forward to going to Florida this winter — Disney World, Sea World, Universal, the whole deal. They have a camp down there for kids who have been through the same stuff as him. Over a hundred kids and that's not even the tip of the iceberg."

"There's a whole generation of broken children; all we can do is protect the ones in our charge. It's all we can do. You can't sit around waiting for the government to protect them. There's just too many people like Irons out there.

"Ever thought of adopting, Carscadden? There are plenty of kids out there and I think you'd be a good dad."

"Well, like I said, I'm not too old . . . and I've met a girl. I'll just take things one step at a time."

Montgomery pointed to the car. "Is Nastos going to come out and say hello?"

"Yeah. He says I'm allowed to have a few drinks tonight so we can put this behind us for once and for all."

Acknowledgements

I WOULD LIKE TO THANK PUBLISHER JACK DAVID OF ECW PRESS FOR giving me this opportunity. The editorial process was educational and could have been pure anguish had it not been for Emily Schultz's and Cat London's clever direction and guidance.

Brian Henry of Toronto provides excellent writing workshops and I suggest aspiring writers check out what he's got to offer. I've been lucky to have good teachers, the kind who prepare you for independence, rather than just reading curriculum at you. Barry Samells, Peter Locke, Peter Koehli, Gianni Owen, Jill Tillman and Diane MacKenzie — any two of them would have made all the difference; I was lucky to have them all.

The Home Team blurs the line between friends and family. Kathleen, Jaida, Mike, Hartley, Karen and Bryan, thanks for the support.